Praise for Joseph Heywood and the Woods Cop Mystery series:

"Heywood has crafted an entertaining bunch of characters. An absorbing narrative twists and turns in a setting ripe for corruption."
—*Dallas Morning News*

"Crisp writing, great scenery, quirky characters and an absorbing plot add to the appeal. . . ."
—*Wall Street Journal*

"Heywood is a master of his form."
—*Detroit Free Press*

"Top-notch action scenes, engaging characters both major and minor, masterful dialogue, and a passionate sense of place make this a fine series."
—*Publishers Weekly*

"Joseph Heywood writes with a voice as unique and rugged as Michigan's Upper Peninsula itself."
—Steve Hamilton, Edgar® Award-winning author of *The Lock Artist*

"Well written, suspenseful, and bleakly humorous while moving as quickly as a wolf cutting through the winter woods. In addition to strong characters and . . . compelling romance, Heywood provides vivid, detailed descriptions of the wilderness and the various procedures and techniques of conservation officers and poachers. . . . Highly recommended."
—*Booklist*

"Taut and assured writing that hooked me from the start. Every word builds toward the ending, and along the way some of the writing took my breath away."
—Kirk Russell, author of *Dead Game* and *Redback*

"[A] tightly written mystery/crime novel . . . that offers a nice balance between belly laughs, head-scratching plot lines, and the real grit of modern police work."
—*Petersen's Hunting*

Praise for The Snowfly

"A truly wonderful, wild, funny and slightly crazy novel about fly fishing. *The Snowfly* ranks with the best this modern era has produced."

— *San Francisco Chronicle*

"A magical whirlwind of a novel, squarely in the tradition of Tim O'Brien's *Going After Cacciato* and Jim Harrison's *Legends of the Fall*."

— Howard Frank Mosher, author of *The Fall of the Year* and others

"*The Snowfly* is as much about fishing as Moby Dick is about whaling."

— *Library Journal*

"Fly-fishing legend meets global adventure in Heywood's sparkling, ambitious novel . . . an engrossing *bildungsroman* . . . part Tom Robbins, part *David Copperfield*."

— *Publishers Weekly* (starred review)

"If *The Snowfly* becomes a movie, it will blast *A River Runs Through It* out of the water."

— *Fly Angler's Online Book Review*

". . . a finely tuned plot and masterful, literary craftsmanship. It will stand with *The River Why* as the finest of its kind."

— *Riverwatch*

Praise for *Red Jacket* (A Lute Bapcat Mystery)

"Joseph Heywood has long been a red-blooded American original and an author worth reading. With *Red Jacket*—a colorful and sprawling new novel with a terrific new protagonist named Lute Bapcat—he raises the bar to soaring new heights."

—C. J. Box, *New York Times* bestselling author of *Force of Nature*

"In 1913, Theodore Roosevelt recruits former Rough Rider Lute Bapcat to become a game warden on Michigan's Upper Peninsula in Heywood's absorbing first in a new series. Outsized characters, both real (athlete George Gipp before his Notre Dame fame, union organizer Mother Jones) and fictional (randy businesswoman Jaquelle Frei; Lute's Russian companion, Pinkhus Sergeyevich Zakov), pepper the narrative."

—*Publishers Weekly*

"Joseph Heywood tells a great story, weaving real and fictional characters throughout his narrative…. [C]risp writing with a sense of humor…."

—*Woods 'N Water magazine*

"Heywood mixes history—the [miners'] strike and the violence it engenders, culminating with the Christmas Eve Italian Hall Disaster in Calumet, Michigan, in which 73 died—with vivid characterizations in a . . . promising series opener."

—*Booklist*

HARD GROUND

ALSO BY JOSEPH HEYWOOD

Woods Cop Mysteries
Ice Hunter
Blue Wolf in Green Fire
Chasing a Blond Moon
Running Dark
Strike Dog
Death Roe
Shadow of the Wolf Tree
Force of Blood

Lute Bapcat Mysteries
Red Jacket

Other Fiction
Taxi Dancer
The Berkut
The Domino Conspiracy
The Snowfly

Non-Fiction
Covered Waters: Tempests of a Nomadic Trouter

HARD GROUND

WOODS COP STORIES

JOSEPH HEYWOOD

LYONS PRESS
Guilford, Connecticut

An imprint of Globe Pequot Press

Lyons Press is an imprint of Globe Pequot Press.

Text design: Sheryl Kober
Layout artist: Melissa Evarts
Project editor: Ellen Urban

Map by Jay Emerson, Licensed Michigan Fisherman Emeritus

Library of Congress Cataloging-in-Publication Data is available on file.

ISBN 978-0-7627-8126-3

Printed in the United States of America

10 9 8 7 6 5 4 3 2 1

For the men and women who wear the green and gray,
and those special people who love them.

CONTENTS

AUTHOR'S NOTE

The stories and characters herein are "fancies," that is, fictional creatures plucked from my internal cedar swamp. If there are unifying themes beyond the wearing of the same uniform, it seems to me they are the quest for justice and search for self-validation and all the strange forms these concerns can take. As the Woods Cop mystery series plugged along and new series began, it occurred to me one day while we were in Deer Park (thirty miles north of Newberry), that in twelve years of patrols with conservation officers I had experienced and learned a heap of things that would never fit into a Grady Service or a Lute Bapcat story. This collection is the result. As always, thanks to Michigan's officers and their supervision for allowing me such access and candid looks at the work they do and the fascinating world in which they live. Theirs is often, by necessity, a secretive existence. Special thanks here to my agent, Phyllis Greenberg, at Harold Ober for her guidance, and to my wife, Lonnie, for her unflagging support; she has to watch the stew brew, which is akin to watching sausage being made, never a pleasant thing. I also want to thank Editor (New-Daddy) Keith Wallman and the team at Lyons Press. This is my twelfth book with the house, and it has been a pleasure all the way. I would like to name all the officers who've endured my presence, but the list is too extensive, and you know who you are. Remember, what follows is fiction. Mostly. Sort of.

Joseph Heywood
Deer Park, Michigan
May 2013

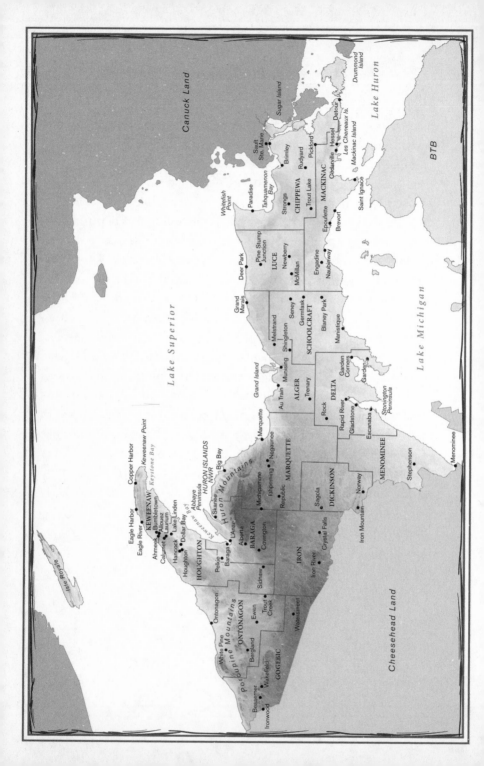

The Second Day

Newly minted Conservation Officer Kirby Halter had been mesmerized as he watched snowshoe hares dancing under a full moon. Only two days on duty on his own, and every moment felt magical, even nature's unexpected presentation of romance last night. Is this real? he kept asking himself. They pay me to do this?

Four years of professional basketball in Spain had been fun, it but wouldn't begin compare to this, he was sure. Not even close. Best of all, you could keep this job until you retired twenty-five years downstream, because this was a real job, not a bunch of pituitarily gifted adults playing a kid's game, dependent on the whims of rich team owners.

Everybody he knew had been bewildered when he passed on the NBA draft to attend the MCOLES police academy and for taking the Michigan state civil service examination, but he already had an offer from Spain and a large signing bonus. When he hung up his Adidas sneakers, he called the Michigan Department of Natural Resources and six months later found himself in a class of nine DNR recruits. A year later, here he was, a probationary conservation officer assigned to Schoolcraft County in Michigan's Upper Peninsula.

For the moment he was living in an apartment over a marina in Manistique, but he had bought a lot on Indian Lake and had a builder working on plans. European basketball had left him with nearly a half-million euros, with more to come over time in deferred payments.

Today, Halter was cruising County Road 436 when Station Twenty in Lansing alerted him to a missing hunter report north of Blaney Park. The hunter had gone out early this morning and not yet come home, the call to 911 coming from the man's wife. The hunter's name was Ben Koski, who lived on the perimeter of the Bear Creek Swamp. Halter immediately headed in that direction.

The house was made of half-logs, a ten-year-old brown minivan parked on a scabrous colorless lawn. A doorless barn held a rusted John Deere tractor. Halter pulled in, parked, and a young woman came out of the old farmhouse with one kid straddling her hip and another trailing close behind like a gosling.

"My name's Asia," she said. "Just like the country. Benny went out to the northwest forty this morning. He owns two-forty total. If you follow the grass two-track, it will take you right to where he parks."

It was April with crusted snow clots still in the woods and no meaningful hunting seasons yet under way. "What's he hunting?"

The woman stood mute, looking confused. She was barely five feet tall and had long, stringy, tinted red-orange hair and big brown eyes, both swollen, the left one nearly shut and discolored. There was a small contusion under her nose, and it looked like she'd tried to hide it with makeup.

"That man hunts everything," she said. "Mind you, he won't eat none of it, just likes to kill. I guess you being a man and all, you probably know about such things," she added, tears in her eyes. Both kids had dry snot trails under their noses.

"What's he driving?" Halter asked.

"Ford pickup, yellow and rusty," she said. "My name's Asia, like the country? Did I already tell you that?"

Halter nodded. "Yes ma'am, you did. It's a nice name." He watched her go back inside, didn't point out Asia was a continent, not a country.

The game warden saw the yellow truck about two hundred yards off, angled nose down on a slight incline, ass in the air like it had been beached, the driver's door open like a small wing. He found a man he assumed to be Ben Koski in the driver's seat, a .410 shotgun stock down in matted trap weed, barrel pointed up, Koski's jaw and right eye gone. The man had somehow gotten his left arm stuck in the steering wheel, pinned in place like a piece of sculpture. Halter checked the man's wrist and neck, got no pulse, pulled out his notebook, wrote down the time, stepped away from the truck, and retched violently into the grass.

Steadying his breathing, the new CO tried to imagine what had happened, guessed the shotgun had been loaded and Koski had dropped it butt first, hurrying to get out. Halter studied the body. Koski looked at least twenty years older than his wife. Had the man beaten her this morning, last night?

Kirby Halter called the Schoolcraft county dispatcher. "DNR Two One Thirty-five has a GSW." He gave the house address.

"Bus or wagon?" The dispatcher asked.

"Wagon," he answered.

Halter debated letting county personnel notify the woman but reminded himself he had been the one to find her husband. It was his responsibility to close the loop.

By the time he got back to the house, the woman called Asia limped out to greet him, a different kid on her hip this time. "Where's he at?" she asked directly.

"I'm very sorry," he said, "There's been a terrible accident."

"Jesus God," the woman whispered in a barely audible voice. "He's *dead*?"

"Yes, ma'am, I'm so sorry."

"That selfish, worthless son of a bitch!" she shouted.

"Ma'am?"

"Know what his last words to me were?"

Halter guessed this might be rhetorical, or she was venting, or something. He decided to let silence stand.

The woman shook her small fist at him: "He said, 'Your poppy will be home soon.' He was talking to his goddamn *dog*, not to his wife or to his four kids, but to his stinks-like-shit, hates-the-whole-damn-world dog. And *then* that dumb bastard stomps outen our house, and he ain't *never* comin' back. You married?"

"No, ma'am."

"Make it stay so," she said with a growl. "Marriage is like hunting; after you pull the trigger, the fun's done, and it ain't nothin' but work from that point on." The woman patted the diapered bottom of the child on her hip and made a face. "How'd it happen?"

"There will be an investigation," Halter said.

"Bullshit. You saw him; tell me what the hell you saw. How hard can that be? You didn't even know him."

"Loaded gun in his truck. Looks like he might've dropped it, and it went off."

"He suffer?" she asked.

"I don't think so," Halter said, having no idea.

"Too damn bad," the woman said. "He was a mean, worthless bastard, bills not paid in four months. I had to take a job over to the casino, and every time that asshole drank, he accused me of fucking out-of-town customers and beat the living shit out of me! I ain't fucked nobody, least of all *him*. What sort of man says goodbye to his dog and ignores his family, eh?"

Halter was sure no answer was expected.

"Hello, are you, like, deaf and dumb?" she spat at him. "What kind of asshole picks his dog over his wife and kids? Am I ugly?"

"No, ma'am, not in my opinion." Actually, she was damn good looking, bruises and all.

"I got a good body?" She twirled like a pole dancer to show him.

"I'd say so, yes, ma'am."

"Then tell me why in hell did he talk to the damn dog?"

"I can't say, ma'am."

She stared angrily at him. "You mean you know, but something is keeping you from saying, or you don't have a clue?"

"No clue, ma'am; sorry." This was worse than the headshot corpse.

"Great, here I've got this awful mess, and who shows up but a clueless clown in a make-believe cop suit."

"Ma'am, is there someone I can call for you?"

"Asia, my name is Asia. Why I want somebody called? You think I'm some weak, quaking little twat? Look at my face! That man beat the shit out of me. Now he's dead. Why would I call someone? My troubles are over, hally-fucking-lujah!"

A Schoolcraft county deputy arrived and joined them.

"Sorry for your loss, ma'am."

The woman said, "What sort of man says goodbye to his dog and ignores his family?"

"I don't know, ma'am," the deputy said.

She laughed. "An honest man! Your partner in the pickle suit said he couldn't say."

Halter left the deputy to deal with her, went to his truck, and began typing a report into the computer. Dancing hares last night, this lunacy today. They didn't talk much about this sort of thing in training. Before he could ponder more deeply, the medical examiner arrived, and Halter led him to the body.

"Touch anything?" the doctor asked.

"Wrist and neck for a pulse."

"Good job," the ME said. "What happened out here?"

"Had a loaded .410 in his truck, and it looks like he must've dropped it getting out."

The ME grunted. "That works for me. Want to type it up? I'll sign it."

"Sir?"

"That's a joke, son. You're the new guy, I bet."

"Yessir."

"Lighten up," the doctor said. "You the fella played basketball in Spain? Saw the article on you in the Manistique paper."

"Yessir."

The ME grinned. "Our dearly departed here was a widely known and much-loathed shitbag."

"I sort of got that impression from his wife."

The ME grinned. "Her? She's worse than him."

Halter got back into his truck and tried to conjure dancing hares. Twenty-five years, he told himself. This is your second day.

Last on the List

They took the Norton–Kramden thing as a left-handed compliment more than a put-down. Not that either man remembered the Jackie Gleason show, *The Honeymooners,* but they knew what it was and decided it was a good thing. COs Edouard Morton (Norton) and Ralf Camden (Kramden) had patrolled Iron County for years, almost always together. The two men had spent so much time together that each felt like he knew what the other was thinking.

By contrast, neither man had a clue what his wife was thinking, but out on patrol they rarely talked in depth about personal matters. On duty, wives and kids were superfluous. Neither man saw what they did as work or a mere job. It was a higher calling, like a doctor, a minister, a hooker, or something.

July 5 was hot and sultry. They were patrolling the Net River country in north-central Iron County, just south of the Baragastan line and north and a bit east of the Wisconsin border in Michigan's Upper Peninsula. Morton and Camden had been young Marines in Hue City, where they had been fire-hardened in combat, seen RPGs obliterate comrades, other men die from sniper fire, still others from grenades stuffed in dead dogs or explosives strapped to seven-year-old girls and detonated remotely. Because of their war (it was always their war, their personal possession), the partners had developed and sustained acute senses of situational awareness. Truth be known, Camden's in-the-moment acuity was a bit better than Morton's, who was by nature more trusting and garrulous.

On patrol when their eyes weren't focused hard outside the truck, they sometimes talked about the possibility of losing the focus and honed edge they had come to call "Big E."

Yesterday had been a busy, long twelve-hour marine patrol, checking boaters and fishermen on Chicagoan Lake. They had written a dozen tickets for various safety violations, short fish, and over-limits, but they mostly issued warnings for lesser violations. While laws were written black and white, enforcement happened more in the gray, where keen judgment and quick reflexes ruled.

"Seems slow," Morton said now, driving slowly. The roads in this part of the county were almost all rock, brutal on trucks and tires, and human spines.

"Yesterday," Camden said. "Busy then, now this. Big yawn."

Both men grunted as they topped a small rise and saw a vehicle a couple of hundred yards ahead of them. Camden had the stabilizer binos in hand. "Passenger's window is open. I count two souls. Driver window's open, too. I can see his elbow."

"Weps?" Morton asked.

"Not visible."

"I'll hang back," he said, "barely keep contact, let them roll along."

"Works for me," Camden said.

The serpentine road was in semi-open country with multiple small rises and dips and now and then a half-mile stretch through a dense hemlock or Norway pine stand or massive popple regrowth.

"Stop!" Camden said to his partner, got out, fetched a shiny new beer can, still with dregs, which he emptied onto the ground, and tossed the empty into the truck bed.

"Road beer," he said as he got back in.

"I didn't see him toss it."

"Passenger let it slip down his door."

"Think they made us?"

"Nah, we're good."

Morton checked his watch. "Shift's pushing eight hours."

"Okay, let's see this dealie through, then head for the barn."

"Plans tonight?" the driver asked.

"Sleep," Camden said. "Too much sun for me yesterday."

"One out of five," Morton said.

A lame old UP joke: 360 days of winter and five days of lousy sledding, the season downstaters called summer.

Camden kept his binos on the vehicle ahead. "Looks like a '59 Buick Electra with fins, a lot of chrome, black ragtop."

"Is there a classic car rally somewhere near here this week?" Morton asked.

"No clue, and this one ahead of us ain't classic or tricked out. It's just old. We're starting to close on them. Fall back a little, or we'll have to tow these assholes out of something," Camden said.

"Projectiles out both sides," Camden then reported.

"Both marked," Morton said, making mental notes of locations. Reaching the spot, Camden jumped out and fetched two more cans.

"PBR," he said, making a face.

"Got a case on the seat between them. Bet?"

"Nope, you're right."

"Littering," Camden said drolly. "Major crime. Jump them now?"

"Not yet, keep watching," Morton said.

Camden looked at his partner. "You feeling something?"

"Not sure. You?"

Morton shrugged. "End of shift: My old lady wants dinner out tonight."

"Quid pro quo?"

"Pretty much," Morton said. "Say when you want me to close on them."

Ten minutes later the Buick stopped and didn't move. Two men got out, pissed beside their vehicle, chugged new beers, and sailed the empties into the weeds.

"Still don't see weps," Morton told his partner.

"Let's get this over," Camden said.

Morton drove fast without lights until they were thirty feet behind the Electra. Only then did he turn on the emergency blue flashers, headlights, spotlights, and give a sharp whirp on the yelper siren. The Buick rolled and lurched another hundred yards before lumbering and jerking to a stop.

"Slow reaction time," Morton said. "Maybe a few too many drinkies for the driver."

The two officers went forward cautiously, Morton to the driver, Camden to the passenger window, where he looked down.

"Got alcohol?" Morton asked the driver.

"No, man," the driver said. "Ya know, just road pops."

Camden's passenger stared straight ahead, his body rigid, head down, chin pulled in, slumped slightly forward.

While the driver was carrying on with Morton like they were asshole buddies, Camden saw the cords tighten in his man's neck, saw the man had his right hand under the seat, groping around, trying to do it without being seen.

Camden grabbed the man's wrist, jerked up the hand clutching an automatic. He could hear his partner still yapping happily with the driver as he got both hands on the passenger's gun hand, yanked him violently through the window, slammed him hard to the ground, dropped onto the man's back with his knee, and smashed the gun hand with his fist into the wrist. The gun came loose, and in one fluid motion Camden wrenched the gun hand behind the man, cuffed it, then cuffed the other hand. Camden popped to his feet, breathing heavily from the sudden exertion. He waved the automatic at his partner.

"Get that sonovabitch out and pat his ass down! The passenger had this under the seat." Camden felt his heart pounding, adrenaline still pumping.

Morton made his man show his hands, got him out, cuffed him, and patted him down. "Clean here," he reported.

Camden yanked his prisoner to his feet. "You have something in mind?"

"Blow your ass to hell, bitch," the passenger said with an uptight wheeze.

"Guess that plan's fucked," Camden said. "Where's your wallet?"

"Don't got one," the man said.

"What's your name?" Camden asked.

"Fuck you."

"That with an F or a PH? Where do you live?"

The man scowled. "Fuck you," he repeated.

"Geez, the name of where you live is the same as the name your mother gave you. What're the odds of that, dirtball?"

Dark now, Camden lit the man with his SureFire and studied his neck. Solid tattoos, crudely rendered. "How long you been out?"

"Fuck you," the man said with a snarl.

"Got home today," the driver volunteered. "Four years in Jackson."

Camden used the sole of his boot to swipe the back of his prisoner's knees and caused him to momentarily lose balance. The man wobbled and twisted his shoulders trying not to fall. "Didn't they teach you manners downstate?"

The man stared straight ahead, trembling.

Morton said, "My guy's Cosgrove, Dawayne."

Camden said, "Who's your partner, Cosgrove?"

"My younger brother, Dusty. He's gonna crash with me till he can get his own place, man."

Camden held the automatic in front of his prisoner. "Nine mike-mike, what were you in for?"

"Meth manufacture and distribute," Dawayne said for his brother. "Marquette County."

"Felon with a firearm: not such a good a day for you, Dusty," Camden said.

The man remained silent.

Camden asked his partner to call the county to request prisoner transport. "We'll meet them at the jail in Crystal, take care of paperwork there."

Morton went back to the patrol truck. Camden looked at Dusty Cosgrove. "Not smart, you with a Wop 9."

"We was just taking us a joy ride," brother Dawayne offered. "To celebrate, you know?"

"What, a ride back to Jackson for your brother?"

"That's real cold, sir," Dawayne said.

Morton came back from the truck and pulled his partner aside. "Officer safety caution on Dusty Cosgrove," he whispered. "When they let him go today, somebody heard him say he'd kill the next cop who stopped him."

"All that was in the warning?" Camden asked.

Morton said, "Affirmative."

Camden asked, "How we supposed to know shit doesn't get passed to us?"

Morton shrugged.

Camden walked back to his prisoner. "How about I unlock your cuffs, put the piece on the ground between us, and see who can get to it first?"

"You crazy, dude," Dusty said.

"I *am* crazy," Camden said, "and you'd do well to remember that, unlike you, I don't get caught. I decide to whack your sorry ass, nobody will ever find you. You ain't inside the publicly funded creep zoo now, partner. Tough talk don't cut shit out here."

"I got rights," the younger Cosgrove said.

"If you get out again," Camden said, "stay the fuck out of our county."

An Iron County deputy took custody of the prisoners, and the conservation officers followed the county car south down US 141 to the county seat in Crystal Falls.

"Goddamn communications," Morton grumbled. "It's not right us not knowing."

"Listen, dickhead. I hauled the passenger out the window, and you were fucking clueless. No E, man; what the fuck happened out there?"

Morton hung his head.

"We don't need a warning to be alert for assholes, Ed. We've got to rely on each other and ourselves. We're all we got."

Morton said contritely, "You're right, and I'm sorry."

"Water over the dam, partner. We'll get this jerk lodged and head for the barn," Camden said, thinking one or both of them could be wounded or dead now had he not been paying attention. He felt his hands shaking and wedged them under his thighs so Morton couldn't see how shook he was. Every close one felt worse than the last one.

Double-jointed Trouble

They were in her ninth-grade homeroom. The fifteen-year-old boy pulled the gun when Jill Flyvie's back was to him; forty sweaty minutes later he surrendered the .38 snub-nose to her, apologizing, nearly in tears. Forty minutes held at gunpoint while the principal and superintendent stood in the hall bug-eyed, doing nothing, staring through the classroom door window like it was a goddamn cable reality show, or a fish tank.

The charter school was new, another half-ass, overpromising, parental ass-kissing cookie-cutter operation, and the super hadn't wanted bad publicity. Result: Jill Flyvie had been knowingly held at gunpoint by a mental defective, and the officials never called the police, a total and complete violation of the school's own lockdown policy.

When Flyvie came out of the room, found out the cops hadn't been called, and then announced she would do it herself, Superintendent Dr. Thela Johnson-Malagassy got close to her.

"This will be a disastrous career move for you," the superintendent whispered.

Unintimidated, Flyvie made the call, and the responding cops had publicly berated both the principal and the superintendent, verbally and in the official police report, which got picked up by local newspapers. In April, Flyvie had been informed she would not be "invited back" for the fall.

Johnson-Malagassy ordered Flyvie to her office for the job-ending sentence. The place was a thirty- by thirty-foot corner room with snow-white carpeting, and all visitors were required to leave their shoes in an anteroom before entering.

The superintendent stared at Flyvie with a greasy smirk. "Whatever possesses you white girls to think they can bring something to our precious black children?"

Flyvie had always been under the impression that children were everyone's responsibility, race being irrelevant, but she only shook her head at the superintendent's ignorance, what her kids called being "ignant." The woman was a self-serving racist and megalomaniac, and Flyvie was glad to be shed of her bullshit, though it hurt a lot to leave her kids.

Flyvie had a B.A. in education, minors in Spanish, entomology, and history. She left the classroom, left Chicago, and graduated from a police academy at Northern Michigan University, took the state civil service test, scored in the 98th percentile, and was hired six months later as a conservation officer assigned to Marquette County.

After half a year she felt her decision to become a CO had been the best she had ever made. Never mind that her CPA ex-husband couldn't tolerate her spending long nights alone with other men and left her after an ultimatum that came down to career or marriage. She chose the former and had no regrets. Bill's soul (if he had one) was missing the joy gene; the man was petty, unimaginative, uninspiring, and unfulfilling in bed. No loss there. Nada.

Flyvie was scheduled to ride with her sergeant, Peggy Kee, in two days. Tonight she had a shiner complaint south of Gwinn. It was off one of the unnamed two-tracks in a maze of trails that paralleled the Escanaba River. A camp owner down that way had called the toll-free Report All Poaching line in Lansing to notify authorities about shots last night after midnight in a cutover south of his camp.

She had been in place less than fifteen minutes when a slow-roller came bumping down the logging road, flicking a spotlight on and off. Both her windows were down. The shot startled her when it came. The truck stopped, and she watched a man fetch a deer, heave it into his truck bed, and continue to drive slowly onward.

Flyvie had her windshield and hood covered with a camo see-through tarp that prevented any bounce-shine off her metal or glass. As the shooter continued north, she ripped her cover away and, running black, followed a hundred yards behind him, watching him spotlighting other cutover fields until he stopped and shot again. This time she saw a muzzle flash, and when the man dragged the second deer back to his truck, she raced forward and lit him up, bolting from her patrol truck almost before it was stopped.

The violator put up his hands and grinned stupidly. He was a little guy, five feet nothing, bearded like a French artist, a ponytail down his back, earrings, Keen walking shoes. His name was Finlayson, Jerome, out of Skandia. The retail sales system computer check showed no DNR licenses for Finlayson to hunt, fish, trap, or do anything else, and three outstanding felony warrants on him with a note to arrest and detain from both counties involved: Menominee and Ingham. Ingham indicated it would send an officer to fetch the man. Ingham was eight hours distant. The man was bad news, but he looked like a wimp, a total nobody.

She made Finlayson gut both deer and load them in the bed of her truck. She noted that he eviscerated the animals quickly and efficiently, no wasted effort. He wasn't new to this work. Gutting done, two deer in the truck bed, Flyvie put her prisoner into her truck in the passenger seat, cuffed and belted him, and called Station Twenty and the county to let them know she was transporting a prisoner to the Marquette County Jail.

As Flyvie turned north from Gwinn, the county dispatcher called. "One One Twenty-four, we have a domestic in progress, 507 Jupiter Street, Sawyer Village. Officer needs back up fast. You close?"

"Affirmative, One One Twenty-four is heading for Jupiter." How many times do you get to say something like that, she thought, and smiled inwardly.

The address led her to a four-plex, four two-story apartments built for the United States Air Force in the 1950s and now used as low-cost government housing for low-income citizens. The base had been closed decades ago, and with the new residents, cops of all ilks were in and out of Sawyer continuously. She pulled up behind the Marquette deputy's patrol unit, got out a triple set of cuffs, which she used as a makeshift chain, attached one end to her prisoner's cuffs and the other to the steering column. A voice in the back of her head was muttering, "Never leave a prisoner alone," but a louder, real voice was screaming over the county frequency, "Where's my backup?"

Flyvie left her prisoner locked in the truck and went into the house, where Deputy Henk Jonkheere was in a wall-shuddering scrap with a massive shirtless man whose fat undulated in rolls like swells on Lake Superior. The man was covered with tattoos, and the house stank of cat piss, skunk weed, vomit, and way too much testosterone. Pepper spray seemed to hang in the air and got into her eyes as she let Jonkheere know she had arrived.

"I'm gonna try to rotate this sonovabitch," Jonkheere grunted. "When I do, put the fucking lightning to the bastard."

The CO pulled her Taser, the deputy turned the man, and she popped him in the back, raising a simultaneous scream and grunt as the man lifted the very large Jonkheere and smashed him head-first into the floor before turning to face her, drool cascading off his chin. She momentarily considered shooting him, but reached instead for her baton, popped it open to full length, put a hard thrust into the man's throat and a second and third to the outside of his knee, which collapsed him and made the floor shake, by which time Jonkheere was back in the fight with his own baton. Eventually they subdued the man and secured him in cuffs.

"Thanks," Jonkheere managed to wheeze. "I thought I was going to have to shoot the bastard."

"Me, too. What's *his* problem?"

"Birth," the deputy said. "Bastard must drink steroids from gallon jugs."

"God, he *stinks*," Flyvie said.

Five minutes later a state trooper, another deputy, and CO Igor Copp arrived. Copp was her colleague, a steady, unflappable longtime game warden who looked at her and grinned.

"A little wrestling, eh?"

No matter how violent, she never heard fellow conservation officers call any physical confrontation a fight. She didn't know why and didn't care. The main thing was, it was over. "He's a behemoth," she told Copp.

"You musta charged right in," he said. "All your truck doors are standing open."

Later Jill Flyvie was sure her heart had stopped at that moment, but she had shoved past Copp, bolted outside, and realized it was true. Finlayson was gone. She began to hyperventilate, partially in anger, partially in fear. Losing a prisoner was a serious transgression, the kind that could kill the career of an officer still technically on probation.

Copp joined her. "Problem?"

"I had a prisoner," she confessed.

"Take deep breaths," he said. "*Had*? Had isn't good. Have is good, not had. It sucks to be you," Copp said, and she couldn't help laughing. "Guess we'd better find the asshole," the other officer added.

Flyvie's radio came on. "DNR One, One Twenty-four, this is Eighty-six, I'm at Mudge and Atlas, found a guy over here wearing bracelets. You missing any?"

Eighty-six was a troop she knew. "That's affirm, Eighty-six."

"Where you at?"

She gave him the address. "I'll fetch him to you," the deputy said.

"Holy Christ in the bakery," CO Copp said when the deputy arrived. "You pinched *Jerome Finlayson!*"

"Shining," she said. "Two kills. Saw both happen."

Copp laughed. "Finlayson hardly ever gets caught, and when he does, he almost always escapes." Copp held up his hands and wiggled his fingers, "Double-jointed or some such shit."

"You know this jerk?"

"Hell, every CO above the bridge knows him. Didn't Peggy brief you on him?"

"I'm working with her day after next. Our first time." Peggy Kee had been a sergeant less than three weeks and was just beginning to ride with her officers.

"Well, you got his sorry little ass back, and that's what counts."

Flyvie spent all the next morning in Marquette with a welder who put together a series of locks and shackles. "You, like, gonna play Torquemada?" the welder asked. "Is this, like, legal? Can cops really use stuff like this?"

"When conditions warrant," Flyvie answered. Torquemada indeed.

"Far out," the welder said.

The next day Sergeant Kee inspected CO Flyvie's vehicle and equipment. When she saw the chain-and-lock apparatus, she held it up. "Personal or professional?"

"Hybrid," Flyvie said. "A personal/professional matter."

"Noted," her sergeant said. "Good initiative, but next time just stay with your goddamn prisoner, and let someone else rescue the other cop."

"You know?"

Kee laughed. "Copp called me from his truck. There're no secrets in this outfit, Jill."

"How was I to know the asshole was double-jointed?"

"Stay with the prisoner, and it won't matter if he's got detachable limbs, superpowers, and an IQ of two-seventy."

"Never leave a prisoner alone," Flyvie said.

"Repeat that a hundred times, throw in a couple of Hail Marys, and consider yourself officially forgiven. But don't let there be a next time, copy?"

"Copy," Jill Flyvie said, "Sergeant, ma'am."

Symbiosis

It was opening day of firearms deer season. CO Steven Burdoni made his way cautiously along an old tote road that split off the Norway Truck Trail and encircled a knob locals had dubbed "Mount Pile of Rocks." Every year on opening morning of deer season in Dickinson County, Burdoni walked into a deer blind here, and the hunter was always over-baited.

The ground blind sat at the bottom of an opening with a clear shooting lane up the hill. But this year Cotton Nebel wasn't in his blind. His pickup was parked where it always was, and Burdoni immediately felt anxious.

Nebel had always been there. A slight, cadaverous man, Nebel wouldn't tip scales at 120 with his old red wool hunting plaids and boots on. The man looked sickly, was a chain smoker with an owl's bark of a cough you could hear 200 yards away.

The man lived in Kentucky but owned a ramshackle deer camp in Dickinson County, used the same blind every season, and Burdoni wrote the same ticket every year. The man always bought an out-of-state license and never shot more than one deer. In all things but baiting, Nebel seemed a law-abiding citizen.

Burdoni got to the blind, saw a fresh Camel butt in the Sanka can the Kentuckian used for an ashtray. There was a single spent .30-30 cartridge gleaming on the ground and a Winchester model 90 lying on top of an old canvas gun case, the lever action wide open for safety.

The conservation officer scanned the hill above him and saw a large buck walking nonchalantly across the open area, easily in shooting range. Beyond the deer, a man popped to his feet and waved. Nebel. The man began coughing, which sent the passing buck into flight.

The game warden worked his way up the hill to find Cotton Nebel's arms red with blood and a fresh gutpile in a dip below a dead six-point. "You see that dandy buck, Steve?" Nebel asked, wiping a hand on his pants and reaching out a bony hand for a handshake.

"You shoulda waited for the big one," Burdoni said.

"Hell, you know I don't care none about no such things. Can't eat them damn horns. Wondered when you'd mosey by."

"How much bait this year?" the officer asked.

"The usual. Hair over two gallons."

Burdoni looked at some apples, corn, two sugar beets. "Looks pretty close to two gallons," the officer said. "And it's spread out real nice."

"Nope, I'm over, Steve, *way* the heck over for sure. Got at least two wheelbarrys full."

Burdoni looked around. "What wheelbarrow?"

"Was a finger of speech," Nebel said. "I used my bucket."

"You want help getting your buck down to the blind?" Burdoni asked.

"Be good," the old man said. "Thanks, Steve."

They dragged the dead animal down the hill, and Nebel lit a new cigarette and held out the pack, which Burdoni refused.

"You gonna write me my ticket now?" Nebel asked.

"Well, you're not that much over, if at all, and the bait's spread out pretty good," the game warden said.

Nebel looked crushed. "I'm over, I *know* I'm over. You *got* to write me, Steve. The law's the law."

Burdoni said, "I don't know. I've seen a lot worse, far more egregious violations."

"Steve," the hunter said, "sir, I've already done marked my rifle." The man picked up the .30-30, closed the lever, and showed the stock to the game warden. It had today's date at the end of a string of nine other dates.

"But you've already got your buck, Cotton."

"That don't matter none. This here's a matter of tradition," the hunter said. "For the both of us. You write a ticket, I get a deer. You get a ticket to start off your law season, and it's good for the both of us. You and me, we do this every year, like partners. I drove all the way from Kansas City. Left my rig there just so I could make the opener."

"I don't know, Cotton."

"How about I make us some fresh coffee?"

"Don't bother."

"Ain't no bother, and your daft talk's a-gettin' me twisterpasted. I'll make coffee, and you write my ticket. We got a deal?"

"I have to tell you I've seen a lot worse baiting than this, even from you, Cotton."

"I know, I know, I didn't have time to do 'er right this year. Grabbed bait, drove over here, hauled it up the hill, walked back down, looked, and there stood that fool six-point. Had no choice. I picked up the rifle and let fly. Dropped right there at the bait. Didn't even have to track the dang fool."

"Well, the bait's just not enough to bother me, especially being spread out the way it is. Got your license?"

"Yut, picked her up in Iron Mountain. Old boy down there stays open all night before the season opener."

"Let me take a look."

Nebel handed his license to the conservation officer.

"Says you bought this at oh four-forty."

"'Bout right," Nebel said. "Thirty minutes to camp from IM."

"You drove to camp, grabbed bait, and came over here. How long from your camp to here?"

"Half hour."

"How long to walk in, put the bait on the hill?"

"Dunno, mebbe 'nother half hour, I speck."

Burdoni scratched his chin, took out his notebook and pencil. "Oh four forty-five leaves store. That's oh five fifteen at your camp. Five minutes there, half hour to here, makes oh five forty-five, half hour to walk in, dump bait, and get down to your blind. That gets us to oh six fifteen, I'd say. You have a smoke before you shot?"

"No time. Looked up, and there he were a-standin'. I put Old Annie's sights on him an' squeezed one off."

"Shooting light?"

"Got 'im, didn't I?"

"How come you're just gettin' to gutting the animal now?"

"Truth is, I'm gettin' old, Steve. Going on eighty. Took a while to get the energy to walk up that dang hill again and do what had to be done. Deer was down. No hurry, was there?"

"I guess I could cite you for shooting early, before legal shooting hours," Burdoni said.

"Fine by me, Steve. Whatever you think is right."

"But I think we'll just call it over-bait and be done with it. The fine's lower."

"That's real good, Steve, just so long as there's a ticket."

Burdoni made out the citation and gave it to Nebel. He explained for the tenth time that the man could pay it by mail, did not have to appear. That it was a civil fine, not criminal.

They drank fresh hot coffee, and the game warden walked away listening to the old man cough. One of these year's Cotton Nebel wouldn't be around anymore, but until then, he'd humor the old man. What exactly a ticket did for Cotton Nebel was beyond Burdoni's ken, but this was the Upper Peninsula, it was the opening day of deer season, and it was what it was . . . whatever *this* was.

Going Viral

During seventeen years as a game warden in Chippewa and Luce Counties, Marlin Rodgers had earned the name "Hemlock" from local violators who insisted he was like poison to their work. Out in the county's cedar swamps and boreal forests, outlaws of all shapes and hues developed sudden palsies when he materialized.

There were some who maintained Rodgers was the most feared man in Luce County.

His fourteen-year-old daughter, Deven, saw it differently. She rolled her eyes, sighed, even walked away whenever he tried to speak to her. Or she told him, "Like, you need to get a life!" Until she was ten, she would hardly let him go off to work alone. Now she had banned him from her school in his CO uniform, even to pick her up after basketball or softball practice. When he did manage to talk to her now, it seemed almost always at her back. The legend in the woods was persona non grata in his own home. Wife Patsy, a guidance counselor at Newberry High School, constantly reassured him that this was a stage, and it would pass. He was dubious.

Deven was a first-rate student and, like her friends, addicted to computers, phones, and various electronic contraptions. She talked about Facebook like it was an alternative world—and a much better one at that. Above all, Deven seemed to measure the importance of everything by whether or not it appeared on YouTube.

Rodgers had looked at all the computer crapazola and rejected it as escapist at best, toys for kids with a little money. It was bad enough how electronically tricked out his own patrol truck was these days, like Big Brother rode on his shoulder, monitoring every move he made.

Having checked his snailmailbox slowmailbox at the district office, Rodgers picked up a new elastic ammo sleeve for his shotgun and slid it over the stock of his .12 gauge. He put eight shells into the sleeve, with the lips pointed down so he could pull them downward into the palm of his hand during a firefight, a maneuver officers called a combat release, something they all practiced.

Rodgers had just slid the shotgun into its case when Central called. "Current location, Two One Nineteen?"

"Just leaving the district office."

"Just got a report of a man covered with blood in the woods, two miles south of your location on a two-track that veers west by a red barn. Troops and our people are tied up."

"I know the place, Central," he said, getting into his truck. "Two One Nineteen is rolling that way."

Man covered in blood. This could be nasty or nothing. You never knew until you were on the scene to assess for yourself. Eyewitness reports, so called, were generally useless and often totally inaccurate.

He found a young woman waiting out by County Road 403, and when he pulled up, she was shrieking, "Help him! Please God, somebody help him, he's bleeding bad!"

"Calm down, ma'am," Rodgers said in a firm but quiet voice. "Who is bleeding?" he asked as he snapped on blue latex gloves.

"I don't know, I don't know! I was, like, walking in, like, you know, like, the woods, and I saw him. Oh my God, there's so much blood!"

"Where is this man?" Rodgers asked. The woman was jacked up on adrenaline and fear.

"Follow me, follow me!" the woman said and started running down the two-track with a grassy hump in the middle.

Rodgers picked up his emergency first aid kit and walking briskly, followed her until she neared a shed, began stabbing with her finger, and screaming, "There, there, there!"

Rodgers got close and saw nothing except a caved-in building with tarpaper walls. "Where exactly, ma'am?"

The woman ran to the ruin and pointed, "There, there, oh my *God!*"

Rodgers felt his heart jump. Bad news: bloody *and* behind cover. He moved in at an angle, got to the corner of the derelict shed, looked around, and saw the man up on his feet: fifties, sixties, wife beater shirt, balding with what remained of a mullet cut, both arms dripping blood, flies buzzing around in hungry armadas.

Secure the scene, the cop voice in his head preached. The man had what looked to be a Bowie knife in his left hand, same arm that seemed to be cut. Big-ass knife, blade bloody. *Oh boy.*

"Sir, I'm Conservation Officer Rodgers, and I want to help you, but first please put the knife on the ground."

"Wha . . .?" the bloody man mumbled, staring blankly.

He was weaving, unsteady, high, drunk, shocky maybe. *No way to assess injuries yet. Secure the scene.* "Sir, *please* put the knife *down,"* Rodgers repeated, standing back.

"So confused," the man said, taking a step forward. "Dizzy…"

"Stop. Look at me!" Rodgers ordered. "Sir, look at me *now!* What's your name?"

"Dunno," the man said, looking up slightly. "What's going on? Huh?"

"Put the knife *down!*"

"*I don't know,*" the man said, stepping forward again. "Where am I, what's going on?" Not just holding the knife, he was now brandishing it clumsily. Dandy, Rodgers thought.

"Sir, put the knife on the ground and step away from it."

· "Knife?"

"In your left hand. Put it *down!*"

The man gathered himself and looked like he was going to charge forward. Rodgers unsnapped the strap of his .40 cal and held his hand on the grip, ready. "Sir, I can't help you until you put the knife *down!*"

Still no compliance. Rodgers drew his weapon and held it behind his leg. "Put the knife down and step away from it, sir. Do it *now!*"

"You can't shoot him!" the female shrieked. "Why aren't you helping this poor man, ohmygod ohmygod ohmygod!" The woman was holding something in her hand, jumping up and down erratically. He snuck a look with his peripheral vision. She had a cell phone. *Just great.*

The man let the knife drop, stepped heavily against the camp wall, and slid to the ground. Rodgers got the knife, threw it behind him, and keyed his radio. "Central, Two One Nineteen needs paramedics. I'm about one hundred yards west of my vehicle on the two-track you sent me to. The road's good. They can drive all the way in."

"EMS rolling, ETA five," dispatch reported.

Rodgers knelt by the man and patted him down for other weapons.

"Ohmygod, are you going to help that poor man or just watch him die, pig?!?" the woman shouted in a shrill tone that hurt his ears. She pointed her phone at him. "I'm getting all of this, and it's going up on YouTube! Everybody's gonna see what you did! If he dies, it's on your head, pig!"

"Ma'am," Rodgers said, trying to remain calm. "Please help us. Go back out to the road and show the EMS where we are."

"While you fucking kill that poor man?!? Ohmygod, when are you gonna help him! I saw you pull your gun. I called for a cop, not some frickin' park ranger. This man needs *real* help." The woman swooped close, held the phone to the CO's face, and flounced away. "What's your name?" she demanded.

"I don't know my name," the bleeding man said with a whine to the woman in a weak and pathetic voice. "Do *you* know?"

The wound was in one arm and ugly but not immediately life-threatening. "Sir, I'm going to help you" Rodgers said, as he leaned down for a closer look at the bloody area. "Can you hold up your arm for me?"

"Okeydokes," the man said in a singsong voice.

The cut was long, down the middle of the left forearm. The blood on his face seemed to be from the arm wound. Rodgers broke open his kit, got a sterile bandage, wrapped the arm, and tied off the bandage to keep it in place. To maintain pressure on the bleeding, he took the man's right hand and held three fingers on the site. "Keep your fingers there. Can you help me do that, partner?"

"How'd I get here?" the man asked. "Who're you?"

"Help him!" the woman shouted as she made another running pass with the phone held out like a weapon. "For the love of our personal savior Jesus Christ!" the woman shouted. "Hey, jerkwad, help the man! He's bleeding to death!"

The woman jarred Rodgers's shoulder on the way past. "Ma'am, you need to back off. If you come close again, you're going to jail."

"A man lies bleeding to death, and this pretend pig is harassing me!" she shrieked at her tiny phone and charged again, this time thrusting the cell phone close to his chest and his metal name tag.

Rodgers told the man, "You're not in any immediate danger, sir. It's going to be okay."

"Where are my teeth?" the man asked, his eyes bulging like ping-pong balls.

Teeth? Ms. Cell Phone swooped in again, and Rodgers caught her arm, stood her up rudely, spun her like a top, and frog-hopped her back to his truck as the EMS came roaring along. He pointed them forward and cuffed the woman to a metal ring on his bumper. "Do *not* move!" he shouted and went back to his patient.

"I holded it," the man said with a nail-in-the-head grin.

"Good job," Rodgers said, looking him over for other wounds as two EMS techs moved in to take over.

"Lots of blood," he reported, "only one wound I can find, knife's over there behind us." He pointed.

"He say what happened?" an EMS man asked.

"Confused, probably shocky."

"Okay, we've got him from here," the EMS woman said. "What's with the chick cuffed to your truck?"

"She reported it."

"Why the histrionics?"

"Don't have the foggiest," Rodgers said.

A Luce County deputy sheriff named Shewbart pulled in and crawled out of his patrol unit, looked at the man on the ground, then nodded toward Rodgers's truck. "The cuffed one do this?"

Rodgers said, "No, she reported a bloody man in the woods. When I got here, she got too rambunctious, and I had to restrain her."

"You want to file charges?"

"No, just take her to the county, chew her ass, and let her go. And let her arrange her own transport home."

"You know her, eh?" Deputy Shewbart asked.

"No."

"Bonnie Lahti, known nutso. Got kicked out of a Colorado police academy her first week, lack of emotional stability. She lives near Engadine. Pain in the patoot, and she hates cops."

"Thanks," Rodgers said, stripped off his gloves, put them in a trash bag, and closed it with a tie-off. He put the knife in a clear evidence bag, labeled it, and headed for his truck. "Meet you guys at emergency at Joy," he told the EMS team. Joy was the name of the local hospital, named after some woman whose history had never interested him enough to learn. Shit got named for rich people's money, and such history bored him.

"You get a name on our patient?" the EMS tech asked.

"It's just like you see. He's too confused. See you there."

It turned out that the attempted suicide had a record of attempts, known bipolar disease, drug abuse, and a heavy booze problem, a loser's trifecta.

Rodgers completed his paperwork and met Deputy Shewbart in the hospital parking lot. "Lahti called somebody to pick her up."

"Thanks."

"She can go mega-whackadoodle in a heartbeat," the deputy said. "Click, and she's off and running!"

"I saw," Rodgers said. He spent the rest of the day in the north county checking trout fishermen, wrote no tickets, gave one man a verbal warning for a short fish, and explained how to safely release a fish: "Always wet your hands before handling a trout. Their slime is their autoimmune system. A dry hand will break the seal, could kill the fish."

It was nearing midnight when he got home, parked in the trees behind the house, removed his equipment belt, took a shower, ate two leftover pork chops in the microwave, and slid into bed beside Patsy. "Dinner in the fridge," she mumbled.

"Found the chops," he said. "Thanks."

"How was your day?" she asked sleepily.

"Uneventful," he answered. "Yours?"

"The usual high school hijinks," she said with a drowsy chuckle.

The next night Deven met him at the front door with an almost violent hug. "You are sooo *cool*, Daddio!" she said and rushed outside.

Patsy was grinning.

"What the hell was that all about?" Rodgers asked her.

"You went viral. You're somebody now."

"I don't feel sick," he said.

"Viral, not virus," Patsy said. "On YouTube. You don't know?"

"Obviously not."

"There's a video of you on YouTube. Posted last night, and there's already forty thousand hits in less than twelve hours. You're the talk of the high school and town."

He stared at his wife, who led him to her laptop, hit some keys, and pointed.

The crazy Lahti woman was calling him every name in the book. "Nice," he said. "CO as storm trooper."

"Uh-uh. All sorts of people think that you should get a medal for helping that poor man and that she should be in jail."

The next morning at breakfast he held out his arms to his daughter, who rolled her eyes. "*Really,* Dad? You were viral yesterday. Old news. Today you're just you," she added.

Patsy smiled, her eyes flashing an emotion somewhere between amusement and sympathy. "Coffee on the table, and there's French toast, Officer Yesterday."

Laws of Physics

They were headed south on US 141 with the intention of cutting north-west on a county road over to Steger Lake, the patrol boat on the trailer behind the truck, sun shining, middle of July, a perfect Upper Peninsula day, warm and mild with a deep blue sky, blueberries already ripe for pick-ing, and the two officers were talking about taking their wives to pick a few quarts, life proceeding normally, pleasantly, uneventfully.

CO Hoyt Blossom was driving, Sergeant Arlon Rubadue sitting shot-gun; the senior man, Rubadue, had three years until retirement, and life was a perpetual grin.

Until a large buck, antlers in green-brown velvet, suddenly materi-alized in the truck's path. Not there, then there, Blossom thought, like magic, and then he squeaked, "Oh shit" as he hit the animal dead center of the steel deer guard, which would usually shed animals left or right. This time, the deer came up *over* the deer guard and into their windshield, spidering it to crackle glass, ticked, and spun across the roof, grazed the top of the truck's tailgate, rose slightly, spun in slow motion the length of the aluminum boat, struck the housing of the forty-horse outboard, and dropped sideways into the windshield of an oncoming Cadillac Seville, all of this occurring in an elapsed time of no more than two or three seconds, after which Sergeant Rubadue said, "You don't see *that* shit every day."

For Finbar and Missy Ribey of Green Bay, Wisconsin, it seemed for an instant like the end of the world as their windshield shattered into their laps, and they slid onto the shoulder, where Missy wrestled the Caddy to a stop, the deer's antler stuck through a hole in the windshield, and blood, tissue, and hair spewed everywhere. They were on the way home from visiting their daughter at Michigan Tech, where she was chasing a doctorate in electrical engineering, a long pursuit that might even end this fall after the girl had spent three tax-sucking years in the goddamn Peace Corps on some South Pacific cannibal atoll the size of Door County. If the girl finished the degree, it would be a long overdue miracle, Missy was thinking, when the deer slammed into them.

Blossom and Rubadue were at the Caddy almost immediately, checking the passengers, expecting carnage, and finding instead a distinguished-looking couple with immaculate silver hair staring straight ahead as blood dripped silently through some cracks in the windshield. Rubadue tapped the driver's window, which came down silently. The woman had been driving. "You folks all right?"

"We're a little shook up, but we're fine," the male passenger volunteered. "No, let us amend that to more than fine, and let us instead proclaim us spiffily fine," he added. "Or call it extremely heavenly excellent if you insist on labels, though I don't hold with supernatural creators, at least not any the average primitive mind can grasp."

"We're fine," the woman said, finding her voice and rolling her eyes. "Thanks to God. Please don't start spouting, Fin."

"Here, you confront my problem head-on, Officer. This gorgeous female creature, whom every man would want, medical doctor, Ph.D., lawyer, and all her high-falutin' intellectual training prevents her from seeing reality, know what I'm saying?" Finbar Ribey told Hoyt Blossom, who had the passenger door open and was checking the man for injuries.

Blossom sort of nodded, had no clue what the man was trying to say, and wondered if he'd banged his head.

"Don't be a fool, Fin," the woman grumbled.

"Therein the prejudice of ologies and isms, the in-place, artery-hardened belief systems of entrenched science and religion," the man said.

"I'm going to call EMS and a hook," Blossom told his sergeant and went back to the patrol truck.

"We're perfectly fine," the driver told Rubadue. "I'm a physician."

"See?" the passenger said. "She claims she's a doctor, and you accept it on face value. But I declare a cervid projectile was dropped by an alien space vehicle, and I am assumed to be a whackadoodle."

Rubadue found himself enjoying whatever this was turning into. "Alien space vehicle? You mean, like a UFO?"

Finbar Ribey smiled benignly. "UFO is a sadly outdated term, shunned by the cognoscenti. To be precise, it was a small Yankee Class Vector 7 that lifted its invisible force shield to discard the cervid. They do this after the experiments are complete. I saw the whole thing. It materialized from nowhere, struck your truck roof and the outboard motor, which spun it down into our path. If you examine the carcass, you'll find they took the animal for interspecies experimentation and, having gotten what they needed from it, dropped it back to earth. Nobody's fault. It's just how the universe works."

Rubadue asked, "If they've got a spaceship, don't they got, like, stuff to, you know, like, get rid of, you know, stuff?"

"Undoubtedly," the man said. "But put yourself in their gravity boots. You're a megajillion miles from your mother ship, or your home planet, and why waste energy? It's a lesson mankind could stand to learn from them."

"Okay," Rubadue said. "You sure you folks don't need some medical attention?"

"Our sheepskinned expert says no, and in this I shall defer to her judgment, despite the fact that she will never acknowledge, much less defer to, my knowledge base."

"Cryptozoology is bunkum," Missy Ribey said. "A sham world for fools without intellectual ballast."

"Then let us examine the carcass," Finbar Ribey demanded and nearly fell out of the Caddy as CO Blossom returned just in time to prop the man up on his shaky legs.

The three men stared at the gore after the officers took photos, pulled the carcass down off the Caddy, and lugged it into the ditch. "You can see bone fragments," Ribey said. "The aliens break them to measure tensile strength and record parameters and other physiological values."

"You *know* these aliens?" Rubadue asked.

"Of course not," the man said. "It's common sense, a simple process of deduction and analysis."

"But you told us we can't understand the aliens with our primitive intellectual development," the wife said from several feet away.

"I guess I heard that, too," Rubadue said.

"Kudos for a fine job of listening, but I do not include myself in that general declaration. You see, I've been trained by the best."

"Who trains the trainers?" Rubadue asked. "Seems to me your aliens had to intervene somewhere along the line; otherwise, how would teachers know now what to teach others?"

"Not to put too fine a point on this, my new friend, but I presume neither you nor your august partner has the training to understand nuclear physics, yet, and this too is an assumption, you must surely accept the existence of nuclear weapons. My field is more arcane than nuclear weaponology."

"What school?" Blossom asked.

Finbar Ribey rolled his eyes. "That question is irrelevant."

Blossom said, "I hope it's not one of those online for-profit schools that run up debt for students. We heard about a woman over to Iron River who spent eighty grand for some advanced science degree but couldn't get a job because the school's curriculum wasn't accredited."

The man sulked. "My program is *fully* accredited," he said, "and all doubting Thomases are like plagues of locusts on the earth."

A long black RV pulled up behind the Caddy, and a muscled young man bounced down, talked to Missy Ribey, and came over to the men. "Finbar, Missy tells me you're becoming contentious."

"Not in the least," Finbar Ribey said. "We are embarked upon a fine and stimulating intellectual discussion here. I'm presently showing these fine officers of the law the clear evidence of alien experimentation on the deceased cervid." He pointed at the carcass.

"The bone splinters I see are typical of any deer hit by a vehicle," Sergeant Rubadue said. "Flesh and bone are no match for a steel mass and momentum."

"But you are no doubt referencing *earthbound* physics," Finbar Ribey countered with a shrill voice. "Such science has no more validity in these circumstances than old wives' tales about vampires."

"I'm just saying what I know after seeing hundreds of deer–vehicle collisions."

"You refute my training and authority?"

"No, sir, just your conclusions—and only in this instance."

"Doctor, you badged cretin," Finbar Ribey barked nastily, his gentle demeanor gone.

The young man said, "Okay, Finbar, that's enough stimulation for today," and firmly grasped Ribey's upper arm.

"Am I to be placed in the mother ship?"

"Yes, sir," the young man said, "straightaway."

"And my wife, the illustrious academic?"

"She wants to remain with the wreck to see to repairs or replacement."

"Not another Cadillac, my darling," Finbar said, holding up a finger. "Clearly these things have been earmarked as targets by our alien visitors."

The RV driver said, "Yessir, Dr. Ribey, whatever you say."

The man gave the two conservation officers a leer and a strange Nazi-like salute. "You see, *this* young man accepts my title and my authority."

Finbar climbed into the RV, and it drove away.

Missy Ribey got out of the Caddy and lit a cigarette as the wrecker pulled up. "Where are the most dealers, et cetera?" she asked Rubadue.

"Probably Iron Mountain."

"Got to call my boss to haul that far," the wrecker driver said.

"Do call him," Missy said. "I'll be paying cash." She turned to the officers. "I hope my husband wasn't too much of a bother. I got him out of the institution in Appleton to visit our daughter." She looked Rubadue in the eye and said disgustedly, "Aliens, for God's sake. The man failed at everything he ever tried to do, so I guess he had no choice but to escape to something where no earthly measurement is possible."

The wrecker driver came back. "Boss says we're good to go."

"Permissible that I ride with you?" the woman asked.

"Yes, ma'am. Hop on up while I get your Caddy on the flatbed. It won't take long."

"Do I need to make a report or something?" she asked the conservation officers.

"Call your insurance company right away," Rubadue said. "We'll make out an accident report."

"You can do that . . . like *real* police?"

"Yes, ma'am," Rubadue said. "Just like real police, we get fully certified from a book-learnin' school and all."

"How unexpectedly fascinating," the woman said and climbed into the cab of the wrecker.

Report done and wrecker gone, the officers got back into the patrol truck, and Blossom shrugged and said, "Laws of physics."

"Or fruits and nuts," Rubadue said. "Sometimes it's hard to differentiate."

Informant

Paul Rajala liked working with his sergeant even when Sergeant Delain Max whined all day about the poor condition of the county roads or Rajala's driving ("Stop! Back up! You missed a rock!"). Max also asked a million weird theoretical questions about his subordinate's decision making; it was almost as if the sergeant wanted to create as much tension as possible to see how he'd handle it. So far, he had done fine, but today was another day, and his supervisor was uncharacteristically quiet as he picked him up at the Michigan State Police Office in Stephenson.

"We have us a plan today, Officer Rajala?" the sergeant asked even before he was belted into the truck. And when he spoke again he said, "We have to make a quick stop at a house down by the dam."

Rajala glanced at his sergeant, who remained mute until they rolled over the bridge below the dam. "Keep going," Max said, "it's the purple house on the left."

Rajala had seen the house before, wondered what sort of weirdo would choose to live in a purple house. "Pull into the driveway?"

"No. Go down one block to the first road and turn left. Right away on the left again, there's a grassy lane behind the house where we can park the truck."

Rajala did as he was instructed, parked in a grove of red maples, and looked at his sergeant. "This okay?"

"Turn off the engine, go up to the back door, and knock. This place belongs to Telford Kinlaw, our informant. I've made countless cases with his help, not to mention those I passed to Wild Life Resources Protection. They made three humdingers with info old Telford laid on us."

"He's *your* informant. Why would he talk to me?"

"He talks to the badge, not the man."

Rajala got out of the truck, and his sergeant said, "Piece of advice. We get hired in great part for our ability to talk and listen to anyone."

"What's your point?"

"He don't bite. See youse when you're done."

He don't bite? Delain Max was pretty damn odd in his own right.

The person who came to the door was tall, at least six-four, skinny as an Ethiopian vegan. His hair was golden blond with long curly tresses. He wore a shimmery purple kimono and gold three-inch satin mules. His fingernails were long and black and if they had been clipped somewhat differently would qualify as illegal double-edged knives.

"I'm Officer Rajala. Sergeant Max told me you wanted to talk to one of us."

"Kinlaw," the man said, extending a hand and commencing to crush Rajala's with a viselike grip that made him want to pull away and shake off the pain.

"Sorry," the man said. "Whenever I meet a new officer, I find it useful to establish some testosteronal credentials at the outset. And with it comes a speech, which goes like this: I'm not queer, not in the slightest, never have been, never will be. I just like to dress this way and always have, all the way back to high school. You have a problem with that, Officer Rajala?"

"No problem, no sir," Rajala said, thinking, BIG problem; this guy's fucking bonkers. Is this one of Sarge's sick jokes, or what?

"Good," Kinlaw said. "We have the basics of an understanding, and now we can proceed like any normal couple, right, sweetie?"

Couple? Sweetie? Did he just say that? Sweet Jesus, what the hell has Sarge gotten me into? Rajala simply nodded.

Kinlaw led him through a frilly, flowery house cluttered with bric-a-brac and gaudy and astonishingly realistic needlepoint animal pictures on the walls. That and one of two half-human, half-horses mouth kissing. At least there was a gun rack, filled with an array of weapons and two black gun safes. "You hunt?" Rajala ventured.

"Just shoot," the man said, walking him into a kitchen walled in the most beautiful pine Rajala had ever seen. "No heart for killing. Alabama pine," the man added. "I think those old boys down in those parts think it's junk wood, but the color about makes me swoon. You agree, hon?"

Hon? Swoon? Was this shit never going to end? "What about the door jambs?"

"Those are striped maple. Grows up by Lake Superior. Virtually unknown these days, but it's hard wood. I like hard wood. How about you?"

Oh, shit. "I'm no carpenter," Rajala said quickly to regain his composure, which was fast slipping away.

Kinlaw did a slow vamp. "You like?"

"Uh, great pine," Rajala said.

"You big green warrior, are you blushing? I have fresh-baked scones, from-scratch razzie or orange-cranny. What's your pleasure?" the man asked.

"Neither."

Kinlaw put his big hands on his hips and glowered. "Listen, mister, nobody comes into this girl's house and goes away without repast. It's always been a human custom to feed visitors, you savage, a matter of hospitality, an extension of the Rule of the Good Samaritan."

"Orange whatchamacallit," Rajala managed to mutter, trying to ignore the other man's words and tone.

"Orange-cranberry scones, hon. Take a seat. Caf or decaf?"

"Caf, please." Or an ejection seat.

"Black or cream?"

"Black," Rajala said. "No sugar." His heart was racing, sweat pooling under his arms. He wanted this shit over so he could strangle his goddamn sergeant.

Kinlaw arched an eyebrow. "Okay, sweetie, you need to take a nice deep breath and calm down. I can tell you're really a sugar-and-cream fella, but types like you come in here, see me, my place, my fine things—and they *are* fine, are they not?" The man stuck a shaved leg through the split in his robe and wiggled his foot. "You get to thinking . . . and it scares you, and you default to your basic masculine black, no sugar, no milk."

"Black coffee," Rajala repeated. "No cream, no sugar."

His host poured coffee into tiny cups and sat down across from him. "You poor man, so insecure in your own gender and sexuality. Sister, do you ever feel confused and troubled?"

Sister? Rajala's voice had fled to parts unknown.

"Delain loves my razzie scones. That's the one on the left. And he also likes his coffee black. Shall we proceed?" Kinlaw picked up a cigarette pack, took one out with a long fingernail, pushed into a long pink holder and slid a golden Zippo across the table. "Light my fire, babe?"

Goddamn that Delain. Rajala fumbled with the lighter, but Kinlaw reached over and steadied his wrist as the flame took hold. "Slow is best in all intimate human interactions, honey."

Rajala could manage only a sort of nod.

Kinlaw exhaled smoke. "Do you think I'm a joke?"

"No, sir, no joke." Maniac, maybe; joke, no. Except to Sergeant Asshole Max.

"Of course you do, you prevaricating hunk. Admit it or get out."

"The concept of joke has not once entered my head, sir."

"Telford, please."

Rajala nodded.

Telford Kinlaw smiled. "Good, I'm not a joke." The man looked to Rajala to be on the verge of tears. "Nobody wants to be a joke. It hurts."

"Yes, I agree; no sir, not a joke, nobody wants that."

"Try the coffee."

It was delicious.

"Your sergeant and I go way back. I thought at first he was the thuggish warrior type, you know, All-American jockstrappado, but it has developed that he's a thoughtful, lovely, open-minded, and sensitive gentleman, a truly beautiful man."

Sergeant Delain Max?

"Yes, love, your delicious supervisor."

Rajala had to press his boots to the floor to keep from running out, but he knew enough to let the informant think he was in control. *The sergeant is delicious? Disgusting!*

The conservation officer sampled the scone. *Wow.*

"You approve?" Kinlaw asked.

"Yes, ma . . . sir."

"Please do call me ma'am. I won't be at all insulted," Kinlaw said. "Humor me."

"Not sure I can do that, sir . . . ma'am." *Did I just call this freak ma'am? Somebody please shoot me, but not until I shoot Delain.*

"That wasn't so difficult, was it?"

"No . . . uh," Rajala said, sensing another blush rising.

"Ma'am," Kinlaw said.

"No, ma'am, it wasn't so difficult, ma'am." *Kill me now, whoever's in charge.*

"And you are Paul. Delain already told me."

Already told him? Damn setup. That bastard. "Yes, ma'am, Paul."

"May I call you Paulie?"

"My name is Paul."

"Yes, I know, properly biblical and all that silly soup, but Paulie is more personal and informal, more endearing."

"I guess Paulie's fine."

"Um," Kinlaw purred. "Do you know Chigger Selberg?"

"Drives snowplow for the county? Yeah."

"That's our Chigger, love, a naughty boy since our days in high school, and the year of our matriculation I shall not specify, for I find it quite depressing."

"What about Chigger?"

"Married a female whose papa owns a sheep farm off the grade down near the Brule. I have it from an unimpeachable source that Papa-in-law has our dear Chigger over for wolf shooting in a friendly competition, with substantial wagers."

"They bury the carcasses?"

"Burn them once a month and settle the tally on the spot. Can you imagine their audacity, Paulie, killing our gorgeous and deliciously glamorous wolves for mere lucre?"

"No, ma'am, I mean, yes, ma'am." *What the hell is lucre?* "You and I both know how some people can be."

Telford Kinlaw giggled. "Indeed we do, sweetie."

"What's the father-in-law's name?"

Kinlaw told him and added, "I believe you fellas have had previous business with the ape."

"We know him," Rajala said. The wolf thing was right down the man's crooked line. "You wouldn't happen to know the burn date?"

Kinlaw raised an eyebrow.

"Ma'am?" the officer said.

"I'm led to believe it happens always at 7:00 p.m. on the last Friday night of the month, which gives Chigger time to get home from the far reaches of the county, if that's where he's been working."

"On his father-in-law's property?"

"Yes, love, on the northernmost corner of his northernmost forty. A lovely friend of mine owns the adjacent eighty and would without doubt grant permission for you girls to enter."

Rajala tried to keep his hand from shaking as he wrapped the sarge's scones in a pink napkin. *Permission for you girls to enter? Jesus, God.*

Kinlaw escorted him to the back door. "Don't be a stranger, Paulie love, and tell dear, sweet Delain this one's a freebie. I am most pleased to have met you, Paulie. Please drop in anytime so I can show you more of my wood."

Rajala stalked angrily to the truck, jerked open his door, and threw the wrapped scones at his sergeant, bouncing the package off his stomach.

"Whoa, Officer Rajala, whoa!" Sergeant Max shouted, holding up his arms to defend himself.

"You fucker!"

"Calm down; you get something?"

"Other than totally fucking creeped out and embarrassed? Yes, and he says it's a freebie, whatever the fuck *that* means dear . . . sweet . . . Delain."

"Good," the sergeant said. "Every time I recommend an informant for RAP money, it seems to take forever for a check to come through." RAP stood for Report All Poaching, a state-sponsored, statewide toll-free phone line manned around the clock. Some callers got rewards, usually at the discretion of the officers they had worked with.

Rajala laid out the information and concluded, "But this one sounds too good to be true, and too damn easy."

"Telford only gives us sure things," said Sergeant Max. "It's a matter of pride about his reputation, his trademark, you might say."

Rajala said incredulously, "What reputation? That he swishes around like some wannabe Lady Gaga?"

Delain Max said only, "Stefani Joanne Angelina Germanotta is fine. Relax, girlie. Time will come when you'll be glad for coffee with Telford, just you girls jabbering your foolish little heads off."

"Who the hell is Stefani Joanne whatever?"

"Lady Gaga. Don't you pay attention to current events?"

"I hate all that showbiz shit."

"Keep that to yourself. It would break Telford's vulnerable heart and cause the department to lose the state's most productive longtime snitch."

"The state's?"

"Multiple agencies. You jealous?"

Rajala could only stare.

"Can you imagine the headlines that will come from this wolf case?"

"Our bust?"

"Hell no, don't be so shortsighted and selfish. We give this to Unit Twenty-five's secret squirrels, let them do the honors, and we'll assist."

Rajala sat behind his steering wheel. "You set me up, eh?"

"Nonsense, sweetie," the sergeant said. "Want a pinch of my scone?" he asked.

Bite me, Rajala started to say, but thought twice and instead said, "No, thank you, Sergeant."

"See?" Delain Max said with a mouthful. "Old Telford's already had a fine effect on you. Man, these scones are *scrumptious!*"

Paul Rajala cringed.

Checkmate

Penny Lositch called Wintermute at home last night. "Edwy," she said in her needy-reedy voice, and right to the point, "Old Man Cramp is supposed to see me weekly, and it's been more than five months since I've heard from that damn reprobate."

Lositch was a parole officer not known for efficiency, effectiveness, or compassion, a floater who sucked the state tit and performed a nominal job at a barely tolerable level and should have been canned years before. People in the cop community called her Penny the Loafer.

"You could check on him," Conservation Officer Edwy Wintermute suggested.

"Don't think I haven't tried. Phone messages go unreturned, e-mails kick back, snail mail is undeliverable, his house stands empty, I'm told, and none of his crooked relatives claim to know where he is."

"Maybe he moved out of state."

"Maybe pigs will fly. Listen, Edwy, we have him on another warrant, sex with a minor, his granddaughter. He won't be getting out this time around."

"Charges alleged or filed?"

"We're on the same side, Edwy; don't go weasel talk on me. You've arrested him more than anyone."

"I'll try to take a look tomorrow. You want me to bring him in?"

"I'd prefer that you shoot that giant drain on my life so I could be done with him once and for all, but use your own judgment," the PO said, ending the conversation. Translation: The man is in violation of his parole, and the rest of you have to figure out what to do and leave me alone.

Wintermute had spent ten years as a game warden, the whole time in Mackinac County, living in Gould City. The man in question, Jacques Cramp, was a lifelong fish and game violator, and over the years he had been frequently accused of incest and various sex crimes, none of which he'd ever actually been charged with, much less been found guilty of.

It seemed to Edwy Wintermute that in this state, once you were down, there were unseen forces that worked together to keep you there and made it impossible for you to climb back to any level of normalcy, never mind respectability. It was an aspect of the state that Wintermute loathed and lamented. In her experience, a lot of the complaints about Cramp came from his competitors, most notably the wing nuts and jamoke violators over in the Garden Peninsula.

Sure enough, Cramp's house looked empty. Wintermute called the county sheriff in St. Ignace to find out if new charges had been filed against the old man. Answer: verbal hand thumps to the bureaucratic forehead, followed by lugubrious silence. Translation: Charges had never been made out or had slipped into the proverbial red tape crack. Or it was all bullshit, which was her guess.

Jacques Cramp had bounced around the county for decades (not to mention parts of Chippewa, Schoolcraft, Luce, and Alger), but the one place he seemed to gravitate toward was a remote camp in Hulbert Township in Chippewa County, reachable only on unmarked, vague two-tracks that wound through monster cedar swamps, north toward the Tahquamenon River flood plain, roads that were impassable much of the year because of flooding and snowdrifts, or whatever.

Once she'd seen the roads covered with five inches of pure ice, and she had gotten a hundred yards in before sliding into a ditch. Not a big deal. By midday the ice melted, and she backed out. There were also deep sugar sand sections to contend with. Years ago Wintermute had hiked in on snowshoes from the East West Road, four miles up the railroad grade and southwest through the swamps to intersect a long finger of hard ground, where the old man's camp sat, built into the side of the ridge, isolated and largely hidden, like a small wilderness keep. Today Wintermute decided to chance the drive and got to the cable gate with minimal trouble (only two blowdowns and one boulder to be evaded).

She left her truck at the cable and walked a quarter mile back to the camp and three hundred yards in found the old man turtling along the two-track, both of his pant legs folded behind what remained of his legs and pinned in place. He was headed the same direction she was.

Wintermute said, "That looks like mighty slow going, Cramp."

The old man stopped but didn't look up. "Good joke. Never woulda thunka that one, Edwy," he said with a series of grunts and gasps.

"Penny misses your weekly *tête-à-têtes*."

"Why God make miserable coose like dat?"

"Variety maybe. You seem to be short some appendages since last we met, Jacques."

"Da sweet blood finally got to 'em. VA over Iron Mountain took 'em off. I told dat PO bitch I had surgery comin' up, and VA even sent letter. She said, yada-yada, yada-yada, sucks to be you."

"You've been in Iron Mountain five *months?*"

"Dere t'ree and some, rest of time seein' old chums. Ya know, like R&R, eh?"

"Like a snowbird to Florida," Wintermute said. "Lositch says there're charges pending, sex with a minor, namely your granddaughter."

Cramp said, "Hell wit dat bullpuckey. You seen *paper* wit charges?" Only then did he finally look up at her.

"No."

"Won't neither. Word out Lositch got her tight ass in sling. I hear she put on warnin' by state for not doin' her job, eh? Way I see it, I disappear, she does, too."

Cramp stopped, twisted to his butt, took a pack of Camels out of his waist pack, and lit one after offering the pack to Wintermute, who accepted and sat down cross-legged, facing him. There was standing swamp water not four feet away, a carpet of Indian sweet grass between them and the water. The ground smelled vaguely of vanilla.

Normally, Wintermute didn't smoke, but today she sensed something momentous in the air and decided to partake. His violating ways aside, she'd always been oddly fond of Jacques Cramp, who never made excuses and always owned up to his faults and crimes once captured.

The two of them sat smoking mindlessly, exhaling, and watching blue tendrils hang in the summer morning air. "Your family know you're out here?" she finally asked.

Cramp showed the game warden his callused hands, which looked like leather baseball gloves. "Pal dropped me nort' of town, and I come up fum dere."

"Crawled?"

"The hull way on old tote roads. She weren't too bad, hey. I seen bugs lots worse for sure, eh."

She calculated the crawl had been twelve to fifteen miles. "Long way," Wintermute said.

"Made it is da point; rest is just jaw-chew."

True enough. "Now what?"

"Get camp, settle in, live high on hog," the old man said, laughing and gasping for air.

Wintermute laughed with him. The old man had always treated her with respect, as if they were the friendly opposition to be outsmarted. "Your camp provisioned?" she asked him.

"Got all I need," the man said, flipping Wintermute a key. "Do me favor? Scoot on up dere, open 'er up, eh?"

"I could carry you," Wintermute said. "Fireman's carry."

"Come dis far on my own, reckon I can finish 'er dat way."

She had no rejoinder and walked to the camp to open the door. Two floors, eighteen by twenty feet, kitchen and larder in front of the ground floor area. She opened cabinets and found nothing, which led to a heart-sinking realization as she heard a single gunshot, ran outside, and saw the old man on his back, not fifty yards from the cabin. He had scratched "thanks" in dirt he had smoothed. He was shirtless, ribs protruding, his shirt tossed up on a raspberry bush laden with ripening fruit. A second note in the dirt read, "My PO wunt see me."

Wintermute thought she understood, and called Lositch, who answered with an irritable, "What is it?"

"No sign of Cramp. I've exhausted all my sources. I think he's disappeared."

"Fuck he has!" Lositch swore and cut the connection.

Wintermute used her boot and a leafy branch to erase the man's "Thanks," picked up their cigarette butts, and carefully put the wiped key into his shirt pocket, where she found a note like the one on the ground. "My PO refewds see me."

Wolves and coyotes would make short work of the old man's body, spread the bones around. Cramp would truly disappear, but the shirt would be found, leaving a circumstantial mess.

The CO took a final look at the old man and his shirt and hiked back to her truck. Some violators weren't all bad, or even bad all the time. And some presumed good guys weren't good at all. Cramp had always been a great violator because he worked alone and planned meticulously, even his final act, it seemed. Wintermute admired the sheer audacity and remembered what some Hollywood star was supposed to have said, that revenge was a dish best served cold. She hoped Lositch would find hell.

Song in the Woods

In two years as a tribal cop on the Keweenaw Bay Reservation in Baraga, three years as a Michigan state trooper, and the last fourteen as a conservation officer in counties below and above the bridge, CO Foresta Quinn had never seen so much debris from a two-vehicle crash, never imagined there could be so damn many pieces, and wondered if manufacturers were doing something differently and hiding it from consumers. It wouldn't surprise her. Little did anymore.

First on scene, she called Central, the multicounty dispatcher who covered city cops, county sheriffs, conservation officers, and state police for Mackinac, Chippewa, and Luce Counties. Quinn asked for assistance with victims and traffic control. She used her own truck to block the westbound lane, then asked a civilian to temporarily signal vehicles to turn around, go back up the hill to Epoufette, and detour north and west through Rexton on the Hiawatha Trail.

Quinn went first to the eighteen-wheeler. The log hauler had been filled with two pups of ten-foot pulp logs, now spread all over the highway like squat pick-up sticks. She found the driver still seat-belted into his cab, multiple facial cuts, but nothing serious or life threatening. Still, he wasn't conscious, and that wasn't good. His pulse felt all right. He could hold for now. She glanced at the red oval Peterbilt logo gleaming on the ground, which she had first thought was blood.

The conservation officer looked for a second vehicle and finally got her mind to reconstruct the remains of what appeared to be a small foreign-model pickup. She used her imagination to guess where the pickup cab might lie in the debris field, went to it, and there found a body still pinned inside. She stretched her arm as far as it would go and got two fingers on the neck, but there was no pulse. A troop came up behind her. "What we got?"

"This one's gone. Rig driver's out cold but alive," Foresta Quinn said as a large houndy dog went to the wreck, sniffed loudly at the body she'd just examined, whined ruefully, and limped across US 2, holding up a bloody front leg. The dog's hindquarters were smeared in blood. The troop was seeing to the truck driver, EMTs from Naubinway were arriving, and a Mackinac County deputy and another troop were turning traffic back in both directions. Quinn saw the dog disappear into a copse of aspens to the north and made a decision. She told the EMTs she was stepping away and jogged after the animal, following a faint blood trail, which she eventually lost in dense ferns. She stopped to listen. In the woods your nose and ears were often better than your eyes.

A voice sang, "I thank God for this amazing day."

The voice was sweet and high, soft as warm honey, and Quinn felt drawn to it, thoughts of the dog momentarily gone. The singing continued, "For the leaping greenly spirit of trees."

Foresta stopped in a small clearing, the floor blanketed with forget-me-nots, and the voice went on, "And a true blue dream of sky, for everything which is natural, which is infinite, which is yes."

The conservation officer saw a woman ahead and approached her. The dog was approaching, too, whimpering ever so softly, and Quinn saw the woman reach out to the animal and caress its forehead and ears. The dog settled down by the woman's leg as she suddenly looked over at Quinn, smiled warmly, and sang, "Some say they're going to a place called glory, and I ain't saying it ain't a fact." The woman closed her eyes and eased the dog into her lap and sang in almost a hoarse whisper, "But we been told we're on the road to Purgatory, and we don't like the sound of *that*."

The woman hummed something Quinn couldn't make out and looked over at her. "We're okay, hon. She made it to me in time, and thank you ever so much." With that, the woman slowly lay back, and the conservation officer moved quickly to her but found only the body of the brown dog. She rubbed her eyes, feeling like she wanted to cry, or maybe to laugh, or to applaud. She knew she'd seen and been part of something special and had no idea what or why.

She guessed she'd never know, and she knew that was often the way among people who dealt firsthand with life and death. Sometimes in the woods in this job you saw things, and there was no explanation. None.

Foresta Quinn took the dead dog into her arms, cradled it, and made her way back to the highway. EMTs had just pulled a woman's body from the wreck and had her on a gurney, and Quinn looked, blinked hard, and lost her voice.

A sobbing man came up to her. "My mom and that damn mutt were inseparable. They were always together, everywhere."

Foresta Quinn couldn't look at the man, mumbled only, "They still are," gently placed the departed animal in his arms, and walked away in tears.

Airzilla

Conservation officers around the state called the man Buck Rogers, but his real name was Ralph Haliday, and he had flown three combat tours in Vietnam and since 1970 piloted for the Department of Natural Resources. Haliday had innovated and perfected tactical flight techniques for law enforcement that had been adopted by states all around the country, but his accomplishments and competence aside, rumors were flying around that all CO pilots would soon lose their flight duties and become full-time ground pounders. There were numerous quiet bets, some of them substantial, that Buck Rogers would retire rather than be relegated to mere truck-and-foot patrols.

Elliot Rose, twenty-seven, with less than three years on the job, had no bets or opinions on Haliday and had never met the man, but this would change today. Rose's sergeant had pressured him into flying as Haliday's airborne spotter. "Easiest job ever. Old Buck can see deer turds from five thousand feet and tell you when they got dropped. Just sit back and enjoy the ride and the scenery."

Elliot Rose had been disturbed his entire life by the prospect of flight. He'd flown, of course, but only when there were no other options. Now, *this* was one of those times. He'd avoided spotter duty for three years, but no more. Looking at the small, single-engine plane inside the hangar at the Escanaba airport, Rose felt his stomach roll. Some smartass had painted *Airzilla* in gold script on the side of the plane.

"You Rose?" a gravelly voice asked from the shadows.

"Yessir," Rose answered automatically.

"I ain't no goddamn sir," a rotund, red-faced, gray-haired man snapped at him. "I'm Haliday, an officer just like you."

"Yessir, I mean . . . I know."

"Afraid to fly, Rose?"

"No, I just don't care much for it."

"Fair enough," Haliday said. "I like mitigated candor. So why'd they pick you?"

"Sergeant Brown thought I should see night ops from topside."

Haliday grinned and nodded enthusiastically. "Cool; this will be a memorable night, Rose. First time always is. Ain't a puker, are ya?"

"Not on boats anyway."

"Boats ain't birds. Your sarge go over the tactical plan with you?"

"Five trucks, ten officers. South and east Marquette Counties, east Delta, west Schoolcraft, finishing down in the Garden."

Haliday chuckled. "Finishing. I like that. You know those douchebags down to the Garden, the DeRoche brothers?"

"Know *of* them. I've done some fish patrols down there."

"Open water or ice?"

"Both."

Haliday smiled. "I always save my A game for the Garden clowns," the pilot said and began walking around the plane, looking at it, gently touching it in places, almost like a lover's gentle caress, like the damn thing was a living creature, a favored pet, or something. Rose found it creepy and looked away.

"Got your parachute?" Haliday mumbled over his shoulder.

"No," Rose said. "Why?"

"Funnin' ya, Rosey," Haliday said and handed him a webbed harness of some kind. "You don't need no damn chute with Buck Rogers and *Airzilla,* son. I always land what I take off. Go ahead and put on your harness and climb in first. You'll be right behind me. You get the big windows, which we'll leave open for the duration."

"What's the harness for?" Rose asked.

"Egress infrastructure," the pilot said, pushing him up. "Haul your butt up there, Rose, and remember, in the sad and improbable unlikelihood we have to get out fast, your port window pops out. Just grab the red strap on top, kick the red mark at the bottom, and out she'll pop, no sweat."

They strapped into their seats, and Haliday started the engine and immediately taxied out of the hangar. "DNR Air One, VFR. Runway, tower?"

"Runway Three Six, DNR One, wind three three zero at six knots, clear to runway."

Haliday raced the plane across the tarmac, and Elliot Rose felt like everything was happening too quickly.

As they neared the runway, Haliday radioed the tower, "DNR Air One approaching runway three six."

"You are cleared for takeoff, DNR Air One. Give 'em hell out there tonight."

"Damn betcha and roger that, tower," Haliday said, then turned onto the runway, lowered the flaps, and slammed the throttle forward.

The power of the little plane's single engine caught Rose by surprise. The plane rolled a short distance and jumped sharply off the runway. Haliday said, "Flaps up, gear up," and banked hard in a climbing turn as he zinged past the tower, saluting as he passed. "Off we go into the wild blue yonder," he added over intercom. "Man, I *love* this shit! Let's rock and roll, Rosey!"

Climbing steadily northward, they leveled off at four thousand feet. The sun was sinking in the west. "Two One Oh One, DNR Air One is airborne, northbound. All you girls ready down there?"

"Air One, we're on stations, DNR Two One Zero One."

Haliday keyed the intercom. "Hey, nav, you got all the call signs?"

No response. "Hey, Rosey, tonight you're my nav, copy?"

"Uh, roger, copy," Rose said. *Nav?*

Haliday laughed out loud, almost gleefully. "Roger? Attaboy, Rosey. Good on ya. Now, let's us go kick some badasses."

They spent two hours over Marquette County and saw nothing suspicious. Rose was amazed by the view, but more by Haliday, who talked patrol trucks down lanes and trails only he seemed to see. It was like he had another dimension of vision from above and the omniscience of God.

Moving south, Haliday radioed Sergeant Brown. "Two One Oh One, we're moving into Delta County. Marquette sure was ugly quiet. Must have us an unprecedented outbreak of lawful behavior."

"Roger, Air One."

"I don't see anything quickly here, we're going to nose on down toward the Garden, copy?"

"Sounds like a plan, Air One."

"Who we got in the Garden, nav?"

"Pedretti and Vairo, Davey and Carter."

Haliday chuckled. "Ass-kickers one and all. This should be a hoot. Where they at now?"

"Pedretti and Vairo are supposed to be by Stable Creek, and Davey and Carter are somewhere up on the grade."

"Okay, switch to our tac freq and tell them to put one vehicle at Hiram Point Trail and the other on County Road 436 below the double ninety-degree turn with County Road 435. No need for them to call in position."

Rose switched to the tactical radio frequency and gave the two teams their orders. It wasn't easy, and for some reason he found himself choking on words, but when he was done, Haliday said over the intercom, "You were born to this shit, Rosey. I ain't seeing diddly squat up this way, so we're gonna press south."

Haliday suddenly began talking in a strange tone of voice. "First time I had to put a bird down was in pilot training at Harlingen, that's down in the unshaved armpit of south Texas. Instructor had a coronary just as our hydraulics went south. Normally, we both woulda punched out, but he passed out, and I couldn't leave that sonovabitch up there alone, and I couldn't get the asshole to talk, so I declared an emergency, swung the bird toward the field, got her lined up on final, and both fucking engines flamed out. It was like flying a flagpole with graham crackers for wings, aerodynamics of a fucking brick, but I damn near got her to the hard top. I landed her in a plowed field filled with rattlesnakes and horned toads. Pilot was already dead, but I didn't know that till we were down. No fire. Mangled the bird some, but I dragged his ass out, and the meat wagons got to us quick-like. No big deal except for him, I guess, but what could be better than dying doing what you love most, next to sex, eh, Rosey?"

Elliot Rose felt his sphincter tighten. "Uh . . . I guess?" *Oh, man. I don't want to hear this shit.*

"My first tour in Vietnam I drove a Misty FAC, a hot and temperamental F-100. Reliable enough, but tricky; had to stay ahead of the power curve with that little fucker. Then some fuckhead Charlie with a popgun put a lucky fricking round through my hydraulic line on final approach. Hell, I even saw the damn tracer. Had to belly that mamu in, but they fixed her up, and she flew again, no big deal."

Just get this night over with and get us back on the ground.

"My second tour I was driving Thuds, Republic F-105s, great old ironhorse birds, well past their prime and not worth shit at high altitude, but great down on the deck. I was out of Takhli in northern Thailand. Got hit by triple A near the old Dien Bien Phu, cripped my ass over into Laos, landed on a road the goddamn NVA and Pathet Lao were building toward a hush-hush CIA station on a mountaintop. The CIA boys and their little Hmongs come to my rescue. That bird got torn up for scrap metal by the CIA and locals. Ass-end of the world, that place. Take my word for it."

Elliot Rose did not want to hear anymore, but Haliday was on a roll. "Aren't we getting close to the Garden?" Rose asked.

"Nah. I just want you to relax, Rosey. My third tour was also in Thuds, Wild Weasel two-seater, our job to go in ahead of the strike force and try to get the bad guys to shoot their SAMs at us so the gaggle could come in when the enemy was out of ammo. Sort of like tonight. We hit us the fucking jackpot one night. Frickin' secondaries all over the frickin' landscape, it looked like the surface of planet Mercury below us, shit cooking off all over the place, flak all around us, and goddamn if a flak fragment didn't hit my GIB smack in his plastic hat, I shit you not. The bird got hit numerous times but kept flying, and I took her back to Laos, hooked up to a tanker, and we siphoned his fuel directly through us until he got us over the Fence, and I put her down hard at Naked Fanny. Two hundred or more holes in the bird, but my Guy In Back got a chunk in the head. He survived, sort of. Lost part of his brain, and now he makes sounds like a baby deer and drools like a Newfy, poor bastard."

Jesus, what is his problem? "Are you trying to tell me we're gonna crash?"

Haliday laughed. "Hell no, Rosey, au fricking contraire, I just want you to understand that hard flyin' and hard landings don't have to be lethal."

"What about the men who were with you?"

"Bullshit. Crashes didn't get them boys; chance got 'em both, bad ticker and a bad-luck frag. You got to listen closer, son."

Rose gulped, couldn't find his voice.

"Here's the deal, Rosey," the pilot said over the intercom. "The DeRoche brothers have a place in the swamp near Three Humps. They run all their illegal shit out of there. Place is on a finger ridge surrounded by a black spruce swamp. I thought we'd drop down, say howdy to those boys, show them we can be real neighborly."

Haliday's voice was calm, rational, matter-of-fact, no big deal, but beneath the chummy facade, Elliot Rose sensed hard steel and pent-up anger.

The DeRoche brothers, Rose knew, were the Garden Peninsula's worst human malfunctions—outlaws whose operations reached to Chicago, Detroit, and even Cleveland. Their specialty was fish and dope with rumors they were also wholesaling illegal venison. The four brothers kept to themselves, had seldom been pinched, and what the department knew of them was largely secondhand and hearsay, neither of much value in getting good warrants, much less making unimpeachable cases for a court.

Dark now, stars above, and the sparsely populated Garden Peninsula was largely black below them, a few lights in Garden Village visible to the west.

"Two One Twenty-one, Air One, blink your headlights once."

Rose saw headlights flash below them.

Haliday radioed, "You know the back road into the DeRoche camp?"

"Negative," CO Tom the Boss Davey radioed back.

"Well, drive about a hundred yards from where you're parked now, and you'll see two giant birch trees in a tag alder line. Pull up to the easternmost tree, and you'll find an old tote road directly behind it. They don't use it much and usually come into their camp off the grade. The tote will take you right into their camp. I walked it last week. Good and hard, no water hazards or sand. Get your two trucks on that road and wait for our signal."

"Air One, what signal?"

"You'll know it when you hear it," Haliday said, chuckling. "I'm guessing thirty minutes from now, give or take."

"Two One Twenty-one copies."

"Two One Thirty-two copies," another voice said. Vairo.

"What's up?" Elliot Rose asked. "I don't remember this being briefed by Sarge."

"This here's our deal, nav, not your damn sarge's—no offense to Brownie."

"How can it be our deal when I don't know what we're doing?"

"Don't be no whinging nitpicker, Rosey. I'm gonna make you almost famous."

"I don't want to be almost famous," the backseater said on the intercom.

"Sure you do. Everybody does."

"Even you?"

"Hell, I'm *already* famous. Listen, as we get close to the camp, I'm gonna turn off our engine and glide down in stealth mode."

Glide? Stealth mode? No engine! Jesus! "Turn off the engine, you mean . . . like turn *off* the fucking motor?"

"Roger. It ain't no big deal."

"You can do this, turn it off and restart it while we're flying?"

"Almost always."

The next thing Elliot Rose knew, they were angled steeply nose down, then suddenly pulling out of the dive, and the engine stopped, leaving them only with the sound of air coming through the open windows. He even heard frogs in the swamp below them, and Haliday was hanging precariously out his window as the aircraft floated along, sinking like a stringless kite.

Rose never saw the pilot light a string of M-80s, but he caught a glimpse of the sputtering fuse as Haliday dropped it. The aircraft continued to float and descend, and Haliday lit and tossed a second string, then turned on the engine, which sputtered momentarily before catching. Haliday took them steeply upward, with Rose looking behind him, watching multiple flashes on the ground where they had passed overhead.

Haliday called on the interphone, "Shacked that shit, eh, Rosey? Now, let's go see if we pissed those suckers off."

"Air One, Two One Twenty-one, those bangs our signal?"

"Negative, wait for the volley."

Rose thought, *Volley? What volley?*

Haliday descended to the treetops, jerking the aircraft muscularly and confidently. "Okay, nav, I think we're lined up pretty good. Two hundred feet off the ground, those assholes won't be able to help themselves."

Rose had no idea what was happening. *At least the crazy bastard has the engine on this time.* Which is when he saw dim orange lights in a building and several blinking white stars and an occasional red or green tracer round. His mind screamed, *Fuck! Kalashnikovs on automatic!*

Haliday said, "Know what them are?"

Before Rose could answer, Davey radioed, "We hear AK-47s on full auto, and we're rolling, Air One."

Haliday laughed. "Ain't you the smart one, Boss. They opened up on us as we flew over. Three weapons, I'd say, could be four."

"Two One Twenty-one and One Thirty-five are going in fast and black."

"Air One copies." Switching to the intercom, Haliday said, "I'm gonna bank hard, come down at them from another angle, switch their attention to us as our colleagues charge."

The pilot immediately descended, the fuselage brushing against tree-tops, shaking the small aircraft.

"Right in their britches this time," Haliday said, laughing.

Bullets came through the fuselage with sharp pings that made Rose flinch and hold his hands over his nuts as the metallic clicks continued. The plane slid left sharply, and Haliday said calmly, "No sweat now, nav, I got this baby. C'mon, baby, c'mon, baby."

The pilot continued to chant as the nose came up, and they got above the treetops. Haliday said over the radio, "Two One Twenty-one, Air One has sustained battle damage, and we have a smidge of a control problem. We're gonna make an emergency let-down on some high-ground humps about a mile northwest of your position."

"Are we *crashing?*" Rose yelled up to the pilot.

"Ain't you been listening?" Haliday yelled back. "Buck Rogers don't crash. What we got us is some teensy control issues, but I got us a dandy alternate picked out. Always remember that, Rosey. In the air or on the ground, with your girlfriend or your squeeze, always have you an alter-nate, every time, every moment, every situation. Pay attention, nav. This here's one you'll be telling your grandkiddies."

"Air One, Two One Thirty-five, say your problem."

"Nav, handle our commo. I'm getting kinda busy up here. C'mon, baby, c'mon, baby, you can do this one last dealie."

One last dealie. Rose felt sick. "Two One Thirty-five, Air One, we've got a situation up here, no details, copy?"

"Good job, Rosey; never let them hear you shit your pants," Haliday said over the intercom.

"Air One, Two One Twenty-one, we have four very, very angry, very surprised, and extremely drunk individuals in custody. County is en route to transport. Say your status and location."

"Uh, still flying," Rose radioed. "I think."

Haliday laughed out loud. "Tell 'em we're on high final and sign off with over."

"Two One Twenty-one, Air One is on high final, over." Rose felt the gear drop down and lock.

Haliday said, "Okay, nav, the moment of truth approaches. See them big-ass trees up ahead?" Haliday wrestled the nose slightly starboard and illuminated the trees with a hand spot as Rose craned to see. "We're gonna set her down right on top. I'm gonna pull the nose up real high and slide through the air bleeding off our airspeed aerodynamically until we lose our lift. Then I'll gently ease the stick forward, and we should plop gently on the treetops like a big yellow bird. You scared?"

Rose tried to say something but only gagged.

Haliday laughed. "Me too, Rosey. Anybody ain't scared in deals like this is psychotic or lives in their mama's basement. Okay, nose coming up, power coming back. Wish us luck, son."

Rose held his breath, tried to remember his Hail Mary, and failed. It felt like his back was pointed at the ground, his face at the stars, and the airframe was creaking and moaning and making all sorts of what he thought were stressful sounds, yet they floated on.

And floated and floated.

Until Haliday said, "Moment of frickin' truth, Rosey. Let's hope I got this right."

The nose dumped forward.

The engine stopped, and the air filled with sounds of metal tearing.

And then it was still, and a whisper breeze was wafting through the windows.

"Keep your headset on, Rosey. You okay?"

Rose opened his eyes. "I think so."

"We're good and secure," Haliday said, making the plane shake to test it. "Let's just sit here a few minutes and let our heart rates normalize. Then

I'll climb out and see where we can get down with our tree penetrators. You ever use one?"

"Never even heard of one," Rose said.

"Piece of cake. Attaches to clips on your harness, two-point connection with one line attached to a pulley secured to a good branch. Release the brake and down you go. Harder you pull, the slower you go. Designed it myself. You get on the ground, release the two connections, and I'll come down behind you."

Rose felt anger welling. "You planned this, you fucking maniac. You *planned* to crash!"

"Don't be a crybaby, Rosey. There ain't been no crash; we just made us an emergency let-down."

"You're a fucking maniac, Haliday!"

"I guess I won't argue a moot point, nav. But I gotta say, you done great! Bean counters in Lansing are dumping us pilots. I got me a job dropping smokejumpers out to Coeur d'Alene. Fuck the bean counters and suit dogs. This pilot is outta here!"

"You could've killed me!"

"You got to get your head out of negative mode, Rosey. It ain't healthy, and you're alive. Look around, man."

Thirty minutes later the two men were on the ground by a two-track, using the 800 MHz radio to bring Two One Twenty-one into position to pick them up. Davey pulled up and looked around. "Where's the crash site?"

"Landing site," Haliday corrected him. "Put your spotlight on the treetops a hundred meters south of us.

Davey lit the top of the trees and whispered, "Holy fuck."

"Get me away from this madman," Elliot Rose said.

Haliday said to Davey, "Ignore the boy. They're always a little unsettled their first time. He ain't got a scratch."

The two patrol trucks drove back to the DNR office in Escanaba, where other officers gathered to await their return. Local radio was already reporting a DNR raid that captured four major poachers with four automatic AK-47s, seventy illegal deer, hundreds of pounds of dope, and other contraband—and the raid resulted in a DNR aircraft sitting atop a grove of trees near the site of the raid. "No word from the state yet on what happened with that—or who's gonna fly the plane off the trees," the local reporter quipped.

Elliot Rose looked at Buck Rogers and made a fist.

Haliday grinned. "Go ahead, kid, you get one free shot. But remember this: You punch me now, you lose the glory that goes with this kind of close call. It's your choice."

Rose exhaled, unclenched his fist, and extended his hand. "Good luck out west, you maniac."

The Dry Spell

Last Independence Day, Lurleen Turco had arrested mental midget Bobo Kokko with 20.4 ounces of skunk weed and fifty-three corncob pipes. Despite all the evidence, Kokko's slimebag lawyer from Oscoda got him released on his own recognizance, and he was free, the trial having been pushed back three times, the last rescheduling set for this fall.

Even with the trial hanging over Kokko, a good tip suggested that the dickhead would be at something called Fender Camp in southwest Alger County. Word to CO Turco was that he was gathering another load of dope, this one grown mostly by local folks, down in the Garden Peninsula.

The tip came from Rocky Tidd, who sold Indian sweet grass to tourists, many of them now stopping to ask if sweet grass was a (wink) euphemism for medical marijuana. Kokko was among the fool callers. He had shown up high and ranting he'd "buy every fucking pound of the good shit" Tidd had. Rocky had to explain to the lunkhead that "sweet grass" wasn't what Kokko wanted, and somehow the dumbass had let drop he was working on "like, a massively massive score at Fender Camp in Alger." What a tool.

Rocky wasn't the straightest arrow in the quiver, or the smartest, but he was mostly honest, and he was clean. CO Turco called the county drug team with the tip, but they said they had something big going on and asked her to handle it. She had agreed, even though she loathed drug cases and felt they were outside what a true a game warden's purview ought to be.

On the other hand, her lack of a personal life was such that more work actually sounded good. It beat the hell out of sitting alone in her house watching fricking reality shows. Twice divorced, she had dated, but she had never been without sex so long, in this instance 388 days and counting. It had gotten so bad that she had to stop herself from trying to size up every stranger she met for his quickie potential.

The array of reasons her dates didn't make love to her begged credulity, and someday she assumed she'd laugh about it, but right now being perpetually horny nearly all the time was not what she'd call fun.

One of her "suitors" always placed two couch pillows over his crotch protectively like the Chinese Great Wall designed to keep invading barbarians out of the middle kingdom. He announced to her that he believed sex was bad for society. She'd countered with, "Syllogistically, no sex, no people; therefore, no society."

He had countered lamely, "You know what I mean." But she didn't, not in the least.

The next would-be paramour had been a room-stopping handsome Mormon, who told her sex with her before marriage would consign his soul to the outer ring of darkness, which she guessed by his tone was a nasty place to be. "Men who make love with me tell me it's heavenly," she tried to reason with him.

"They're not Mormon," he shot back.

No argument there.

One of the strangest ones was a recovering sex addict, and she distinctly remembered upon hearing his confession, "Thank God, finally!" But he'd been three years without sex and didn't want to "fall off his bed of nails. Otherwise I'd have to go back to scratch one," he told her, explaining, "You have to understand, I was a total satire."

Obviously, Mr. Scratch One/Total Satire was a literate recovering sex addict. Even so, missing out on that one probably hurt the most, as much from pure curiosity as sexual need.

More work would be just fine, even if she donated time to the state, which had no budget for overtime. Boyfriends came and went. Only the job persevered.

She telephoned CO Jock Gillian in Munising. "You know the Fender Camp?"

"Ya, it's the one owned by family claims they're related to the guitar people, but that may or may not be bull-pucky. You know how camp owners love to bullshit. Something up?"

"Could be. People who own it are named Fender?"

"Nope, Gavrilaitis, Greeks or Turks, I tend ta get those two mixed up. The story I heard was that old man Gavrilaitis worked for Dow Chemical and sold car lacquers to Fender for their gitfiddles. The old man got rich and retired. One that owns the camp now is a grandson, I think, lives out to Rancho Somethingorother in California, spends May through October at the camp. Word is he has a full electronic recording studio out there."

"You been out there on business?"

"Nah, all I know is local gab. Not sure the Fender Camp bunch fishes, hunts, or even walks in the woods. Why?"

"Musicians in and out of there, West Coastals and drug suckers and the like?"

"I'd guess, but that's all it would be is conjecture and bar talk," Gillian said. "I once heard old man Gavrilaitis owned the world's largest collection of Gibson Les Paul guitars with Seth Lover humbuckers."

"Can that be parsed into English?" she asked.

"You don't pick?"

"Only my nose and the occasional nag," she said.

"I played some. Humbucker's a sweet gizmo takes the hum and white noise shit out, you know, pulls the buzz and interference out of the background. Fenders and Gibsons are real cool."

Gillian had a Dubya/Alfred E. Newman look to him, with massive elephant ears, not the sort of person whose countenance sang out musician, never mind guitarist. "Bump you later, Jack."

Rocky Tidd said he heard from Kokko there was to be some sort of big get-together at Fender Camp over the Fourth and that the gathering was "primo for dumping his shit."

The night of July 3, Turco located Fender Camp and walked the perimeter as a steady flow of vehicles drove down the ungated two-track. No wire fencing, only a few no trespassing signs, and the absence of a gate suggested the owner wasn't over-amped with security concerns. Not that getting into the camp would be a piece of cake. It wouldn't. She couldn't charge in on the say-so of a single informant, and she had no evidence as probable cause other than Kokko's track record and Tidd's tip. She had pretty much concluded about the best she could do was show up tomorrow with a smile, say howdy, and look around. It was lame, but it was all she could come up with.

Shooting erupted suddenly, so many rounds that she lost count, but she could plainly hear bullets coming down through the trees and leaves as their upward trajectories lost momentum, and gravity pulled them home. *Good grief!* Every day some segment of the American public becomes more and more like the damn PLO, whipping out their AKs and cranking rounds straight up in celebration or sadness, and never mind the unlucky schnooks who happened to be standing under a plummeting spent round.

Shooting provided reasonable cause. Turco went back to her truck and drove out to the camp road, where she got wedged between pickup trucks, PT Cruisers, four-wheelers, and motorcycles, all of them raising a humongous cloud of fine reddish gray dust. When they finally entered an open area, she could see even through the dust a field filled with haphazardly parked vehicles of every imaginable description and make.

As she parked and got out, more rounds went off, and one thunked down on the roof of a new VW bug beside her. Turco got down on her hands and knees and felt around until she found the spent round, which she stashed in her pants pocket.

Standing up, she blinked wildly as she found herself trapped in a surging crowd of Elvis Presleys, all in checkered leather suits and shiny boots, all streaming toward a huge circus tent, which suddenly illuminated with floodlights and a sign that proclaimed, UPPER GREAT LAKES REGION TOP 100 COMPETITION: LOYAL, PRAYERFUL ORDER OF GOD'S LIFTING UP PROFESSIONAL FEMALE, MALE, AND TRANSGENDER ELVIS IMPERSONATORS.

"Oh my," she said out loud. She couldn't decide whether to laugh or scream, but one thing was clear, that among so many oddly garbed folk, she stood out. If she walked into the big top, Kokko would surely see her and split. Better to scour the parking lot, find the asshole's cherry red Chevy pickup, and surveil it until he showed. For the ideal pinch she needed to see him deal drugs, but this was a detail that would sort out or not. Such were the vagaries of law enforcement.

Multiple bands were warming up in the humid night. She could hear squeals and screeching amps, drum thumps rattling like distant heartbeats, chords being strummed. She always kept several changes of clothes in her truck for emergencies and was in the process of deciding how to dress (favoring a short white sundress with spaghetti sandals to show off her legs) when someone grabbed her neck with a sleeper hold, and she felt herself tumbling into lalaland, no decisions to be made there, but with all these men there had to be a few straight ones, and maybe going braless would make good bait, yeah, that would work good—if she could get past this asshole who was in the process of assaulting her. Her final thought before sleep was: *This frickin' jerk knows his stuff.*

She awoke in the dark, propped against a tree, her butt on the ground, a pine needle stuck in her buttock. She could hear music thumping somewhere off in the distance, and she had a low-grade headache. A dark figure sat near her. She immediately tried to gain control and mumbled, "Who are you, and where am I, and why am I here, and all that shit?"

"What are you doing in this damn Elvis mob?" a vaguely familiar voice asked.

"Bite me," she said, adding, "Did we have sex?"

The figured laughed. "Charley Vincent," he said, "you hard case *you.* Hell no we didn't have sex. Are you suggesting that's an option, Turco?"

"C.V.?"

Vincent was a detective in the Wildlife Resource Protection Unit, the Department of Natural Resource's undercover investigative branch. "Sex is never an option with you, asshole. The drug team asked me to handle a case."

"Which case?"

"Bobo Kokko, drugs."

"No shit. We're on his case, too. The group here is having a venison roast in honor of Elvis. Guess who's providing the fare?"

"What an idiot," she said and saw by the silhouette that her colleague was in neither civvies nor uniform. "Good God , C.V., is that asshole getup you've got on really necessary?"

"You are obviously unfamiliar with the principles of undercover blending in, ma'am."

"Is that like passing?"

"Pretty much. Listen, Lurleen, anybody not in costume here gets the heave-ho. No costume, no can stay. They're real hard-asses about it."

"Who, Elvis trannies?"

"Don't levy value judgments, Officer Turco. Away from here these are some normal productive folk."

"If you say so," Turco said, her words dripping sarcasm.

"We have to get you made up," the detective said.

"We?"

"Our people, Fish and Wildlife, FBI, Homeland Security, Immigration, BATF—hell, the whole law enforcement mob is here. The feds have information leading them to believe Arab terrorists have infiltrated the Elvisian community."

"Why would they think that?" she asked, and it occurred to her that mob was a good term for the gaggle of law enforcement personnel. What this was going to be, she knew, was a memorable goat rodeo.

"Elvis swap meets. These folks sell guns to each other, *lots* of guns."

She thought for a moment. "Okay, I'm in, but you got to get me into an outfit."

"Other agents may not like this," Vincent said.

"Fuck them, C.V. I'll find Kokko's truck and stay with that."

"He'll be dressed as Elvis," Vincent said.

"No duh. Which flavor?" she said.

"Not sure, ma'am, but thank ya varra, varra much," he said in a crude rendition of Elvis speak.

"You know Kokko's got a court date on last year's drug case?" she asked.

"We're aware."

"Why the hell didn't you tell me about this shit?"

"Need to know," he said. "You know how feds think."

Actually, she didn't. Nor did she want to. What she said was, "Uh-huh, where's my damn costume, C.V.?"

"I'm on it," he said, "ma'am."

"I'll wait right here," she said.

"Thank ya varra, varra much."

As soon as Vincent was gone, she followed him, which wasn't difficult. C.V.'s white leather jumpsuit illuminated like a chemical light stick. Back in the lot, she veered off to find Kokko's truck, and as providence would have it, she bumped into a person in a checked leather jumpsuit who mumbled, "You wan' score weed, blow, speed, pixie dirt?"

What the fuck is pixie dirt? "One-stop shopping, that your spiel?"

"You want to eat it, snort it, or fuck it, I got it for ya, ma'am."

"How much for your best weed?"

"Garden Green's primo with supermax THC, little lady."

"Price?" *Dillweed.*

"Twenty for two lids."

Too weird to be real. She *knew* this voice. "The good shit, right?"

"The best," he said.

"Good, hit me," Turco said, and when Kokko handed her two small bags, she gave him $20 and slapped a cuff on his wrist, grabbed the other, and got that one, too, all before he could even react.

When he did, what he said was, "What this is, *motherfucker?!?*"

"Clean up your vocabulary, son. Our Elvis didn't use that kind of language."

"Ya, what would you fags know about the real Elvis?" he challenged.

"Well, he was heterosexual, unlike you and yours, and he was a person of color."

Kokko tried to pull away. "You bitch, you callin' Elvis a colored boy!"

"No, a person of color. Where's your truck, asshole?"

"Fuck you," Kokko said.

"Easy way or hard way, Bo?" Lurleen Turco asked her prisoner, who stood a foot taller than she.

The man answered with an elbow, which she calmly stepped under as she drove a fist sharply upward into his armpit, which dropped him to his knees, where she struck the heel of her hand against the side of his head and toppled him into the dirt. She hauled him back to his knees. "Glad you chose the easy way, asshole," she told him as he moaned. "Behave or you'll ride the lightning, dude."

"You carry a Tasmanian?" Kokko mumbled.

Moron. "You bet."

"I'm allergic," he said.

"To what?" she asked.

"Life, I guess."

She stifled a laugh. "Take me to your truck."

"Fuck, I'm 'pose to find it in the dark?"

"I have a flashlight, dimwit." She started to walk with him but changed her mind, took him to a tree, undid the cuffs, and redid them with his arms around the trunk. He was too dazed or high or both to resist. "You can stand right there, and we'll let the Elvii tribe sing in the sunrise for you," she said.

"How such a bloated up hillbilly get all that money and poontang?" Kokko asked her. "I ain't never understood *that* shit."

"Ask the people here; I expect they could tell you."

"They ain't normal."

"We are each unique in our maker's eyes," she said.

"What the hell's that 'pose to mean?"

She noticed he was tall and sort of ruggedly handsome in the low light. Until this moment she'd never noticed. "I don't have the slightest idea. You got a wife, Bo?"

"Hell no, nor a girlfriend. I don't like being chained down. Something about me scares women."

"You mean you turn them off."

"Hell, I get some every day," he bragged. "Pound them cooters regularly."

He was totally gross and disgusting. "Yeah, what about *today*?"

"*Ever'* damn day," he bragged.

"Don't bullshit me, Kokko."

"Okay, it's been a while maybe, you know, with all the court shit and such you got me into, Turco."

"You got yourself into it. How long exactly, a week, a month, a year?"

"I ain't been keepin' count," Kokko said.

Lurleen Turco blinked and gasped. God, I can't be this desperate. This is totally sick! I disgust myself.

Detective Vincent intercepted her in the woods. "You get lost?" he asked.

"Momentarily," she said. "Kokko's handcuffed to a tree over that way." She handed the detective the two plastic bags. "I bought these from him. He and the evidence are all yours."

"Where are you going?"

"Away, out, home"

"But it's *your* bust."

"My gift to you. How many people are here?"

"Three hundred, and a hundred impersonators."

"Everybody makes the top one hundred, that the deal?"

"Brilliant marketing, eh? Seriously, where are you going?"

"Home."

"Alone? There'll be a big party later today."

"Count me out."

"You antisocial?"

"Might just be," she admitted, thinking all evidence pointed toward a lot more days in the dry spell.

Over near the big top a voice blared, "All backup bands, ten seconds until the Group Elvis Anthem, say again, ten seconds." Guns began to fire into the air, and Turco ducked instinctively and plodded toward her truck as the crisp morning air flooded with countless electric guitars and drums and three or four hundred voices singing more or less together "Any Way You Want Me." And Lurleen Turco thought, *At least I still have some standards.*

Henry VIII

The day ahead was the kind Amiziah Imus loved best: no complaints to follow up, no warrants to serve, no nothing, just strap his butt into the truck, pick a route, and go see what's happening. And in thirteen years as a conservation officer in Marquette County—the biggest county east of the Mississippi, filled with ne'er-do-wells and violators of every stripe—Imus figured he'd seen it all.

He called in service to Station Twenty in Lansing and to the county. The county dispatcher immediately asked him where he was.

"Leaving my residence. Diorite."

"One One Twenty-two, we've got a traffic situation on County Road 496 and M-28."

"What sort of problem? One One Twenty-two."

"Situation is all we know, deputy requesting assistance from a conservation officer."

"Which end of CR 496, east or west?"

"East," the dispatcher said.

"ETA five minutes." *Now what?*

When Imus reached M-28, he found traffic stopped and backed up to the horizon in both directions. He drove up the shoulder to a Marquette County sheriff's cruiser and parked as a blue goose pulled in behind him. The problem was immediately clear: a black bear of no more than 120 pounds sitting with splayed legs in the westbound lane, sunning himself and enjoying the attention of people with cameras. Not too smart: Unwary bears invariably became deceased bears.

"What's his problem?" Imus asked the dep.

"They teach you guys to talk bear, eh."

Imus immediately concentrated on the animal but saw nothing obvious. "He hurt?"

"He ain't much of a talker," the dep said.

"Sometimes words aren't needed," Imus said.

"Tell me," the deputy said. "I got a wife."

Imus knelt near the bear, careful not to get too close. Bears were quicker and more agile than they appeared to be. "What's your problem, Henry?" No idea why *that* name came to mind or why he'd be thinking of Herman's Hermits and their classic song. He hated Herman's Hermits, the mop-head British twinks.

He went back to the dep. "Get us a couple hundred-yard gap to let the little guy make a move. When he's gone, we can let people go on their way."

"We've already got a lot of pissed off motorists," the troop said.

"Let's deal with what we have to deal with first. They'll get over it."

Imus pulled his shotgun out of its case, unloaded the slugs and buckshot, and replaced the killing ammo with cracker shells. When the traffic was rearranged, he walked over toward the bear and fired a round. The bear pawed listlessly at him. Three more shots earned only an irritated chuff. Imus took off his hat, spread his arms like a scarecrow, and ran yelling at the animal, which hopped off the road but only onto the grass just off the shoulder. Imus drew his .40 caliber Sig Sauer and fired rounds into the dirt on either side of the animal. Nary a flinch. *Shit.*

"Just shoot the sucker," the deputy said. "It ain't like we got all day here."

In thirteen years Imus had been forced to euthanize two problem bears in school zones, and he had trapped and relocated five others, all of which had later been treed and killed by houndsmen. This was his eighth bear, and no way was this little guy going to die. In the past he'd made the mistake of telling people where he released animals. Not this time. He knew this might not be a cause-and-effect deal, but it felt that way. Not this time. "*I'll* take care of it," he told the deputy with a snarl.

"You ain't got the stomach to put it down?" the deputy asked sarcastically. Imus's icy stare shut him up. "Joke, man," the deputy said weakly and turned away.

"Would be easier to shoot the damn beast," a troop argued.

"We are not shooting En-ree," Imus said assertively.

"Who the fuck is En-ree?" the troop asked.

Imus ignored him, watched traffic normalizing into two lanes, and headed for the field office to fetch a culvert trap, which he hooked to his truck. He stopped at Fernie's Pizza and got a half dozen of last night's fare from the morning pitch pile sale, gassed up his truck, and bought a bag of bite-size Baby Ruth candy bars.

The bear was exactly where he had left it, contentedly watching traffic from his roadside vantage. Deps halted traffic again, and Imus backed the trap toward the animal, stopping it twenty feet away on the road shoulder. He lifted and set the rear hatch, connected the bait trigger, and dumped three pizzas inside. When the animal stepped on the trigger, the hatch would slam shut behind it and lock him in.

The bear watched his every move, and when Imus tossed a piece of pizza toward it, the animal stood up, waddled lazily over, and wolfed it down. Imus backed up toward the trap throwing pizza chunks and finally pitched the biggest chunk into the cage, stepped forward, and held out a piece to the bear. When the animal stepped forward, he pitched the piece into the trap, and the bear sailed past him, went to the pizza, and stepped on the trigger. When the door came down, the bear was busy scarfing down pizza, drool cascading from his tan snout.

A TV crew from Channel 6 News had arrived on site and had recorded the whole sequence. When the bear went into the trap and the door came down, onlookers whistled and cheered and whoop-whooped, and drivers honked horns, like Imus had just scored a touchdown. A female reporter came over pointing a boom microphone at him, but he begged off any kind of interview. There was still a traffic hazard, and he needed to get the animal relocated pronto.

"How far you taking him?" the reporter asked.

"Far, far away," he said.

"Second star on the right?" she countered, getting into the spirit.

"Not that close," he said, getting into his truck.

Imus drove back roads all the way to east of Munising, connecting with M-28 south of town, and headed east on the two-lane highway toward the Seney Stretch, debating whether to make the drop north or south of the roadway. When he saw a good road, he went north, crossed Walsh Creek, drove three miles down a beat-up and sandy two-track, past a decaying, abandoned hunting camp, and stopped. He peeled a candy bar and pushed it through the bars to the animal, which inhaled it happily, clacking its teeth for more.

"Okay, En-ree, boy, this here's your new home." Imus put two whole pizzas on the ground thirty feet from the trap, stood on the fender of the trailer, sprung the door, and expected the animal to leap out for the food. But the small bear sat in the cage, tilted its head, and looked up at him. "Bear, you got a screw loose or something? This is world-class blueberry country. The cage ain't got none."

Imus frisbeed more pizza at the pile. The bear yawned, circled, and lay down.

"No nap, En-ree, me-boy," Imus said sharply, as he took out his baton and poked the animal. "Hit the road, fella."

No response. Imus poked again, and the animal reluctantly jumped down and ambled over to the pizza pile.

The officer leaped into the truck and sped away, not stopping for a mile. When he stopped, he looked back. No sign of En-ree. *Good,* relocation complete. He'd noticed that the animal had very little hair on its rump. Disease? Not sure. Henry looked good other than that small flaw.

Ten minutes passed. *No En-ree.* Imus felt good.

• • •

Next morning at the district office near the state prison, El-tee Alvin Crate joined Imus getting coffee. "About ten days ago a man called, said he legally purchased a bear he used to train his hounds, but training was done, and he wanted to give us the animal. I told him since he purchased it legally, he could dispose of it the same way. He wasn't real happy," the lieutenant added.

En-ree had been all over the news and Internet last night. Suddenly the bare spot on the animal's rump made sense. "Cement floor in a cage," Imus said. "I'm guessing your caller dumped the animal west of town. He was totally unafraid of people."

"Where'd you take him?" Crate asked.

Imus took the lieutenant into the conference room to the wall map and showed him.

Crate chuckled. "That ought to do 'er, but why drive so far?"

"Wanted to be sure."

"You know better, Amiziah, there's no certainty in our line of work."

• • •

Three months later El-Tee Crate grabbed Imus as he was coming into the building and steered him back to his office. "Coffee's on my credenza," the lieutenant said.

Highly unusual. Crate was a fine man and a good leader but not the chummy type. "I do something wrong, El-Tee?"

"I just wanted to share something. It seems a troop of Boy Scouts were camping and canoeing at the Little Bear Lake Campground in Pictured Rocks. They were making s'mores over a campfire, and a bear came into camp and ran at them like a big dog, right at them. They panicked and ducked under their canoes. The bear tried to get underneath with them, which totally freaked 'em, adult leaders included. The group's scream was so loud that it brought a Pictured Rocks ranger on the run with a shotgun, and he killed the animal. The scouts and their leaders fell on the dead bear with knives and hatchets and chopped it to pieces. The ranger said it was surreal and savage, like *Lord of the Flies* or something. It made him sick. Next morning he told them to pack up and get the hell out of the campground. His report says the bear's backside was nearly bald."

En-ree, Imus thought, gulping.

The conservation officer went into the conference room and measured the distance from where he'd put the animal to the campground in question. It was less than twenty miles as the crow flies. *Should have put him south of the highway into the Seney Wildlife Refuge. Poor Henry. Not his fault. Mine. Oh-fer-eight. Shit.*

Funnest Man Ever

The scene was grisly, the man sprawled on the railroad track, cut in two. But there wasn't that much blood, all things considered. Conservation Officer Meglizabeth Vesco had gotten a call from the dispatcher and been first on the scene. The vic looked to be in his forties, sort of small, though it was impossible to judge with the two parts about three feet apart. Oddest of all, there was a smile on his face, not a smirk but a full shit-eating grin, a Joker-size smile.

Vesco had been a conservation officer for eleven years and seen death in all its forms: suicides, vehicular accidents (the snowmobiles tended to be the worst—many beheadings), death by violence (guns and knives, even fists, one with a broomstick carved and fire-hardened into a spear). Mostly the rictus of death left a shocked look on the faces of the dead, never a smile or a grin. Not like this.

The accident took place near Menominee, about a mile from any main intersection, and by the time Vesco got down the tracks in her patrol truck, she found a crowd of about thirty gawkers, all intent on seeing the body. She had no idea what sort of psychology attracted the living to the bodies of the dead, but the pull for some folks seemed undeniable.

Vesco checked the mangled corpse and began herding people away to make room for EMTs and the county medical examiner, an old gal named Gwendolyn Goldie Golt, whom everyone called Three G.

The conservation officer stood with the gawkers. The stiff had no identification in his clothing. "Anybody see what happened?" Vesco asked.

"Hitted by a train," a man said. "Thud, then flump!"

"Thud, then flump," several voices said in unison, and Vesco turned and looked at the gawker chorus. There was one group of perhaps seven or eight, and they all had small, distant eyes that sparkled.

"Thud, then flomp?" Vesco said.

"More *FLUMP!* than flomp," a man corrected her.

The small group nodded in unison and shouted, "*FLUMP!*"

Vesco took an involuntary step back and turned to look at the body. The group scream sounded eerily like something of substantial solid mass was striking something of flesh and bone. Onomatopoeic, a voice in her head said, and then she began to have a hard time getting it to go away, an earworm. *Geez, what a pain.* "One of you folks see this . . . flamp?"

"*FLUMP,*" a man said with a hiss. "Not flamp, not flomp, not flimp!"

The group shrieked *FLUMP!* and caught the officer off guard again.

The man standing in front of her was a wide body, with gray hair combed over, thick glasses with black rims, an earring in his right ear (gay or not gay, Vesco couldn't remember), University of Michigan sweatshirt, Detroit Tigers baseball cap, and weird red lips, like pasted-on licorice strips. "What's your name, sir?"

"Not telling the man," he said happily and waggled a forefinger like a metronome.

"I'm not the man, I'm Meg Vesco. You can tell me."

"I don't *think* so," the man said. "*FLUMP!*"

The chorus echoed the *FLUMP,* and Vesco looked at them and began to wonder exactly what the hell she was dealing with. "Anybody here know the man on the tracks?"

"*FLUMP!*" the group cackled in unison.

"The funnest man," a woman said.

"Anything for a grinsky," someone added.

"*FLUMP!*" the chorus said, and they all began to applaud enthusiastically, flippers over their heads like trained circus seals.

Clearly there was something off bubble with these folks, and when Vesco looked more closely, she decided they were all mentally deficient.

Not a diagnosis, but a quick cop-take on reality. Droolers, she thought, and having had this thought she felt ashamed and turned away from the group to face the other onlookers. "Anybody here actually see what happened?" Vesco asked.

A woman with a ring in her lower lip and another in her left nostril pointed at the group. "They were all standing here when I got here, and I was first of all the rest of these dudes," she said, indicating the other people around her.

"They were here?"

"Right where they are now."

"Doing anything particular?"

"Like now, just standing there staring with their mouths hanging open."

Vesco asked, "Do you *know* those people?"

"Don't know them, but by the look of them I'm guessing they come from the House of Joy, back across that field behind us. It's a group home for some kind of short-bus brigade," she said matter-of-factly, pointing.

Vesco turned back to the group. "You folks from the House of Joy?"

"*FLUMP!*" they answered.

A single female voice said, "We stayed right here, Little Joe. Just the way you said."

"And we laughed. This was the funnest," another person said, this from a man of thirty, though the more Vesco looked, the less certain she felt about guesstimating ages.

"You saw the train hit your friend, and it was the funnest?"

No group yell this time. The group nodded solemnly as one.

Unbelievable. "But he's dead."

"Dead as dirt," somebody said.

"Always had a split personality, now his body matches," a woman called out.

"He said he wanted to go play train," a man said, and Vesco homed in on him.

"Your friend wanted to go play train, he *said* that?"

"Joe-Joe said."

"Okay, Joe-Joe wanted to go play train, is that it?"

"No, we all played. *TEAM*."

"*FLUMP!*" the group roared.

"What do you mean, you all played?" she asked, not sure to whom to direct the question. Vesco selected a man at random and pointed at him. "You all played. What's that mean?"

"Joe-Joe got his. We told him."

"Told him, *FLUMP!*" the group called out.

"I don't understand. Joe-Joe was the funnest man?"

"And meanest," a woman said meekly.

"Not nice, not nice," a man said, and began rocking from heel to toe on both feet, staring up at the sky. "He's gone, he's gone, the funnest man is gone."

"*FLUMP!*" the group shouted and began to whoop and whistle and clap their hands.

Vesco said, "You're glad he's dead, is that what you're telling me?"

They all smiled.

Vesco felt queasy. "Was this Joe-Joe's idea, to come over here and do this?"

"Yah," a woman whispered. "Was *his* idea."

"But you came to watch?"

"No law against watch," the woman said with a hint of defiance in her voice.

Vesco tried to sort out the gibberish. "So Joe-Joe was mean and fun?"

"Two Joe-Joe's then, two Joe-Joes now," a voice called out.

The group shouted "*FLUMP!*"

"Joe-Joe's idea to come over here?"

Silence from the group.

"But you knew he was coming, and what he planned to do?"

Still silence.

"Did you know he was going to jump in front of a train?"

"Stand, not jump," one of the group said, and the rest of them turned to glare at the man who said it, and together they said "*FLUMP*" in a throaty, low, growly tone. The man put his head down and began to sob.

"United we stand, divided we hang," a female voice said from the edge of the group. It was getting dark, and Vesco was having trouble seeing who was saying what.

"Who said that?"

No answer.

"There's no capital punishment in Michigan," she said.

"Lansing is the capital of Michigan," a voice said.

Vesco rubbed her eyes and wondered when the damn medical personnel would arrive.

"Okay, just between us. You all came over here and watched Joe-Joe step in front of a moving train, and now he's dead and you're laughing . . . why?"

"It was funnest to see," a young woman said.

"Somebody dying is fun?"

"If it's Joe-Joe," she said.

The group thundered, "*FLUMP!*" and began to jump up and down.

A local deputy finally arrived. "Sorry it took so long to get here. Had a damn domestic call other side of the county, and I'm the only one on." The man looked at the body, made a face. "Yuck, fricking gork, what the fuck is that all about?"

"The group behind me may be from the House of Joy, and I get the feeling they watched the poor bastard commit suicide."

The dep looked over at the group. "*That* bunch?"

"Not just that, but I get a real bad feeling that somehow they may have forced the vic to do it."

The deputy looked at them again. "Are you *kidding*? Rubber room rangers? That lot can't plan where to take their next dump, much less engineer homicide."

"Nevertheless," Vesco said.

"These ain't homicidal maniacs," the deputy said. "They're just a little slow on the uptake."

A new man showed up, tall, young, freshly shaven. "Dr. David Peterson. I run the House of Joy."

"Is the victim over there one of yours?"

Peterson exhaled slowly. "Alas."

"I've been talking to your people."

"You can't trust what they say. They don't lie, they just don't have full contact with reality. They're somewhat slower than the rest of us."

Vesco said, "Listen, Doc, I think they watched the whole thing, you know, came over here to watch their pal step in front of a train."

The doctor sighed. "That was Joe-Joe, anything for a laugh."

"I get the feeling this was more than a joke."

"You don't understand," the doctor said.

"Everyone keeps telling me that, and still I keep trying."

"These are not the criminally insane; in fact, these gentle folk are not insane at all."

"Well, something smells here," Vesco said.

"I think you have an overactive imagination," the doctor said. "These are sweet, peace-loving, harmless folks."

Vesco felt like a heel. The doctor was probably right.

The EMS and medical examiner arrived, along with a state trooper, and Vesco explained what she knew and suspected and stood by the group. They all whispered "*Flump*" in an almost inaudible single voice, and someone added, "The tortoise brains won *this* race." The group said "*FLUMP*" again, and Vesco looked at them and knew that they had somehow engineered the death of Joe-Joe and that this would never be pursued, much less proven.

"Must be tough to lose your funnest man," Vesco suggested to the group and shone her SureFire on them. There were all smiling, a united front, undefeatable.

As she took a step toward the truck, a woman from the group said, "We're sooo slow," and giggled out loud.

The Third Partner

A LUTE BAPCAT STORY

Twenty inches of snow fell last night, concluding its business around dawn, the latest storm in a long winter of muscular wallops. On Bumbletown Hill above Allouez, where the Keweenaw Peninsula's two deputy fish, game, and forestry wardens lived, snow had piled up to the roof line on the north and west faces of their log structure.

Over the winter the deputies had dug three tunnels through the frozen drifts, one from the porch of the house to the shed, where they parked the state-owned Ford; another from the shed out to Bumbletown Hill Road; and a third directly from the porch out to the road.

"Starting to look like catacombs here," Pinkhus Sergeyevich Zakov had remarked as they were clearing new snow.

Lute Bapcat had no idea what a catacomb was and had been too busy shoveling to ask at the time. The Russian-born Zakov, a former colonel in the czar's army, was brimming with vocabulary and trivia, some of which were interesting and occasionally useful, but many of which were downright odd and seemed insignificant to Bapcat.

They were inside now, Zakov brewing tea, and Lute Bapcat, former cowboy, hunting guide, miner, trapper, and Rough Rider, was navigating the labyrinthine forests of a law text called *Tiffany's*, the law bible for game wardens and other lawmen across the state. Bapcat liked to learn but found reading difficult and tedious. Written law for him was often like a cedar swamp where no light touched ground.

"I hear something on the porch," Zakov announced. The former Russian soldier had keen ears, though it seemed to Bapcat that the man was most keen to hear his own voice. Come May, the two would have been partners for almost a year, and over the months, Bapcat had learned how to tune out his colleague, a difficult feat.

"Are you not listening to me?" the Russian pressed.

"I am reading," Bapcat countered. "Only you seem able to talk and listen at the same time."

"There is no need for that tone of voice, *gospodin*. I am merely sharing an observation."

"Open the door if you think someone's there."

"My ears suggest some*thing*, not someone."

"By the time you get around to the door, it will be long gone, this thing you think you hear."

"You are so quick to belittle my hearing acumen?"

"Talk is no strain on you, only for the rest of us forced to listen."

"It would serve you well professionally to learn to talk more. Partners should share their thinking, their dreams, ideas, fears, everything."

Bapcat sighed. He too now heard the heavy sound outside the door, put the book aside, walked to the door, opened it, and found himself face-to-face with a long-necked red mule of gargantuan proportions, breath blasting from its fire-red face and spurting small clouds in the icy air. Bapcat touched the animal's soft muzzle. "Why, what're you doin' here, Joe?"

The mule, which stood almost eighteen hands at its withers, towered above its Swedish owners, the Skojoldebrand brothers, fishermen out of Eagle Harbor, who were nowhere to be seen. In winter, Goran and Palle Skojoldebrand rented an old mining house a mile north of the deputies across the Houghton County line and inside Keweenaw County.

Bapcat and Zakov sometimes visited the Swedes. Goran was morose and seldom spoke. Palle was gregarious by Swedish standards but spoke English in a nearly unintelligible accent. The brothers made their own vodka and flavored it with various spices and fruits. The giant mule lived in the fishermen's house in winter and invariably greeted Bapcat like a long-lost friend.

"Joe's here," Bapcat said over his shoulder to Zakov.

"Alone or with the Swedling mutes?"

"Appears it's just him."

"Perhaps he is fleeing Goran. In his position, I would no doubt do the same, only I would have done so many years ago."

"There's too much snow to take him home," Bapcat said, opening the door wide and encouraging the animal to enter. Joe ducked his massive head as he confidently stepped inside.

Zakov observed, "We had many *muls* in the czar's army, but nothing of our Joe's proportions. Even medieval Russian battle horses would be dwarfed by this creature. I must duly commend my partner's hospitality but also must point out we now have an outsize four-legged creature *inside* our cozy abode. Am I to assume our dear friend Joe will take his meals at the table with us, and do you think you could you share the next step in this developing plan? Or will the next step be as much a surprise as dear Joe's arrival?"

The mule bared its teeth and issued a horselike whinny and soft bray. The two men laughed.

"It would seem," Zakov said, "that our friend also wallows in suspense over what comes next."

Bapcat began to dress in winter clothes.

"Where are we going?" Zakov asked.

"Feels like something's really wrong," Bapcat said.

The Russian pushed aside his tea makings and also began to dress. "The vehicle is out of question after this snowfall."

"We have snowshoes."

Zakov grunted displeasure. "I welcome the time when such dreadful devices will be relegated to a museum of wilderness oddities instead of everyday winter conveyances."

"No need for both of us to make the trip."

"Are you so arrogant as to think you are the only one with the power to sense trouble?"

Bapcat ignored the comment. "I think we should backtrack Joe as far as we can."

"There seems a lull in the wind at the moment, and I concur."

"If we lose the tracks, we'll head directly from that point to the Skojoldebrand brothers' house."

"Shall we alert Sheriff Hepting?"

"Too soon. This may amount to a simple matter of Joe wandering off. Maybe he got lost in the storm and couldn't find home."

"It appears you know little of mules, my friend. *Mul*, as we call this animal in Russian, like a horse, does *not* lose its bearings, but unlike horses, they seldom panic. The *mul* is a practical animal with immensely more common sense than its human masters."

Bapcat knew mules from his time in the Dakotas. He had ridden a steady animal named Reggie when he guided Teddy Roosevelt on several hunting trips. And he knew horses from his cowboying and Rough Rider days, though the troop in Cuba had been unhorsed and reduced to foot cavalry when they assaulted the San Juan Heights and became famous in the process.

"What about our friend Joe?" Zakov asked.

"He can stay here."

"A decision obviously begging disaster," the Russian argued.

"I'm not leaving him alone outside, and I don't want to try to lead him home with the two of us on snowshoes."

"Zakov grudgingly accepts this logic."

"That sure makes my day complete," Bapcat said sarcastically.

"This peninsula is Siberia exaggerated," Zakov said when they got under way. "Same cold, same winds, but far more snow."

The deputy wardens followed the giant mule's tracks back to its owners' small house. The animal lived in a stable built along the wall of the house, but there was an opening that allowed it free entry to the house, which the brothers had bought on credit from a mining company. Bapcat had no idea where the mule had come from. It seemed the brothers had always had Joe.

No smoke was coming from the chimney. Bapcat shucked off one of his beaver choppers and tried the door: unlocked. He stepped inside, found a lantern, and struck a match to give them light. No sign of Goran Skojoldebrand, but Palle was in a chair next to the wood stove, which was cold. The man's face was waxy and blue.

"Get wood," Bapcat told his partner. "We need heat fast."

"The woodbin is empty," Zakov reported.

"Break something and burn it. Palle is barely breathing." Bapcat went into a bedroom to gather quilts and blankets and saw blood and tissue all over one wall and the bare wood floor.

He wrapped the barely conscious Palle like a mummy.

A fire was soon going and throwing off heat. The two men pushed the Swede close to the stove and rubbed him, trying to increase circulation. "Palle, we're here. Where's Goran?" Bapcat asked, getting no response.

Zakov repeated the question; same result.

The heat increased. The man began to move under the blankets, his eyes flickering.

"Palle?" Bapcat said. "It's me, Lute."

Zakov went around looking into cabinets and drawers. "Nothing here," he reported, "no wood, no food, nothing, like Mother Hubbard's cupboard. The larder is in name only."

"Heat water on the stove," Bapcat said, and the Russian set to work immediately.

The deputies always carried packs with tea, sugar, extra provisions, and clothing, never knowing what circumstances might conspire to threaten them. Or where. Up here on the Keweenaw, weather was an unpredictable and ever-present predator that found ways to kill humans year-round. Bapcat tapped cayenne pepper into the hot water, an old remedy that beat brandy for cold and chills.

Palle Skojoldebrand fluttered on the edge of life. "Joe found you, did he, Lute?"

"Tea," Bapcat told Zakov, and they held a cup close to the Swede's lips and helped him sip.

"Joe came to our place."

"Good, he'll be happy dere witchus. I put Goran oot beck for dose wuffs. Dey gott eat same we do, eh."

Bapcat and Zakov exchanged glances. Zakov raised an eyebrow and moved away.

"Out back, Palle? You put Goran out back?"

"Yeh, we lose dat fish bees'nees, dis place, ev't'ing she gone, no food neither. Goran cry two day, take gun to mout'. I tole him we got hard time before plenty, donchuknow, we start with nothings once, do again, donchuknow. Goran said give Joe youse, and I done it."

"If you need money, you can sell Joe," Bapcat offered.

Palle Skojoldebrand made a pained face. "Joe's famblee. Can't sell famblee, Lute. Gott wunt want us sell famblee."

Bapcat didn't know what to say.

"Joe, he yore mule now. Gone die, Lute. Ticker bad. Wanted go like Goran, go togedder, like we live are whole dem lifes, but I got no guts, me. Joe, he yours. Goran said he always like you best."

Zakov came in from outside, sweeping snow off his clothes, made a pistol shape with his hand, put his forefinger in his mouth, and shook his head.

"Palle, we'll call the doc. We know a good one. He's a pal."

"Iss no damn good, Lute. What he gone do, make me new heart?" The Swede grinned crookedly.

"I'm no doctor," Bapcat said, "but I hear they can do all kinds of things nowadays."

"Not stuff I need; damn sawboneses iss like dose damn benkers, eh. Money, money, money," Palle mumbled. "Take lots money, dose guys. We buy beesnees, what benk call dat moralgauge, twent year, pay so much end every fish year. This year not so much fish, donchuknow. Benk says, 'Sorry, boys, our house, our boat, our bisnisst, not yours no more, you not pay, we take back, too bad not enough fish dis year.' Den dey call company stores, tell dem no more credit for dose Swede fitcher boy, and dat's end of us, donchuknow. Like I tell, Goran cry two day. Was good brudder, him. Lute, you take good care Joe. He good brudder, too."

Palle Skojoldebrand died with his eyes open, gawking into an unseen void.

The deputy wardens felt helpless and did not speak until Zakov declared, "Laissez-faire capitalism: You have here its fruit, men as means, with less value than machines, the identical callousness we observed during the strike. The two brothers were killed by capitalism."

The violent miners' strike lasted July of last year into early this year, with lots of victims falling along the way. The copper mine operators, fueled by East Coast money, were kings in the Keweenaw, and when the miners walked out, the operators had gone all out to break the back of the union and everyone who supported it.

"The French," Zakov proclaimed, "were fond of snatching savages and barbarians from the New World back to France, under the mistaken assumption that they could inculcate in such beings a veneer of civilization."

The Russian's changes in subject and direction could be dizzying. First he's talking about the copper strike, then French and savages? It was often impossible for Bapcat to keep up with the man's thoughts and words. "And?"

Zakov looked at his partner. "I have had the pleasure of reading on one occasion a tome by the French intellectual Montaigne, who reported Brazilian Indians captured by the French and brought to France as captives. They were paraded around the country and finally to the king's court and afterward asked what they thought about what they had seen. They said they had seen white men eating and drinking and gorging themselves and mating and outside those places thousands of poor and starving men, and having seen this, the Indians could not understand how the downtrodden should accept this and not kill their rich tormentors, take the possessions they needed, and burn the rest."

"Your point is beyond my horizon." Bapcat had learned this phrase from the Russian and liked it.

"Imbalance invariably brings eventual violent reaction."

"Like Bunker Hill and all that?" Bapcat's knowledge of his country's history was limited at best.

"No, your country's revolution was fomented and orchestrated almost exclusively by the rich, who didn't want to pay more taxes to England. The rhetoric was woven around the concept of freedom, but make no mistake, it was and is about the colony's rich protecting their money. If true human freedom had been the goal, the originators of the separation would have made sure there were no more slaves. It took you another war and millions of dead to make this happen. America says many fine words about freedom, but they are just often a mash of words. Money is what drives your country, Lute. All countries."

"The strike here was a kind of revolution," Bapcat offered.

"If widely construed, that is perhaps true, but at least the strike came from the bottom, from the workers themselves, not from the top. Those suffering the conditions and privations themselves fought to change them."

"The miners lost," Bapcat said.

"They all lost. Mr. Ford down in Detroit will steal labor from here by offering more than mine operators are willing to pay. The die is cast, and there will come a day in this country when the imbalance between rich and poor, have and have-not, will become so extreme that the little people of this country will rise up and take what they think is rightfully theirs, or more precisely take away from others what the masses view as not rightfully theirs."

"This has happened in other places?" Bapcat asked.

"France, and I think it will soon happen in my Russia as well."

"A Russian revolution," Bapcat asked. "Who will win, the czar?"

"No, the czar is impotent, uncaring, and will be easily displaced, but it is impossible to predict what will replace royalty in the short term. Long term, all Russians will suffer and lose. It has always been so. We Russians have no experience in determining our own fate, individually or collectively. We are a political vacuum, naïfs awaiting disaster. First came Genghis Khan and his Mongols, later Bonaparte. Who and what will come next?"

"You came here," Bapcat said.

"An exception proving the rule, my friend."

"Like our Swedish friends, then?"

"Perhaps."

"We need to call John Hepting and the coroner and get them down here," Bapcat told his partner.

"They will shed few tears," Zakov said. "Death in these surrounds is an unwanted but familiar neighbor. More importantly, what of the good mule, Joe?"

"I think we will build a shelter for him, mebbe where the truck is now. We can build something else for the truck."

"At least the creature will be outside," Zakov said.

"But it will take us a while to build his shelter for him. We'll have to keep Joe with us until breakup comes, and he can be outside."

"I foresee extremely unsettling domestic conditions," the Russian carped.

"I've been saying the same thing since the first day you showed up," Bapcat quickly countered, thereby ending the interchange and discussion. He rolled a cigarette and lit it. The violence of last year's strike had never left him. On Christmas Eve more than seventy innocents had died, and he and the Russian and their friend Dominick Vairo had helped recover the bodies, mostly young children.

Cuba had been about principles, it seemed to Bapcat, fighting a foreign enemy for your country. But the strike had been about money and power, and nothing more, and this fact left him with an annoying edge that he was having trouble blunting. Having little formal education made the deputy warden self-conscious about his deficiencies and created in him a determination to improve himself. He wanted only to do a good job by doing the right thing and enforcing the law, but how did a man decide what right was? Who determined this? He didn't know.

Bapcat exhaled. In this case, right was taking care of the mule. That was an easy one. He knew most situations would be far more complicated and jumbled, and he hoped he would be up to the many tasks ahead.

"Have you considered that the state may adjudge this mule to be its property, not yours?" Zakov asked.

He had not. "Well, good. If Joe's theirs, I guess they can't complain about the money we spend on him, and if he ain't theirs, he's ours, and they won't have much say in what we do with what's rightfully ours."

"The dispatch with which you speed to the simplest solution is forever astounding," Zakov said, "and quite commendable."

"Go find a telephone and call the sheriff. I'll stay with the brothers and think about all the things we should be doing for our new partner."

"You propose a lowly mule as our partner."

"Well, he *is* living with us, ain't he?"

"Temporarily, that is, for the time being."

"Well, I don't know about that," Bapcat said. "I done some thinking on the subject. Did you look around and sniff the Swedes' place when we were inside? I think our Joe, unlike them Brazilian boys, your Frenchmen, seems pretty civilized and fits right into our place. The house hardly stunk at all."

Zakov looked as if he had something to say, but instead he took his snowshoes and announced he would go find a phone and call Sheriff Hepting. He turned after a couple of steps and looked back. "If our civilized mule suffers failings, I will not be cleaning up after him."

Bapcat smiled. "Aren't you always lecturing me to see the best in people?"

"A mule is not people."

"Well, I guess we're gonna find that out," Bapcat said.

Black Beyond Black

A GRADY SERVICE STORY

Doctor Vince Vilardo was standing beside his new 1974 Ford Country Sedan, gnawing his meerschaum pipe, which Conservation Officer Grady Service had never seen him light. Service eased shut his door and walked over to the internist-turned-county medical examiner.

"What's going on?"

There were four sheriff's cruisers and a state cop blue goose all parked in front of the small house, and first in line was Sheriff Hugh Vale Swick's gold Buick station wagon with its outlandish white five-point stars on the doors, roof, and hood.

Vilardo said in a hushed tone, "Bear carried off a three-year-old girl about an hour and some ago. Took her right off the back porch as her mama watched."

"Who's on the trail?"

"Nobody. Swick called Imago Moiles to bring his dogs."

Jesus. "Moiles couldn't find a Percheron in a pony stall."

"That's why I had the county call you," Vilardo said.

Thinking out loud, Service said, "Let's hope Beany Moiles leaves her old man to home. He'll be deep into his cups this time of day."

Beany was Barbara Jane Moiles, Imago's wife, and the actual tracker-hunter-dog breeder in the family if you ignored her bigmouth husband. The peculiar couple bred special bear dogs that reputedly brought top dollar from houndsmen around the eastern US.

"Beany shows alone, point her at me, and tell her to leave the dogs in her truck until we can talk," said Service, who feared dogs, all sizes, all breeds, all temperaments.

His concerns aside, Service knew that Beany had a strike dog named Stagger Lee, said to be the top bear dog in the state. But he didn't want any dog on the scent until he and Beany could map out a plan.

"If Imago shows up alone, play dumb. I don't want that drooling asshole anywhere out in the woods with me."

"I alerted Rudi Venable, too," Vilardo said.

Venable was a longtime area veterinarian, a native Yooper, and someone who spent most of his spare time hunting and fishing. Service knew that the young medical examiner was thinking about what would happen after they killed the bear. Venable could perform a bush autopsy and organ necropsy to verify stomach contents. Service didn't dwell on this aspect. He needed to find the animal and the child first.

"Thanks, Vince," Service said. "Good call on Rudi."

Service retrieved his Remington .12 gauge shotgun from the soft case in his 1973 Plymouth Fury, checked to make sure the weapon was loaded with slugs, including one in the pipe, and dumped a handful of shells into his pocket. He pulled on his rucksack, shrugged it into position on his shoulders, and headed across the small grassy backyard behind the house.

"Hey, *you*," a voice yelped. Service saw the corpulent Sheriff Swick sashaying toward him. "Just what do you think *you're* doing here?" the man demanded officiously, puffing with exertion from having crossed the small backyard. Hugh Vale Swick was blockily built with blue veins spidering out to his cheeks from the bridge of the piggish snout on his booze-drenched puss. "Halt," the sheriff wheezed.

Service turned to face the man he considered contemptible—a cheat at worst and an unprofessional clown masquerading as a peace officer at best. Word was circulating that Swick would run for another term as sheriff, then retire to the general contracting-vacation real estate business he had built over the years, much of it on the county's time and dime.

Some of the man's own deputies called him the Thief of Police behind his back.

"Who's got the track?" Service threw out gruffly.

"Put a call in to Moiles."

Service grunted his displeasure. "I were you, there'd already be somebody tracking. Response time counts here."

"You aren't me, and I don't want to spoil the site or the track for the professionals."

"*Moiles?*" Service said, his voice dripping sarcasm. "I'm taking the track now."

"I haven't authorized it," the sheriff said by way of mild protest.

"Exactly," Service said and turned his attention to the challenge ahead.

"Damn state, damn DNR," Swick grumbled.

Service tuned out the man, who had built dozens of houses in bear habitat that had once been isolated and where there had been little chance of human contact. Because of the isolation, the sheriff had bought the land parcels on the cheap, and his pals on the county zoning commission had been good-ol'-boyed into approving his housing plans and building permits.

"Take it up with my supervision," Service said over his shoulder to the self-serving sheriff.

"Goddamn antiprogress obstructionists, the whole damn lot of you state people," Swick grumped, causing Service to smile. The DNR was trying to get the county zoners to reverse their rulings where land plans disrupted animal habitat, or at least block future projects that might disrupt wildlife. Swick and his pals were not happy with what they saw as unwarranted state meddling in a purely local issue.

Service was on the edge of the yard and moved east to west, looking down until he found two drops of blood on a fern. With this finding, he began to push everything but tracking out of his mind.

He moved almost lazily. Not a lot of blood, no splashes. He could see where the animal appeared to have put down the child briefly, perhaps to get a more secure carrying grip. Adjustment made, it moved south toward the massive Bread Creek Swamp.

Service's mind churned: Three-year-old girl? Shit. Clear your mind, pal. Focus. She's a goner. No berries this summer and a damn poor fall mast crop looming, all from a long drought. The animals need to fatten up for winter, and there's nothing to eat. Some are going to get desperate and stupid. But you don't *know* the child's a goner, he corrected himself.

Ten minutes later he found where the bear veered south, roughly paralleling the swamp perimeter, and minutes later he came upon a bear run used so heavily it was worn down to mineral earth. He looked back up the hill. Not 250 yards to the house, and here was a virtual bear interstate, the largest he'd ever seen in the UP.

The houses on the hill were a disaster in waiting. *Damn it, Swick!*

Blood sign remained sparse, and the CO advanced slowly, moving his eyes from just in front of him up to the terrain ahead and on all sides. Bears were like blobs of India ink in the forest, black beyond black, easy to spot. Usually.

He tried to will himself into the animal's head. Maybe an old bear with bad teeth, starving and desperate. Putting the girl down to get a better hold could be evidence of this. Or maybe it was a young animal cashing in on opportunity. Young bears were erratic, impulsive, and hard to read, much less predict. Young males in spring could be real pains in the ass, coming out of their dens. But this was August, not April.

He leaned his thinking toward an old animal, whose sole focus would be on food, and Service guessed it would cache the meal in a place where it would be difficult for other animals to try to take it away. Theory was worthless, of course. He needed evidence, especially a fresh track, to help him understand what he was dealing with. When he reached a small trickle from an underground seep, he got what he wanted—a clear, fresh track in wet, black dirt. Big track, *really* big track. Old animal, probably desperate. Not good for the child, not at all. Service felt his heart racing, took a deep breath, and exhaled slowly.

Less than a quarter mile farther along he found a splash of blood the size of the palm of his hand. It appeared that the animal had again stopped to regrip its prey. If the child had been miraculously alive before this, that seemed highly unlikely now. The blood was dark red, almost black.

The officer increased his pace and his vigilance, crossing the stream and following the blood sign downhill to a dense copse of young gray-green popples. The sign seemed clear. The animal was heading into heavy cover to protect its prize and to not be disturbed.

Decision time: Wait for the dogs and let them push and tree the animal, or go in and find it. Crappy choices. The kid, he thought, she's first. What if she's still alive? No choices here. Do your job.

Service eased his way to the edge of the aspens and froze, using his eyes to scan, careful to not move his head and give the animal a visual clue. In heavy cover there would be no reaction time if the animal came after him. Service felt sweat beading on his face, tried to control his heart rate, his breathing, straining to summon a cold heart and the quiet nerve of the dispassionate hunter closing on prey. He saw blood on a diaphanous flap of a young paper birch, a wine-colored stain on unsullied bark. It made his stomach flip.

Another step in, and he saw a tiny white sandal tipped on its side, like a small abandoned boat. No blood, only the orphaned shoe. Leave it for later. He sniffed the air, breeze slight, wafting softly over his face like a gauze tail, direction in his favor. He reasoned: This bear wants food, which means it won't be so fussy about wind and scent. Normally, bears were easily spooked creatures. Just like a human violator, this animal was locked on the prize, its tiny brain probably causing thin streams of saliva, small jolts of all-encompassing anticipation.

One more step. Stop. Keep a tree to your front to help block a charge. Listen. Sniff. Look. Listen. Wait.

Step again.

There! He could smell it, the fetid stench pinching his nostrils closed. It's damn close. Ease off the shotgun's safety, bring barrel up. Move again, follow your nose.

Another step, smell stronger, wind holding in his favor. And another step.

With each step, deeper, closer.

Heard it before he saw it—

—a peculiar sound like a heavy boot stamped once on gravel, a crunch of quiet yet somehow epic proportion, small in volume, big in his imagination, all his alarms blasting full on. He raised the shotgun barrel toward the sound, stared ahead into a small round of grassy space buried in the trees, bright sun beaming thin devil's smiles from above, the light angled slightly from the west.

—found himself looking directly into gleaming, intense brown eyes set back from a rusty snout. The animal softly woofed annoyance, clacked its teeth loudly: Keep away. Mine. Just mine. Grady Service took aim, drew a deep breath, and let it out slowly. How many times had he and Treebone done this in Vietnam, but with a man on the business end of the barrel? Too many times. *Don't think about the girl, just the bear.*

He expected the animal to stand on its hind legs to get a better look, or better air, but it remained on all fours, a black blot occasionally looking at him, its jaws working silently.

His mind was racing. In such thick cover, he second-guessed himself, momentarily wishing he had double-aught buck in the boiler. Thought: But the child's still there. *Can't hit her, in case she's alive. Buckshot might tear into her and leave lots of damage.* He let disturbing thoughts dissolve and put the bead sight on the animal's forehead, lining up between the eyes, but it suddenly lifted its head, presenting the top between the ears, and Service's inner trigger whispered, "Fire."

He was so focused on the target, he didn't feel the Remington's recoil. His only focus was the bear, which rolled backward as if it had been swatted by the hand of an invisible giant, somehow recovered its feet, and bounded southward.

Service stepped sideways with the animal, like the bear was his dance partner, and calmly pumped two more rounds just behind the animal's front left leg. It went down onto its jaw and skidded perhaps three feet, its legs still, but the head pushed up.

The bony time now, the waiting. Service stood with the barrel leveled at the animal. No movement, no more sound, just the stench. He stepped forward and used a stick with his left hand to touch one of the animal's eyes, while his right hand was on the shotgun's trigger, holding the gun on the animal. No response or reaction, no breath motion. Dead. The stink was disquieting. Fresh blood on the dead animal's snout. The girl.

He moved quickly to the child, felt lead gathering suddenly in his legs, but willed himself forward. Her face was unmarked, strangely white, an alabaster doll on a green bed, four ticks crossing her cheek under her right eye, looking to escape to better prospects, her blond hair spread out in a halo, sticky with her own blood and animal saliva, a flat, matted crown. Service forced himself to check for a pulse he knew wasn't there, probably hadn't been since the first time the animal put her down. No pulse. Shit. But you had to check, right, do your duty? Nothing. Skin still warmish. The bear was still, the child was still, the breeze stopped, all sound died all at once to create a stillness few other than the dead would ever experience. Silence was nothing, was death.

Service left the child and returned to the animal. Back of the bear's head gone, much of the brain with it. What had it used to move, a single cell somehow still connected to its nervous system? Weird. Shots two and three had hit where he aimed, hammering in quick succession into the heart area, leaving behind a gaping crater on the far side. When they opened the animal, its vitals would be obliterated. He hoped this wouldn't screw up the science. The officer went over to a windfall, sat down heavily, and lit a cigarette, placing himself so he wouldn't have to look at the child.

"Service?" a female voice called. "You okay?"

"Down here," he said listlessly, his body dumping adrenaline now that it was no longer needed.

Beany Moiles walked past him directly to the animal. "She charge youse?"

He shook his head. "Clacked her jaws once."

"One more and she'da come rightachyouse," Moiles said. The tiny woman knelt beside the bear and bent close to inspect her. "You see white star on her chest?"

"No." He'd seen only the eyes, the head. White star flash on the bear and white stars all over the sheriff's gaudy station wagon. The two images merged in his mind, made his stomach sour, made him reach deep to remain focused.

"I know this animal," Moiles said quietly. "Ten years back she had three cubs, went four hundred pounds easy. Lived her whole life down there in the Bread Creek wilds. Shoulda died down there too, eh." She paused. "Back in her prime dis star bear prolly push at least six hundred, eh. Now look at her: starving to death, teeth rotted and falling out, ribs showing; poor old gal. Nature's way: Eat or die. Her and us. Doc Venable's up to da house. Youse want him down here now?" She added, "Damn builders anyways."

Moiles moved over to the child, didn't touch the body and didn't linger. "Animal on the kill when you come upon her?"

Grady Service nodded.

"Got a smoke?"

He handed her his pack and ancient Zippo, asked her, "Imago with you?"

"Kicked his ass out a month ago, filed divorce papers. He ain't told nobody, been sittin' over there on a stool at the Frozen Dog since den, like ever't'ing hunky-dory. Piece of shit, he is."

The Frozen Dog. Service knew what that was all about. A local watering hole favored by the hopelessly addicted, including Service's late father, a drunk, and also a career conservation officer.

Moiles finished her smoke, GI'd it, stuck the butt in a pocket. "I'll fetch Doc Venable."

"Vince, too, but not Swick. Tell that toad we're not yet sure what we have down here, and tell him you didn't see anything, that I want the area preserved for the doctors."

"I'll bring 'em. Youse sit tight and try to relax." She handed the lighter and pack back to him and rubbed his upper back. "Youse done good, Grady."

"Hard," he said.

"I know," she said and walked away, angling up the hill in the direction of the child's home.

Rudi Venable was white-haired, in his sixties, a hard-working, no-bullshit veterinarian who didn't milk his clients with pet-owner complex built on ownership guilt. His hair was white-walled into a buzz cut that needed a trim. Venable knelt beside the bear, and Vilardo went to the child and stood there, slowly shaking his head, absentmindedly chewing his bottom lip, blinking hard.

Service got off the windfall and joined the vet.

"*Old* girl," Venable remarked, his hand under the sow's jaw, elevating it so he could look. "Find her on the kill?"

"Yah," Service said.

"Her teeth are a mess. Can't figure how'd she even chew. Probably pinched stuff off with the crushing power of her jaws." The doctor opened a large plastic tool box, put on a rubber apron, got out a wood-handled fillet knife, honed it with a few whacks on a leather strop, and pulled on elbow-length rubber choppers. It took the combined strength of all three men to roll over all the dead weight and get the animal's upper body slightly elevated so gravity could assist the evisceration process.

The veterinarian delicately punctured the abdomen, just below where ribs came together, and using two fingers, one on either side of the sharp blade, slid his hand downward, opening the cavity, moving smoothly from top to bottom. Steam spewed from the body, the stench overwhelming Service, who pretended not to notice. Game wardens were supposed to have cast-iron stomachs. His was. Mostly.

"Not much fat," the vet reported, pointing. "Pretty sure she wunta made it through this winter."

Service watched the vet remove organs and place them in black rubber bags. Venable stopped and used the back of his forearm to wipe sweat away. "Brain's in bits. Heart, too. Whereju hit 'er first?" he asked the CO.

"Top of the head."

"And she ran?"

"Tried."

"Brain surge, speck she wunta gone too far. Got enough brain tissue I can run some tests, but her heart's a lost cause," Venable told the men. He used the knife to sever the stomach at the top and tilted it down and out, flopping it in grass in front of his knees like a bulging laundry bag, used the sharp knife to deftly slice open the sac, releasing more cloying smells, and reached inside with his gloved hand.

"Not much in her," he said, leaning over and fishing deep in a pool of liquids and slime. Venable looked up at his colleagues. "Check the right hand on our vic, Vince."

"Isn't one," Vilardo said quietly.

"Okay, good. Got it here in her gut. We'll do blood tests, but this is our killer," Venable said.

The three men were silent. A breeze ruffled leaves over them. Service lit a cigarette, his hand shaking slightly. Vilardo chewed on his pipe. Venable rubbed his forearm against his head again, rested his buttocks on his boot heels as he knelt.

"I don't think I have words for this, fellas," the veterinarian said. He looked up at Service. "Good thing you found her, otherwise damn yahoos would be out here shootin' every darn bear they come across."

"Still may," Service said.

When an animal killed a human, Yoopers tended to go overboard, ostensibly to find the killer and put it out of the way of harming others, but as much out of pure revenge as any other reason. As often as not with bears, the vigilantes killed a whole lot of animals and never did confirm the guilty one. Rudi was right about his finding the animal with the child, good luck for the bear population tacked on the ass end of tragedy. He also knew some hardheads would still not believe he had the right killer, suspecting the DNR was holding back from the public. He could never understand why people felt this way, but it wasn't uncommon here.

"Only the sheriff hears about the hand," Vilardo told them. "I want to spare the mother whatever horror we can."

"Swick needs to tell reporters this is the right animal," Service said.

"*I'll* handle that," the vet said.

Vilardo took out his 35 mm Leica and began snapping photos, first of the child, then of the animal.

"You want the hand for the mortician?" Venable asked the medical examiner, "You know, so they can bury all of her together?"

It was the sort of bizarre conversation cops and other emergency personnel often had, and it left Service feeling more grouchy than anything else. Vilardo handed a rubber bag to the vet, who placed the hand in it and said, "Let me fish around, see if there's anything else in there to salvage."

A minute or so later, the vet said, "Looks like we've got all of her."

Vilardo sealed the black rubber container and placed it in his medical bag so no one would see it.

"Reporters will want to photograph the animal," the vet said.

"Not this time," Service said. "Will you need more off the bear?"

"No, I should be good," Venable said.

"I'll call other officers. They can winch the remains out of here, take it somewhere, and dispose of it. That okay?"

"That's not okay," Vilardo said, intervening. "We need to store the animal's carcass until the inquest is done.

"There's an evidence cooler in our Gladstone office. There *has* to be an inquest?"

"You know that's the law," the ME said, turning to Service.

"Doesn't seem right," Service replied.

Both doctors shrugged. Vilardo radioed his people back at the house and asked them to come down, using a code word for recovering a body.

Service and Venable left Vilardo with a technician and a state cop and went up to the house, where they met Swick.

"You find her?" the sheriff asked the veterinarian.

"I examined her. Service found her."

"The bear?" the sheriff huffed at the CO.

"Dead," Service said.

"How far from him were you?"

"She, not him, a sow; she was on the body, and I was less than thirty feet from her," he reported. "She went two or three steps, I shot again and dumped her."

"You'll swear to that under oath at the inquest?"

Service nodded, felt like backhanding the man.

"Being on the kill don't necessarily means youse has got the right one," the sheriff asserted.

"This the right one, Hugh," the vet said. "Absolutely no doubt."

Swick looked to Vince Vilardo, who had come up to get more muscle to help move the animal. "You'll talk to the mother, Vince?"

"That's your job," Vilardo said.

Swick frowned. "I ain't never been too good at that next-of-kin notification bullshit."

Grady Service turned to the sheriff and smiled. "I'll take care of it for you, Sheriff."

Swick brightened. "Thanks, man. Between us girls, I don't got a heap of boohoos for a mother lets her tot play alone outside in bear country."

Service looked at the man. "You don't hunt. How the fuck do you know this is bear country?"

"Found that out when I bought the land for these houses," the sheriff said. "Helped me leverage a better price, eh."

Service said, "I'll talk to the mother," and walked toward the house. He turned off the new tape recorder in his pocket as he stepped onto the back porch. Next of kin *bullshit?*

He knew an old *Evening News* reporter who might find the recording very, very interesting, but now it was time to compose himself and give the sad news to an already grieving mother.

Cuffed to a Truck, Left to Die

After twelve years in southwest Michigan, Conservation Officer Shana Lafave finally got her transfer to Watersmeet in Gogebic County. She'd even found a decent little house to rent her first trip up and moved in after trout season had kicked off. It would be weeks before she was actually settled into the place.

Locals had so far treated Lafave with distant respect—the one-step-back politeness Yoopers reserved for all outsiders, newcomers, and people perceived to have some power, not to mention the enemy, which meant any game warden or cop.

It was Friday night, humid and sultry, the best sort of night for brook trout fishing. Long ago her grandma Franck had taken her to Ten Mile Creek every summer, where they loaded fresh brook trout into canvas creels and shared a beer afterward, from the time Lafave was eight. In those days she and Grandma Franck paid no attention to DNR rules and considered the creek's fish to be their personal eating stock, an attitude shared by many denizens of the Upper Peninsula.

The spot she used to fish with Grandma was a half-mile walk along an eroded razorback ridge. If others were fishing the area, Grandma would park at a little cul-de-sac, currently empty, and walk a couple hundred yards down to the stream. The old gal had told her a lot of locals liked to hike in from County Line Road, which put them upstream of where Lafave intended to stash her truck tonight after a quick look at the stream.

Lafave hiked south, and fifteen minutes later she heard vehicle doors slam at the parking area. She wished she'd brushed away her in-and-out tracks, but it was too late for that, and all but the most serious violators didn't pay that much attention to anything except what was smack in front of them. She backtracked over a hill, heard voices, and stepped into some trees as the group passed, six men, beer cans in hand, the usual male verbal jabbing and bullshit. She heard them reach the creek and separate upstream and down.

The conservation officer moved toward them and watched one of them drifting worms under the skeleton of a cedar blowdown. Very quickly he had a fish on, removed it from the hook, and dropped it into a clear plastic bag tied to his hipper belt.

The size limit here was eight inches. This trout was maybe half that. The man moved downstream, catching one tiny trout after another, keeping them all. One of his upstream compadres yelled down to say he was "slaying these bitches!" and the man closest to her yelled back, "Same here, dude!"

Dillweeds, one and all, traveled in packs.

The closest man finished a beer and tossed it on the bank, sat down on a log, and rolled a cigarette, which he lit, inhaled deeply, and held. She smelled the skunk weed, real cheap dope. She guessed the men would rendezvous at the parking area after dark and decided to wait there to make contact. She was certain they'd all be over the keep limit and have short fish.

It was nearly eleven when they stumbled back up to the truck, still drinking beers. She waited until they were right at the trucks before stepping out on them.

"Conservation officer; you guys have any luck?"

Silence was *not* the reaction she hoped for. Yoopers in the face of authority generally defaulted to denial or fudged an answer, no matter the question, anything short of a bald-faced lie out of the gate. But all she had was an ominous quiet, and she immediately guessed what would come next. *I wanted to avoid this crap.*

"Yo, honey, we heard about youse," one of the men said in a ten-year-old boy's singsong bully voice.

"Put your fish bags on the ground in front of you," Lafave said.

"Or what?" one of the men asked. "Way we heard it, you ain't so tough."

"You can't believe everything you hear," Lafave said. "Put your fish bags on the ground, boys." "

"Bitch," a man said. "No wonder you got yours."

"Fish. Ground. Now."

When they didn't move, she unsnapped her holster and waited.

Time for a little game. She had not yet checked licenses with Lansing, but she made a hobby of memorizing most popular baby names by year, and she guessed these toads at about twenty or a hair older. "Fish down. Which one of you birds is Lucas or Jason?"

One by one they put the fish on the ground. The man to her right was tall and big with a thick bullneck and mullet, decked out in a black wife beater and a nose ring. He held up his hand. "Lucas."

Lafave said, "Line up your fish, longest on your right, shortest on the left, in order of size."

"Do it yourself," Lucas said and looked down at the Taser in her hand. "That the lightning?"

"Yeah; you wanna ride it?"

"No, ma'am," he said, kneeling and arranging his fish.

The other five followed the first man's example.

She said. "Operator and fishing licenses."

"Left my fish license to home," one of the men said quickly.

"Convenient," she said, "but it doesn't matter. Just guessing here, but when I run you through RSS, I'll find none of you has a license this year, and I'm guessing you haven't bothered to buy a license for several years. Anybody want to disagree?"

"Bought mine this morning," the man countered. "There's a lag before it'll show up in your computer."

"The law says you have to have it with you. If you bought it this morning, where is it?"

"Just told you I left it to home in my wallet in my other pants."

"You have two wallets?"

One of the men sniggered.

"You've got a wallet in the pants you have on, right?" she said.

"Why you doing this shit to us?" the man complained.

She turned to the other man she had named. "*Your* story?"

"Never got around to buying a license. I meant to, but I didn't, and that's the plain truth. That'll make it easier on me, telling the truth, right?"

"It won't make it worse. Count off your fish, out loud." She held out her digital recorder, repeated the called out counts: ten, ten, twelve, sixteen, seven, eleven. "Limit's five, boys," she said.

"Didn't use to be," one of the men complained.

"Measure the fish," she said.

"With what? We ain't got no ruler."

"Hey, Foley," one of the men chirruped, "whip out youse's four-inch hog and tell her it's eight inches, like you tell all the bar bunnies."

The insulted man took a roundhouse swing at his comrade but missed and cartwheeled harmlessly to the ground.

Lafave tossed a tape measure to the man on the ground. "So you don't have to embarrass yourself. Call out each length. The rest of you get out your operator licenses."

"We ain't driving; why we need them?" one of the men asked.

"Because the law says you do." She wrote down fish lengths as the man called them out. "The lot of you are getting tickets for littering, being over the daily limit and possessing short fish, and fishing without licenses. I'm ignoring the dope."

"That's a buncha chickenshit!" Lucas howled, puffing with rage.

"One more word from you, sir, and it's jail tonight for interfering with a police officer in the performance of duties."

"No way that will stick," he said.

"Won't matter," she countered. "There'll be a trial, it'll be in the news, on the radio and TV, and Facebook; you'll have to take time off work, and you'll lose the case. How will it look for everybody in town to know you got busted by the split-tail fish cop? Think about it."

The others laughed.

"I ought to . . . ," Lucas said.

"*What?*" she asked sharply, stepping toward him. "How about you ought to keep your trap shut. I start inspecting trucks here tonight, there'll be no end to the possibilities, and your pals will suffer all because of you."

"C'mon, Lucas, listen to her, eh?" one of his friends said.

She looked at them. "You guys heard how some assholes gang-raped me and used my own handcuffs to attach me to my own patrol truck and left me there to be found, and because of that the DNR transferred me up here because they feared I'd lost my ability to be effective there, or I might get hurt. That or something like it is what you heard: Now, here's the truth—I caught a guy spiking my tires, beat him half to death, and told him when he got out I'd finish the other half of the job. I cuffed him to the truck while I whaled on him. Questions?"

None. An hour later she had all the tickets written, had them collect their empties, and reduced the littering charge to a warning. By then they were all joking and laughing and carrying on with each other. Tickets handed out, she said, "Git," and they jumped in three trucks and were gone.

Lafave got a cigarette out of her truck, put down the tailgate, sat down, and lit up. Every female officer in the state who transferred or came into a county as a new officer had the same myth attached to her arrival. This round of horseshit would pass. In time, some of tonight's fools would become her snitches, and she would slowly strangle the illegal activities of the county's wingnuts with their help. She'd asked for this transfer because this is where she spent summers with her grandmother.

She could imagine Grandma Franck smiling from heaven.

Guts Young

Six-foot seven Sergeant Jeffey Bryan was supposed to meet Jingo Sedge to check a deer camp south of Eckerman filled with Detroit and Toledo swells, but his curiosity finally got the best of him. For several years a garish blue Astrovan had been parked next to the East Branch of the Sage River on M-28. It was there again. He'd never seen the hunter. The van was plastered with Alaska stickers and right-wing slogans like CHRISTEN, THEN ARM: START THEM OFF RIGHT. Bryan smiled and shook his head. Right, indeed.

The hunter's trail led south into heavy tag alders. Bryan put on his hippers, grabbed his ruck and ticket book, and began tracking. Once into the tag jungle, the trail was clearly beaten down. He guessed the man came in from different points, always converging on this place. A mile south, the trail veered to the riverbank, where the tannin-stained water shallowed to a gravel bar and led southeast through heavy swamp with a couple of old, deeply rutted bear runs and very little sign of deer.

A mile beyond the crossing, Bryan crossed another branch of the river, or a feeder creek, he wasn't sure which, and the trail swung south through more tags toward rising ground.

Bryan stopped to have a sip of water from a bottle he carried and used his binoculars to scan the gradual slope ahead. Two or three hundred yards ahead the ground was a greensward sloping upward to a thick conifer wood line. He scanned the line, saw something clumped at the bottom of a tree, caught a glint higher up, and kept looking until his lenses hit upon on a hunter thirty feet up a tree, scoping *him*.

Sonovabitch!

The hunter was head-to-toe in camouflage. Until this moment Jeffey Bryan had been admiring the man's field craft and obvious desire to hunt alone. If he hadn't stopped and looked ahead, he might have walked into the greensward as vulnerable as a duck on a dock. Instead, he now hiked west and circled, moving at a trot through the heaviest cover he could find. The hunter had no hunter orange and was damn near invisible up so high. He hated to be scoped or have weapons pointed at him, and he took it personally. Even his nephews, whom he adored, were not allowed to point their toy pistols at him.

Next question: Had he really been seen? No way to know. Sergeant Bryan moved to the tag alders again and surged south-southwest, arcing his way to the west to intercept the hunter's ridge line, and come up behind him through heavy cover in the tree line. Every tree blind had at least one total blind spot. This one was no different.

It took a while to get up into the maple and oak stand, and here and there he saw old apple and cherry trees, guessing this was a onetime homestead gone wild. Such places were all around the Upper Peninsula.

Locating and approaching the hunter's tree, he saw a small tent inside the tree line. There was also a camo tarp over a gear pile at the base of the tree. Climbing steps had been screwed into the tree trunk. They were camo, chipped, and looked old. Probably using this same blind for years.

No smoke. Silence. Bryan sniffed and listened. The hunter was disciplined, quiet, serious about business. Most who came north would hike no more than a hundred yards from their vehicles, or they'd get dropped at their blind by four-wheelers and fetched for lunch and dinner.

"Hey up there in the blind," Sergeant Bryan yelled. "DNR."

No response.

"I'm at the bottom of your tree, dipstick. I can see your tent and your cache. Get your butt down here *now*. This is Sergeant Bryan, DNR."

The figure came down slowly and deliberately, descending confidently, rifle slung over the back.

"Keep your hands where I can see them," the sergeant said. "Unsling your rifle and hand it to me."

The hunter wore a camo face mask, nodded, unslung, and passed the rifle to the officer, who checked it. Remington 2700 caliber bolt action, with a 6X scope. Empty, clean, well cared for. "You got orange?" he asked.

"Don't need it on the stand," the hunter said.

That voice? What the hell is this? "Take off your mask and hat."

A girl, twelve at most. "How old are you?"

"Thirteen this week," she said.

"You have your hunter ed card and an adult with you?"

"I had hunter safety. Officer Sedge taught the class."

"She tell you that you have to hunt with an adult until you're sixteen?"

"She told us."

"Yet here you are alone. What's the deal?"

"I'm hunting is all. What's the big deal? I know what I'm doing."

Jeffey Bryan sensed pluck in the girl, some inner steel, and he liked it. Guts young was good.

"That your van out by the highway?"

"My pop's."

"Where is he?"

"With Jesus," the girl said. "My ma, too. She went when I was seven. Just pop and me since then; now it's just me."

"You live around here?"

"Near Hulbert Lake."

"Thirteen and driving illegally," Sergeant Bryan said, towering over the child. "Has the DMV issued new regs I don't know about?"

"It's too damn far to walk," the girl said forcefully. "Me and Pop always hunted here. Pop taught me to drive."

"Did you scope me?" he asked.

"If I had, you wunta found me up this tree," she said candidly.

"Do you *have* orange?"

"My pop didn't believe in it."

The sergeant took off his ruck and pulled out a hunter orange wool chook, which he handed to her. "Put it on," he said. "What's your name?"

"Turley, Anastasia Turley."

Bryan called Sedge on the 800. "You remember a hunter safety student named Turley?"

"Anna Turley? You bet. Great kid; why?"

"No reason, thanks."

"Turley," the sergeant said, facing the child. "Go back up there and hunt, but keep that damn orange chook on. When you drive home, get the hell off M-28 fast as you can after you cross the Hendrie River. Use the truck the rest of this season, but after that you're grounded till you get your license. Who are you living with?"

"My aunt, Lattis Earle. She don't hunt."

"Does she drive?"

"When she has to. She's real old and cranky."

"Like I said, finish your season. I'll make sure the cops leave you be. You hike back here every day?"

"No sir, I'm in till the season's over, just the way Pop and I did it. I got plenty of grub."

"You're thirteen? What about school?"

"What *about* it?"

"You make good grades?"

"Home school. I'm in all advanced high school courses and a college-level English course."

"Who oversees your home schooling?"

"Was Pop, now me. Computers make it easy."

"You ever tempted to cheat?"

She puffed up indignantly. "People of honor don't cheat."

"Except when it comes to hunting," he said.

"Your definition, not mine," she came back and hung her head.

"Why'd you stay up in the tree?"

"High ground, sir; never surrender the high ground."

"Your father teach you that?"

"Yessir."

Sergeant Jeffey Bryan stuck a business card in her hand and extended a huge paw. "Pleasure to meet you, Miss Anastasia Turley. I hope you get you a dandy buck."

"Thanks for the hat," she said. "Do I get a ticket?"

"Nope."

"Could you get in trouble for this?" she asked.

"We both could," he said, "but not if you don't screw up."

"I won't," she said. "I promise, sir."

Two weeks later Jeffey Bryan got a telephone call. "Sergeant, this is Anna Turley. I got my buck, a ten-point, and I've got meat for you. My aunt says you should come to dinner so she can meet you."

They made a date. Jeffey closed his phone and smiled. Some gambles were worth taking, especially out in the way back.

Man in the Woods; Man on the Road

Loren Degu was headed south on M-77 to join a dozen other officers for the annual group patrol and goat rodeo on Big Mass Lake, an event conservation officers called the Redneck Mardi Gras. It was a gathering of beer guzzlers and dopers with mullet cuts and multiple body tattoos, multiple body piercings, hats facing south, untied boots and shoes, the uniform of shiftless twenty-somethings who would all converge on a sandbar in the middle of the lake, hook their boats into a large flotilla raft, and commence an en masse alcoholic rock-dive into the kingdom of stupid.

It was not a patrol Degu looked forward to. Sure, it produced some astonishingly stupid behaviors, events, and great stories year in and year out, but he'd rather stay in his own county where he had his own reliably unreliable troublemakers. The truth was that stupid people disturbed and annoyed him more than he could adequately express in words, and to see so many mouth breathers gathered together was the stuff of nightmares.

But duty was duty, and he was headed south, having come across bad roads from Deer Park. Normally, he had his eighteen-foot aluminum boat, but his sergeant had wrecked it a month ago. North of Green Haven on M-77 a jaybird in a rusty red Volvo wagon jetted around him, swerved wildly, and nearly went off the road, nicking the gravel shoulder, throwing up a rooster tail of dirt and crap, and unceremoniously dropping a beer can on the road.

Was this guy *blind*? Degu stopped, picked up the can, accelerated to catch up, got behind the Volvo, and turned on his blue emergency lights.

The vehicle continued to sail south toward Seney. Amazed that the man seemed not to have seen him, Degu pulled alongside the other vehicle again. The pigtailed driver looked over, grinned, and waved. He appeared to have a giant spliff stuck to his lower lip, his insipid grin suggesting a cocktail of beer and cannabis. Degu motioned for the man to pull over, but all the driver did was to salute, smile, and continue driving south.

Reaching Lavender's Corner, Degu used his siren to try to wake up the man, but as they approached a long bend in the road, the driver kept going.

Degu knew it was pretty much a straight shot from here to Seney, lots of space. The man chucked another beer can, and Degu hung close behind him, lights going until they crossed the bridge over the East Branch of the Fox River. Time to act, Degu told himself.

The conservation officer again pulled alongside the Volvo and signaled for the driver to pull over.

The man rolled down his window and tossed a plastic bag, which Degu was certain would contain his drug stash. The officer hit the marker button on his Automatic Vehicle Locator to mark the drop-spot, then called the Schoolcraft County dispatcher. "Two, One Eleven is southbound on M-77 in pursuit of a red Volvo, one occupant, fleeing stop."

"You want backup?" the dispatcher asked over the radio.

"Affirmative. I'm still north of the big curve, and I'm going to PIT him here." The Precision Immobilization Technique was Degu's safest bet to knock the fleeing vehicle off the road and end the flight.

Degu lined up his front right bumper with the target's left rear wheel and cut hard into him, causing the Volvo to spin into the ditch as Degu braked, stopped, threw open his door, charged the red car, jerked the driver out, rolled him roughly onto his face, and cuffed him.

A troop in a blue goose arrived as Degu was getting the man to his feet. "He tossed a bag about a half mile back," Degu told the state policeman. "Should be right on the road."

"Drugs?"

"My guess. Beer in the car. He was all over the road."

The troop left to retrieve the evidence.

This was the area where Schoolcraft, Alger, and Luce Counties all sort of touched each other, and Degu had to think about where he wanted to take the prisoner and decided on Munising. By the time he got the man lodged and did paperwork, he could beg off the group patrol on the lake.

A second troop arrived on the scene and asked, "Call a hook for you?"

"Please."

Degu administered a preliminary sobriety test, and the man agreed to take a Breathalyzer, noting, "Ain't had but a six-pack, dude."

The man blew 1.3, his pupils were dilated, and Degu counted a dozen empty cans on the floor of the Volvo's passenger side. There was a new twelve-pack in a Styrofoam cooler on the seat. "Smoke a little?" Degu asked.

"Don't ever'body?" the Volvo driver answered.

"You're under arrest. You're over the blood alcohol content limit."

The man shrugged.

When the Volvo was on the way to Seney on a flatbed wrecker to be impounded, Degu loaded his prisoner into the truck and started west for Munising.

"*Dude*," the prisoner said, "you done run me offen motherfuckin' road. You, like, scared the shit outen me."

"You wouldn't pull over."

The man rolled his eyes. "Like, I had to get south, dude."

"For what?"

"Replenish my stash. I smoked the last coming down here. Dude, you were, like, totally pissed when you pulled me outen my wheels."

"You could have killed yourself, me, or others," Degu said.

The man rolled his eyes. "Road beers, man. Was only some road beers. No big deal, sayin'? Road beers ain't, like, illegal; road beers is, like, patriotic, you know, help fight the rechestion and such shit. I'm spending my cash, dude, just how our president Big George want us to do."

Stupid people, stupid, stupid, stupid, Degu thought. On the other hand, now he was free of the goat rodeo where this guy's clones would show in spades. Not a bad trade. "You should have pulled over when I blue-lighted you," Conservation Officer Degu said.

The man looked at him, obviously groping for words. "Dude, I *knew* you was the man in the woods. How was I to know you also the man on the motherfucking road, too?"

Degu squeezed his steering wheel until his knuckles turned white, but he said nothing and kept his eyes on the road.

Fences

Ex-wife Paula had swept up the kid last night and headed to the Mall of America, wherever in hell that was.

"You think maybe the kid's a hair young to learn a shopaholic's habits?" he had asked.

Paula, with a million-dollar book-learning mind and not ten cents' worth of common sense, fluffed her thick hair and said indignantly, "Her name is Star, and I am not now nor have I ever been a shopaholic."

"Our credit cards and bank accounts tell a different tale."

"I told you the first time you dipped your wick out to my old man's camp I wasn't good with the numbers."

"You're a CPA and a lawyer! I thought you were joking."

"Now you know," she said curtly, took Star's tiny hand, and flounced out to her new red Hummer.

"At least I'm not paying for that piece of shit," Conservation Officer Ivan Bouffardi said to her back.

The only pain in the divorce was having Star only half the week. To her credit, Paula had asked for no assets (there were none) or alimony. Her own income was six figures, multiple zeros over his own salary after ten years working for the state in uniform.

What ate at him most was the faint possibility of his being transferred to the eastern Upper Peninsula. Living here in Kingsford, she was too damn close to the Mall of America in Minneapolis and to the big malls in Milwaukee and Green Bay. He had filed the request before the divorce, hoping that the lack of shopping to the east would reform his then-wife, though deep in his heart he'd known it probably wouldn't work. Now if he got transferred, Paula wouldn't be going, and she would make it impossible for him to have Star at all.

It was too bad, because he really wanted to move. The family hunting camp on the South Branch of the Two Hearted River was his and about as isolated a spot as one could hope for, but the chances of transfer to Mackinac, Luce, or Chippewa seemed slim to none, and after ten years in Dickinson County the truth was that he was worn out. There were days when he had dozens of contacts per day, more than some officers in the UP encountered in a year, and knowing this, it would be nice to have a more human pace, though he wasn't sure he could adapt to it. Over here there were more lawbreakers, more assholes per capita, and the bottom line was that Bouffardi liked enforcing the law, right over wrong, no gray, yes-no, binary decisions, up-down, one way or the other, and life went on. Above all else, he loathed the differences in legal outcomes that people of wealth seemed to buy for themselves. The inequity drove him crazy, but what could he do about it? He didn't make the laws or adjudicate them; he simply enforced laws on the books.

Today's patrol would take him out to Perry Anka's 400-acre impoundment in the extreme north of the county near Wild West Creek. Christ Perry Anka was Ironwood-born but had made a fortune in the business of home health care and durable medical goods. Anka, now pushing eighty, had been on the state's Natural Resources Commission for the past twenty years and was hailed as the state's premier conservationist, so much so that newspaper headlines around the state had only to refer to "Perry" for readers to know who the piece was referring to.

Anka was said to evaluate his life based on the number of enemies he'd accumulated. He brooked no fools, toadies, suck-ups, or slackers.

Once a week in the fall, Ivan Bouffardi took a drive out to Anka's private hunting ground. Not that the patrol would produce results: Perry had his own private security setup to protect his scientifically managed, fenced-in deer herd. But Bouffardi loved the property and seeing all the humongous animals prancing around.

Once in a while some local jerkoffs from Norway, Channing, or Sagola would try to get through the wire, but it was futile. Perry's fence had electronics that would be state of the art even at the dang Pentagon. Anka once told him, "That system tells me when a chipmunk farts," and chuckled until he was red in the face. The chance of finding an intruder on Perry's property was close to nil, but it would make for a relaxing day in the truck, some time to not think about Paula and Star or the transfer deal.

Leekie Annisdottir was on duty at the gate. A onetime downstate Pontiac cop, for several years Leekie had been on Perry's security force, which consisted of six people, three men and three women. The compound was guarded and monitored twenty-four/seven.

Annisdottir buzzed open the gate and ambled over to the truck. "Walking or driving today?" she asked.

"Driving." Bouffardi looked at his watch. "You on till fourteen hundred?"

"Had the nights last month, twenty-two hundred to oh-six. That shift's not for me. How's your kid?"

"Went with Paula to the Mall of America," he said, groaning.

"I feel your pain," the attractive guard said. "Sounds like your ex is starting your little one early."

"Seems like," he said.

"How long the girls gone?" she asked.

"Four days, back Monday."

"Got no plans myself, case you're up for a diversion," she said.

Surprised, he said, "I'll keep that in mind." Several times over the past months, it seemed to him that she had hinted at the possibility of seeing him, but this was different, blunt, right to the point. He always answered in the negative, begging off. This time he said, "Your place or mine?" *What the hell; I'm divorced, right?*

She arched an eyebrow. "You sure?"

"Yes, ma'am."

"Don't make me no never mind," she said, "but I got a fully stocked fridge and kitchen, I love to cook, and there's even a king-size bed, not necessarily in that order."

He felt himself blushing. "Your place, then."

"Two miles out of Foster City on C.R. Five Oh Nine . Bright red house, the only one for miles," she said. "

"That's close to work," he observed.

"What Perry demands."

"For you or for everyone?"

"*Everybody* on the security team lives within twenty miles."

"How come?"

Annisdottir shrugged. "The rich don't explain themselves."

"I hear you," he said.

"Till later, take care, Ten Days."

"Say what?"

"Everybody in the county knows, Ivan. How you caught some filthy rich shithead from Green Bay with two illegal does, and he hired big-shot lawyers who kept getting postponements after you got to court, and that started eating up your duty time. Ten times, dude. That was damn stubborn, the stuff of legend. Word is the judge called you into his chambers the tenth time, but nobody knows what got said."

What the judge had said was, "Son, this damn defendant's got pockets so deep his hands brush the heads of Chinamen. He can outlast you and me, and the whole damn state, if need be."

"Not me, he can't," Bouffardi told the judge.

"Gonna irritate your management some, I guess, all that field time lost."

"The man wants his day in court. And I do, too," he told the smiling judge.

The trial began on the eleventh date. The jury was out exactly sixteen minutes and found the man guilty on all counts. "Not important what got said," Bouffardi told Annisdottir.

• • •

Ten minutes later, Bouffardi found himself unable to focus. All he could think about was Leekie and her alluring voice. Shouldna said nothing, he chastised himself. *Shoulda left things the way they are.*

Perry had twin trout ponds on the property, one of them planted with big brown trout. Bouffardi liked to walk to the larger trout lake, have a pipe, enjoy the solace at a shed Perry called the Gillie Hut. Here he would take off his boots and socks when the weather was nice and relax.

His family on his father's side descended from one Corporal Jean Nepoma Bouffardi, a soldier in Napoleon's Grande Armée. At the battle of Friedland, his ancestor had both arms and legs blown off by artillery, but a day later one of his arms had been found, still clutching his pipe. From then on French soldiers called their pipes *bouffardes*. Ivan liked to think Jean Nepoma's singlemindedness came down to him genetically, as did his love for a good, relaxing smoke.

Ivan's pipe had been made for him before his old man passed on. His grandfather had made his father's pipe, and he hoped one day to make one for his own son. He couldn't imagine there wouldn't be a son. Paula was gone, but he was still young.

His *bouffarde* was large, made from hundred-year-old French briar root, *Erica arborea*, the word briar a bastardization of the French *bruyère*, for "heath tree." His pipe had been fashioned from *bruyère blanche* and brought home from World War II from Saint-Claude, where the world's finest pipes were made. His pipe was in the pot style, with a fat bowl. His father had taught him to puff, not inhale, the latter causing health problems. The French government had raged against the evils of smoking as a poison and a drug—until the government nationalized all tobacco businesses in the mid-seventeenth century. Since then? Rarely a government criticism, revenue being altogether more relevant and real than theoretical, pie-in-the-sky, or real health risks.

Bouffardi wiggled his toes in the morning air and puffed contentedly, wondering if this was what it felt like to be old and tired in retirement.

Movement across the pond caught his attention as a large doe came bounding along the north shore and collapsed in the water with a dramatic splash. Bouffardi saw blood pooling in the shallows, hurriedly put on his socks and boots, and tapped the dottle into his hand with two sharp taps of the bowl. He pressed the tobacco remains into the dirt with his boot heel, making sure there were no lingering embers. He carefully put the pipe in its leather carrying pouch and hung the cord around his neck. In the truck the pipe had a special box. He grinned at how the tobacco business in France paralleled marijuana here. By 1635 Parisian policy allowed the sale of tobacco only with a physician's prescription. It was said that Napoleon in 1810 was at a party in Paris and saw a woman festooned in diamonds. He asked an aide who she was and was told she was the wife of a tobacconist. At the time, the government tobacco monopoly had been more or less "resting," but Napoleon drafted new regulations reestablishing the state's power over such sales, and little had changed since then.

The conservation officer pulled the doe to shore. A crossbow bolt protruded slightly. Hard to believe the animal hadn't fallen when it was hit, but the desire to live, whatever the species, often overrode theoretical and sometimes even real physiological limits.

Bouffardi suppressed a smile. A date with Annisdottir, a fine smoke, a nice day, and finally what appeared to be a violator *inside* Perry's fence, all of this contributing to a rush that left him feeling almost giddy.

Having examined the deer, Bouffardi moved immediately into the wood, offsetting a few feet from the animal's blood trail, which was clear in places, sporadic in others. The shooter would no doubt eventually follow the animal or move to another target. Bouffardi stopped and decided to wait.

Soon came a man in full camo creeping low, carrying a crossbow. Bouffardi stood up. "Conservation officer."

"Motherfucker," the man said with a groan.

"Discharge the bolt into the ground by your right foot," Bouffardi ordered.

"I can just take it out," the man said.

"Do what I say," Bouffardi said. "Now."

The bolt made a thunk as it struck the hard ground. "Crossbow down, and off with the camo mask."

The man complied.

Oh, shit. It was L-Sun Banks, one of Perry's longtime security men. Banks pretentiously spelled his name L-Sun, which made Bouffardi roll his eyes, and he had no idea why he reacted so. The man was black. Maybe that was why. He couldn't be sure.

"Banks."

"Your eyes is good."

"Got an explanation?"

"How about I got six kids, and they like to eat meat."

"You have a job."

"You know what Perry pays? Minimum fucking wage is what, no benefits, no cost of living, no change for inflation, I'm talkin' barebones, and he dictates where we live or can't. And here he got all this damn meat right here, all these old bucks making his old Johnson stiff, and I don't bother none of his damn trophies. Can't eat antlers."

"You've done this *before*?"

"Ya think?'

"Jesus, Banks, that animal is your boss's property."

The man countered, "What that doe is, is food for my old lady and kids, nothin' more, nothin' less."

"You can get one legally elsewhere in the state season."

"That old man got us tied up all the time. Not slaves, see, but indentured servants, and like that."

Bouffardi started to say something about finding another job but held back. There weren't any jobs these days.

Banks said, "Okay with you, I gut this old girl, head to shack, relieve Leekie."

Banks rode with Bouffardi to the guardhouse. Annisdottir looked surprised to see the men together. Banks went into the change room to dump his camo, put on his uniform.

"He do this often?" Bouffardi asked her.

"He takes wonderful photographs," she said.

Photos? "What photographs?"

"Wildlife. He wins awards, hopes to go pro, make a real living, not this hand-to-mouth gig we have with Perry."

Banks emerged in uniform. Annisdottir went to change into her civvies.

"Photographs?" Bouffardi asked.

"That girl don't know what fum what," Banks said.

"You really take pictures?"

"Yeah. That against the law?"

"Your cover?"

"My passion, man."

"Don't bullshit me L-Sun, we're both brothers of the suck in the way back when. Both of us are ex-Marines."

Banks had served in Iraq, been wounded, and won a silver star.

Leekie came out in a diaphanous sundress, paper-thin sandals, tanned legs. "Have a fine day, boys," she said, heading for her white Toyota.

"I ain't taken no trophies," Banks said, diverting Bouffardi's attention from the woman's shapely legs.

"It's still theft."

"What you call how Perry treat people?"

"Legal," Bouffardi said. "His property, his rules. America."

"That good enough for you? *Legal?* What about fair, what about moral, you know, or what's right?"

"I enforce laws, that's all."

"That's bullshit, man. If the law told your sorry ass to shoot all dogs you see on patrol, you'd do that?"

"I don't see a way around a ticket here, L-Sun."

"Perry's gonna fire my ass quick-fast, sue me for redress, you hear what I'm sayin'?"

"Hey, you'll be free of him."

"Man, you ig-nant. Perry try put my ass inside. The way he is, he crush everybody, death to all motherfucking enemies. That old man would kick a six-year-old's ass in checkers just to show who's best."

"Be a chance for you to pursue your photography," Bouffardi said.

"This economy? I lose this sorry-ass job, I be dead, and my family, too. Whatchugonnado, Ivan? Semper Fi, man. That shit means something, right? Once a Marine, always a Marine. We brothers, right?"

Bouffardi tucked his ticket book under his arm. "This time, this once. Do it again, all stops are out."

"You the man," Banks said. "Watch the gate while I load meat in my vehicle?"

Bouffardi thought: In for a penny, or whatever that saying was. He got out his pipe, loaded it, and lit up.

• • •

Annisdottir met him at her door wearing her workout clothes, barefoot, and handed him a beer. "Red Jacket," she said. "Microbrewery in Houghton, eh?"

"You a Copper Country girl?"

"Michigamme-born," she said, beaming.

She took trays out of the fridge. "I took the liberty of starting the grill. Weber, plain-old charcoal, good by you?"

"Simple is best," he said.

"You want to chef the meat?"

"Sure."

He took the platter outside, removed the aluminum foil that covered it, and found backstraps, thin, beautiful backstraps, fresh, not store-bought, no freezer burn. He turned toward her, found her examining him.

"I've seen this meat recently?"

"Fair chance," she said, the hint of a grin on her lips.

"You guys are in this together," he said after a long pause.

"Just this one, Ivan. L-Sun, he said your tight ass got no flex. I told him you are cool, thoughtful, fair. And I was right," she added.

"You like being right?" he asked.

Leekie Annisdottir laughed and took his hand. "Beats the alternative," she said.

Special Powers

The two conservation officers lay hidden on the shore, using their binoculars to watch two men in an aluminum boat, not fifty yards away in the water. They had counted at least fifty fish brought over the gunwales, none released. The only species in Holland Lake was brook trout, the daily take limit five per person, artificial baits only. The men in the boat were using worms, and they were passing what appeared to be a large spliff back and forth, laughing maniacally.

At one point, one of the violators picked up a revolver, pointed it at shore, and yelled, "Pow, you motherfuckin' bears and motherfuckin' Martians!" This set off another laughing fit as they had another puff and pitched empty beer cans over the side.

Conservation Officer Jespert Ivory leaned against a tree, took a chew of tobacco, and smiled at his partner, Sergeant C.A. Collar. "Ripe," Ivory said, "very pregnant indeed."

The sergeant wasn't sure what his partner meant. "Clarify?"

"The situation, the timing, the opportunity."

And the word *Martians?* This Ivory kept to himself.

"You sure?" Collar quizzed.

"Eighteen years gives one a certain sense," Ivory said.

Collar had less than eight in uniform, not six full months as a sergeant. He seemed as befuddled by his promotion as others. He had applied, of course, allegedly just for the interviewing experience. He didn't actually expect to be promoted his first time in the system.

Ivory, on the other hand, had long ago rejected promotion, liked where he was, loved what he did, and did not want to get drowned by paperwork and other bullshit flowing downhill from Lansing. An officer in the field had enough to do; he couldn't imagine a sergeant's burden. Supervision, it seemed to him, meant taking on all the major and picayune dramas of the people you supervised, like some kind of sin eater, though he had no idea where this notion had come to him from, or even what it meant, other than somebody absorbed the burdens of others.

Meanwhile, there was no doubt about the men in the boat. These fools were primo candidates.

Ivory had told Collar about a "certain" approach he wanted to try, and all his sergeant had said was, "Are you kidding?"

"These two are perfect," Ivory said. "You don't believe this works, just watch, but you still have to help."

"I'm not so sure," Collar said. "Seems, I don't know . . . unorthodox."

"It *is* weird, that's the beauty of it. Think of it as a learning moment. Believe me, C.A., these opportunities are rare."

The officers were here because the girlfriend of one of the fishermen called to report the strange stuff her boyfriend and his pal were doing. Arriving at the lake, the COs had talked to the girlfriends, both of them young and attractive chemical blondes. Hell, the two morons had taken a loaded .44 Magnum in the boat with them out of fear of bears. In the middle of a sixty-acre lake? Did they expect a bear to swim out and attack the damn boat? And, the girls said, there had been pills, though they weren't sure what kind. "You know, like, you know, meth or something?"

"Yah, this pair for sure, C.A. You in or out?"

"In, I guess," the sergeant said.

"You recall the order, right?" Ivory had explained it all in advance, just in case, outlined what would happen, the order, and so forth.

Collar said, "Fish, then dope, then gun. But shouldn't we get the gun first, you know, for officer safety?"

"If we start with the gun, lines of resistance will firm up right-quick, and we'll be adversaries with a line drawn on the ground between us. It's easier and safer to mesmerize them, calm them like kittens."

"You've done this before, right?"

"Affirmative, but you've always got to evaluate the situation first. Sometimes I use coon bones on the hood of the truck and read them like magical tea leaves, but this is better, less time, happens so fast they get stupefied."

"Geez, I don't know, Jes," the reluctant sergeant said, using his subordinate's first name, a technique all cops were taught to depressurize stressful situations and contacts.

"Sarge, I fuck this up, and you can always reprimand my ass and cover your own."

"I'm not like that," Collar said quickly.

Jespert Ivory had been around. All supervisors covered their asses, more these days than when he first joined the force, but even back then CYA automatically came with the three stripes on the arm, one chevron for each letter. It was worse for lieutenants and captains, who wore shiny gewgaws pinned to their collars.

"Launch our boat?" the sergeant asked.

"Nah, we'll let them come to us and step out on them on dry land, use the element of surprise."

"But they have a gun."

"It's for the damn bears and Martians, C.A. Did you not listen to their blimbos?" The two women, he'd noted earlier, were not the kind he associated with such lowlife male companions, and he wondered how and why the hell they'd gotten mixed up with them. Still, over the years he'd seen odder matchups. There was no judging the human heart, never mind logic. Highly educated, classy women sometimes inexplicably chose scuzzlebags for partners. Accept it and move on. He couldn't ask his new sergeant about such things because his goody-two-shoes new wife thought Lions and Packers were some biblical characters and so far seemed to have not an iota of street sense about anything.

"Not sure I agree with this," Collar said.

There it was: naked CYA. "Well, decide now. You're the boss man, and this gambit needs two players. In or out, game on or game off?"

"Okay, I guess I'm in," Collar said, almost in a whisper. "With reservations."

"Yeah, I got that." Ivory spit out his tobacco and lit a cigarette.

Collar said, "They might smell it."

Ivory winced. Fifty yards out in the lake, drinking beer, smoking dope, howling and laughing, dead fish in the boat. "Guess again, Sarge. These guys are in their boat on the interplanetary express. They wouldn't smell a rotting moose in the back of their boat."

"What about our *image?*" Collar came back. "You know, the division, the department."

"We're alone," Ivory reminded his boss. "Rules say no smokes in patrol vehicles or in front of civilians when we're in uniform. Neither condition pertains here, eh. Stop being so goddamn uptight."

It was an hour before the two anglers stood up in the boat and pissed off both ends, making the boat wobble erratically. Shakes done, they pulled up two anchors, started the outboard, and headed slowly shoreward.

"Let's go," the sergeant said, excitement in his voice.

"Relax, let them get to the ramp. Call them up to you, and when you have them close, I'll step out below and start my deal."

"Start what? You haven't been exactly precise on what's gonna go down here."

"Fish, dope, gun. I have special powers. Take your lead from me."

"This feels like a questionable idea."

"New things usually do," Ivory said. "Don't be such a wuss."

• • •

He watched the boat approach. The assholes were heaving empty beer cans in their wake, like an arrow of aluminum turds pointing right at them. One man stood in the bow, like Washington crossing the Delaware. Ivory thought it was Washington, but he couldn't remember for sure. He thought there was a painting, or a cartoon, something like that. History wasn't his long suit. What he was good at was catching dirtbags.

No state registration number apparent on the boat, probably no personal flotation devices, littering. He'd already run the two through the Retail Sales System and learned neither had a license, this year or any other year. One of them had a couple of busts for drugs—holding, but no current wants or warrants on either man. The second fool had one DUI, four years ago. Clearly, these were minor league losers on a one-day howl. Not unusual. Basically, they were ignorant and harmless, though the gun bothered him. *Bears and Martians? Jesus with a jump rope!*

The boat bumped its nose on the sloped concrete ramp, and the two men stumbled out. Sergeant Collar stood at the top of the ramp, but the men didn't notice him. "Conservation officer; any luck today, boys?"

"Oh, fuck yah!" one of them shouted. "We killed the perch, man." The spokesman had purple and green hair. The other man had white hair in a shoulder-length mullet, high PWT fashion in the mouth-breathing community.

"Secure your boat. You can just put the anchors on the ramp," the sergeant said. "Step up here so we can talk."

"We ain't done nothin' wrong," Technicolor Hair offered.

"Didn't say you have. Step on up here so we can talk. You *can* talk, right?"

The two men looked at each other, shrugged, and walked up the ramp.

Ivory waited until the two men were near Collar, stepped out of the tag alders, and began to whimper like a jacked-up hound.

The two men gawked as he stood panting, his tongue hanging out.

"Our special officer," Sergeant Collar said. "He's got special powers."

"Like fucking Batman, or something?" Mullet Boy asked.

Ivory started to howl and point at the boat.

"Got fish?" Collar asked.

"Dude, we just told you, we killed the motherfucking perch," Purple Hair said, watching Ivory with wide, unbelieving eyes.

"My partner's bark says differently."

"His *bark*? Dude!"

Ivory howled again.

"No perch, my partner says."

"Perch," Purple Hair insisted. "I know fish, dude!"

Ivory's howl went up at least an octave. "Better get the fish so we can take a look," Collar said.

One of the men went down to the boat, keeping an eye on Ivory, grabbed two stringers, and dragged them up the ramp, leaving a line of wet slime.

Collar looked at the stringer. "Not a single perch, boys. They're all brook trout, the limit's five, and the size minimum here is ten inches, of which not more than a couple of these are that. Let me see your licenses."

"Left mine in the tent," Purple Hair said.

"Mine's back home," White Hair said.

Ivory began barking again. This time the sounds he made were urgent and low, deep-throated, almost angry.

"We'll deal with the licenses in a minute, boys, but my partner says there's drugs in the boat."

"No sir," Purple Hair said. "Uh-uh."

"No dope," White Hair said. "We don't do that shit. Not us, no way."

Ivory's barking shifted again, escalating to an extended hair-raising howl, so much like a wolf Collar almost turned to look for an animal. "Here's the deal," he said. "Fetch the dope now, voluntarily. If we search the boat and find contraband, we won't be so easy to work with. Last chance, boys."

Ivory's remarkably realistic canine snarls punctuated his sergeant's words, and the men stared at each other. Reluctantly, White Hair trudged down to the boat and got out a red plastic container with a blue cap. The can read Folger's Classic Roast.

"How much is in there?" Collar asked.

"Not much now. Asshole there smoked most of the shit today. I only do it once in a while," White Hair said.

Ivory's barking grew louder, and he began to run on the ramp, circling back angrily, drool bubbling out of his mouth and cascading down his chin.

"Is he, like . . . rabid?" Purple Hair asked the sergeant as Ivory charged the two men and bared his teeth.

"You men," Collar said firmly, "please tell me you don't have a *firearm* in that boat."

White Hair said, "You fucking moron" to his partner. "I told youse."

Ivory's barking became more aggressive.

"Show me," Collar said.

Ivory ran to the boat, picked up a .44 snubby, turned it around, examining it, looked up at the men and said, "Somebody got a CCW for this iron hose?"

"It ain't concealed," Purple Hair said. "We don't need no permit."

"It was under a towel," Ivory said. "That makes it concealed."

"Protecting it from the rain," the man tried to argue.

A white sun was overhead, the sky entirely blue. Jespert Ivory shook his head. "Serial number's been filed off."

"No shit?" Purple Hair said. "Guess I didn't notice. A pal give it to me for p'otection."

"From bears?"

"Here bears, back home it's niggers, sayin'?"

"No registration numbers on the boat," Collar said. "Friend give you guys the boat, too?"

"Matter of fucking fact," Purple Hair said, nodding.

Collar said, "No PFDs. Let me see your fishing licenses and your driver's licenses."

"Ain't with us," White Hair said, "'Member?"

Ivory snarled so realistically that even his sergeant took a step backward. "Don't bullshit us, you. Neither of you bought a license. We already checked the computers."

"Bought it this morning," White Hair said. "There's a lag. I used to work at Meijers in Flint."

"You guys came here with your girlfriends last night. You haven't left the campground."

Purple Hair turned to his partner and sneered. "Let's just drive us up over the fuckin' *bridge* and have us a good old time," he said mockingly. "Don't nobody pay attention to nothing up there among them cedar savages. Christ, they got fucking cops up here with superpowers."

"Littering," Sergeant Collar added, pointing at a can in the boat and the trail on the lake.

"Ain't no fucking litter if it's *in* the boat," Purple Hair said.

"I'm talking about nearly a case of empties floating on the lake, from the empty carton in the boat. A plus B equals littering."

"Jesus," Purple Hair said, "this one got superpowers, too! What is this shit?"

"Them ain't our cans," White Hair said. "Ain't gonna lie. Lotsa companies use blue cans."

"We'll just compare serial numbers, the ones in the boat against those in the water," Sergeant Collar said.

"*What* serial numbers?" White Hair asked, stammering.

"Take the boat, go on out there, and get in those cans. *All* of them."

Purple Hair started to follow his partner, but the sergeant caught the man's arm and pulled him back. "It's a one-man job."

• • •

The next week during a break at the district meeting in Newberry, Jespert Ivory heard Sergeant Collar telling a group of COs about how he and Ivory had barked their way to a stolen handgun and stolen boat, littering, no PFDs, no fishing licenses, much less all-species, and sixty trout—only three of which had met the ten-inch minimum.

Ivory stood back out of sight and lit a cigarette. *That ought to keep him out of my hair for a while.*

Humane Disposal

Arno Skell got into Jack Elray's Silverado, slid his gear bag, rifle, and shotgun cases in back, handed his partner a thermos of coffee, said, "Cream and sugar, what's the plan today?" and snapped into his safety belt.

"County just called, complaint from Lunatic Pond," Elray said.

"Oh, joy," Skell said. "They share any details?"

"Something about a pest removal dispute."

"Goody, a rat wrangler rodeo. Think the city fathers will ever get around to renaming the city?"

Lunatic Pond was the label COs applied to the town, which had a different name on maps, a small college with high tuition, a small, rich student body, a smug, affluent faculty, a disinterested administration, and a small mental health infirmary that served patients from a three-county area. It seemed wherever officers went there they encountered people who babbled with vocabularies miles above the average man, or with damaged brains that made for the strangest sorts of conversations.

"I think the city's stuck with the old name. Intellectual paper pushers hate change. Hell, they're still badmouthing some poor asshole who came back from the outside and had the audacity to open a store catering mainly to students. They called him everything but a goddamn Commie. The prevailing local business attitude back then was to leave the little snots and their uppity profs to themselves, and if they needed something, let them come crawling to town from the campus. Which they did, in trickles. Classic town and gown," Elray said. "The new guy got rich real fast, and now they all cater to the rich kids."

"We got an address?" Skell asked.

Elray said, "The Charles Edward Emerson Bone House on Lunatic Pond."

"What the hell kind of address is *that*?" Skell asked.

"My wife says Bone was a Georgia architect in the '40s and '50s; he became famous and wealthy, built custom houses all over the country."

"Geez, Jack, why would Lois know all *that*?"

"I don't know," Elray said. "But maybe we can get us some breakfast after this. Tata Café maybe."

The Tata was in reality the Morning Coffee Diner, but it employed four female waitpersons with enormous bust lines and tiny waists.

"We'll see," Skell said.

"It ain't an actual address," Elray said.

"Guess we don't need one," the other officer said. "Let's just get there and take us a look-see. I'm gonna guess such a chi-chi house ain't gonna be too hard to pick out. There a name on this complaint?"

"Mr. and Mrs. Emerson Charles. The missus, name of Juvamelia, was the one who called the county."

"What flavor's that name?" Skell asked. "Latin? This is all weird. Complainant is Emerson Charles, and the house is Charles Emerson. What's that all about?"

The house was indeed easy to locate, not because of the uniqueness of the structure, which Skell considered a gray cinderblock bomb shelter, but because of a gaudy panel truck parked in a driveway, the signage on the truck declaring GOD'S HUMAN DISPOSAL CORPS: ALL CREATURES LARGE AND SMALL, SCALY, VENOMOUS, FURRY, AND YUCKY. OUR QUOTES ARE OUR WORD!!!

"Boy," was all Elray said before resuming his train of thought. "I'll go to the front. Why don't you swing around back, see what's up."

Elray just arrived at the door when his partner came up on the 800 MHz. "We got us a deal out back."

Circling the structure, Elray saw that the house was on a hill overlooking Lunatic Pond, which was ringed by cattails, tag alders, Russian olive, honeysuckle, and other invasive species. While the main house was a hundred feet up the hill, there was a smaller cinderblock building halfway down to the water. There stood Skell, who waved Elray toward him.

Elray estimated fifteen live traps on the grounds, each with a dying animal in it, plaintive-eyed creatures looking for some sort of divine intervention and mercy.

"At least a dozen more traps over the lip of the hill," Arno Skell said, rolling his eyes.

Elray saw woodchucks, coons, two skunks, possums, rabbits, and a small badger. Both skunks had panicked, loosed their gas. The area reeked.

A man and a woman stood with a second man, whom Elray guessed to be six-six. He had the turkey neck and countenance of Abe Lincoln, whiskers and all, and wore a pale blue jumpsuit with gold embroidery that read GHDC and underneath those letters SHARLETON, BOSS MAN #2.

Skell joined the trio. "Conservation officers. You folks the Charles's?"

"Juvamelia," the woman said. "Juvamelia Charles." She thrust her tiny hand in Elray's direction.

Firm grip, he noted, maybe a little *too* firm.

"My husband, the eminent Chinese anthropology scholar Professor H. Emerson Charles, Ph.D., will observe. Unlike we mere mortals, Emmy's mind takes him to faraway places that we shall never know, much less comprehend."

The woman tilted her head toward the man in the jumpsuit.

"This creature here, this . . . charlatan, this dishonest, money-gouging bunco artist, has trapped all these poor animals and refuses to remove and dispose of them until we pay. His quote was $50 per creature, but now he wants more than $250 per head!"

"I have a copy of the quote," the man said. "I am the Right Reverend Acmetha Sharleton with an S, not charlatan with a C."

Skell stared at the man's embroidery. "If you're number two, who's Boss #1?"

Sharleton pointed up at the sky, and Skell wondered if there had ever been such a thing as a wrong reverend but kept it to himself. "Why don't you show us the paperwork, Reverend," Elray said.

"Yessir, indeed, I obey the letter of the law, all of them, here and . . . " he pointed upward again.

"That man," Juvamelia Emerson said, "is the poorest excuse for a human being I ever did meet, and we once lived in Spain. Right, Emmy?"

The professor put a finger on his chin and rolled his eyes. "*España*," he said. "*Hola.*"

"See?" the woman said. "Even Emmy can see it, and he's rarely in our dimension."

The man tugged at his own sleeve and said, "Okay, my darling, see you later." His eyes rolled back until only the whites showed. He stood with his hands at his side. Elray thought at first he'd fall over, but he seemed stable, even statuesque, rooted into the earth, with dying, gasping animals surrounding him.

"He's at work now," explained the woman, whom Elray guessed was fortyish. She was short, with purple toenails, flip-flops, a deep tan, possibly chemical.

When the reverend returned with paperwork, the woman thrust hers at the officers. The reverend's read $250 a head, the woman's, $50. Skell shook his head.

The conservation officer held up the $50 quote. "This what you gave her, Reverend?"

"Yessir, before He spoke to me on it."

"He? You mean God spoke to you?"

The reverend tapped the higher quote paper. "Changed the number, which is His prerogative. That is God's handwriting on that page, and we must do what our creator orders."

"But *you* revised the original number?" Elray asked. "God didn't have his own pencil, right?"

"God dictated the original, and He simply amended it appropriately upward through my hand, no doubt because there are so many of His creatures here and all the suffering they've been through."

Juvamelia Emerson suddenly punched the reverend in the chest so hard that he took a step backward.

"Suffered because of *you*, you, you . . . *false disposer!*"

The woman turned to Elray. "He put these traps in nine days ago. We've called him every damn day and left a message, and he never called back and never came out to check the cages, which, according to his sales pitch, the goddamn sonovabitch promised to do once *every* twenty-four hours."

"My dear woman," Reverend Sharleton said. "Anger over temporal matters is no reason to use God's name in vain."

"Bite me, you ugly, cheating, incompetent turd!" the missus screamed.

"I forgive you," the reverend said quietly. "And so, too, does our Lord."

"Fuck you," the woman yelped. "The animals on the lower hill are already dead, and those up here are close. We've tried to feed them and give them water, but they refuse it."

Jack Elray knew the past week had seen 90 percent humidity and five days of temperatures over one hundred. "You asked the reverend to take these animals away and kill them, yet you fed and watered them?" he asked. "I just want to understand the whole picture here."

"Not kill," the reverend said. "Humanely dispose of . . . for two fifty a head."

"And how exactly do you accomplish that, Reverend?" asked Elray.

"With the blessed sleep of water," Sharleton said.

"You drown them?" Skell asked, intervening.

"Humanely, amen," Acmetha Sharleton said, joining his hands.

"You have a church, Reverend?" Skell asked.

"Between assignments," Sharleton said. "God gave us this work to carry us through."

"Where was your last church?" Skell asked.

"I don't see the relevance, but I am seeking my first church, my initial service to Him."

"How long's your so-called seek been on?" Elray asked.

"A long, long time, amen. I can assure you, it renders a man humble."

"So you drown them humanely to not mar the pelts, right?" Skell asked.

"Of course, waste not, want not, God's loving directive to help us find The Way."

"I don't think that's biblical," Skell offered.

"You have biblical training?" Reverend Sharleton asked.

"No, sir."

"Well then."

"Yoohoo," the woman said. "I am not paying this pompous asshole. I'd go to prison and become a jailhouse lesbian before I'd give this creep a nickel!"

"Been in this business long?" Elray asked the man in the jumpsuit.

"Seven years, approaching eight."

"You've disposed of a lot of animals?"

"Yes, but I maintain no running total."

Elray looked over at Skell, who nodded and walked away.

"Where do you perform this humane disposal, Reverend?"

"Upper Moth Creek. I have a camp there."

"Moth Creek, huh? That's pretty far north of here. You drown them, then what?"

"I won't listen to this shit!" the woman shouted before marching away, while her husband remained in his trance.

"Eviscerate and skin," Sharleton said.

"Sell the pelts?"

"Prices have been mightily depressed," the man said.

"So you stockpile and collect them until prices go up?"

"You might say that. All proceeds go to God."

"How's that?" Elray asked. "You don't have a church."

"They go to me. I represent Him. I'm not-for-profit. My heart is pure and true."

Skell came back and told Elray, "He's never bought a fur harvester's license."

"A man of God does not need an earthly license," the reverend said. "It is written, amen."

"How many furs you got at your camp now?" Skell asked.

Sharleton tried to step away, but Elray blocked him. "Answer him."

"God wants me to take care of His suffering creatures," the reverend said.

"Take the skunks down to the pond and drown them," Elray said. "Leave the others where they are."

They watched the man struggle and gag with the two cages, the cloud of skunk stench around him almost visible.

"Nasty shit," Skell said. "He charges people with a problem whatever he thinks they'll pay and takes the pelts, too. The old double dip."

"God as entrepreneurial muse," Elray said.

"We won't argue that," Skell replied. "We'll get a warrant for his house and his camp. He admitted that he's stockpiled furs."

"Now?" Elray wanted to know.

"No, we'll let him walk now and get after him later."

"He'll dump the evidence."

"Look at him," Elray said. "He's a cheat, greedy, and a nutcase. He'll hold onto them. God's on his side."

"But *Gawddd* is not on his side, nosireebob," Professor Emerson Charles announced, popping out of his trance. He ran his fingers through his thinning gray hair, blinked repeatedly, started to walk away, stopped, and looked back at the officers. "I just visited God. He wishes to inform us that the reverend is a fake and not one of his true appointed agents on earth."

"Like you?" Skell said.

Professor Charles grinned demonically. "Don't fun me, son. God and me are tight. We *get* each other."

Skell and Elray looked at each other.

"Make a note, gentlemen," said the professor. "I am a licensed fisher of the state of Michigan. You can check your RSS." With that, he followed his wife up to the house.

Sharleton came back up from the pond, his flesh red and flushed. "I left the cages in the water," he chuffed.

"We'll help you with the others," Elray said.

"Furs?"

"You can leave the animals for now, come back later."

"The traps are my legal property and these pelts will spoil fast in this heat."

"You've caused enough trouble here, friend. Leave the traps," Elray said.

"And my bill?"

"Civil court if you want to push it. We can't settle that. But, Reverend, to be frank, I doubt any judge or jury will buy a sales agreement being changed by God."

"Huh," Sharleton said. "Unbelievers in a country led by men intent on removing God from our nation. I guess this is a hard and costly lesson for me. Must be part of God's design and His plan to lift me up."

"No doubt," Skell said, having no idea what the man was referring to, nor particularly giving a damn.

•••

The final animal count was thirty-three. The reverend departed in his panel truck, without pay. The conservation officers found the complainants on their screened back porch making blueberry martinis, which they called Bluetinis.

Skell looked at his partner as they got back into the truck. "Remind me again why we can't just dispose of some people."

"Against the law, partner," Elray said.

"Too bad," Skell said.

Life in Grays

After a decade married to Juney, Conservation Officer Colfax Mingo still had a difficult time deciphering her, the irony being that as an investigator he could interview people and extract information few other civilians or fellow lawmen could get. This skill set held for virtually anyone in almost any set of circumstances, just not at home, where his Methodist preacher wife kept him in a near-permanent state of kerflummoxation. *What the heck was missing?* Kids were great, sex life astounding, friends as loyal as your best dog, finances solid.

But understanding his wife? Not so much, despite her claims to the contrary. She was always telling him not to worry.

"Hey, Flat Line," a voice said, interrupting Mingo's personal ruminations. Flat Line was his nickname among the officers, given for his ability to show no emotion, even under a falling sky. "Your boy wants a parley."

Mingo had been called to the Newberry state police post at oh dark thirty. A troop named Brenda Joyntlet had picked off "Stonehand" Valiant, going 95 in a 55 mph zone, and by the time she got him pulled over and stopped, she saw blood and hair around the trunk lid and back bumper of the well-known violator's '88 Camaro. Mingo had no idea how many times he and other cops had arrested Valiant, but even with the man's vast rap sheet, courts had so far refused to brand the man a habitual offender and send him away for a long stay.

Harry Valiant's handle came from his youth, when his natural and only instinct in the face of authority or arrest had been to fight. Back then, he'd been pretty good at it, too, usually giving as good as he got. But now the man was old and presumably wiser.

The game warden stepped into the small blue interview room, and Valiant grinned. "They get youse out of bed, you old fart?"

"Yah, I was busy putting it to your old lady," the CO said.

Valiant guffawed. "Might as well be youse. She sure don't give me none of that no more."

Colfax Mingo had looked inside the Camaro trunk and found a sow bear and three cubs, each shot with slugs, probably a .20 gauge. "Your old lady don't give you none, so what, you developed a hankering for bear stew?"

"Don't know what youse're talking about," Valiant said. "My son Chuckles been using my Camaro. Just picked it up from him tonight. Go ask the little shithead."

Mingo held out a pack of cigarettes and tapped one out. Valiant took it and tapped it on the table. Mingo slid over a lighter, and the man lit up and inhaled deeply. "C'mon, Harry, you and me go way back."

Valiant nodded like a bobblehead. "Even porkin' same ginch, yah."

"The thing is, Harry, no matter what you say, no matter what dingle-berry lawyer you hire, we have you cold and sealed for delivery on this one."

"Can't bullshit no bullshitter, Mingo," Valiant said, grinning, puffing his cigarette, making small blue rings.

"Seriously, Harry. Every murderer leaves a minimum of twenty-seven forensic clues behind."

"What kind of clues?" Valiant asked, stabbing with his cigarette.

"You know, scientific clues, forensic evidence, measurable, verifiable stuff." Mingo picked up Valiant's cigarette butt, put it into an evidence bag, said, "Excuse me, Harry," and stepped out of the interview room.

Brenda Joyntlet was sitting in front of the two-way glass. "You really porkin' his old lady?" she asked.

"Brenda, it's an interview, a *pose* for God's sake. Just chill and watch me roll."

"Hey, I *know* that, Cole, but you being married to a drop-dead gorgeous preacher-lady, I figured you're all about the path of righteousness, the old straight and narrow. But, dude, if you're, like, into some occasional strange, where's the sign-up sheet?"

"Dadgummit, Brenda."

The Michigan State Police Officer gave him a wink and vamped, pursing her lips and making an obscene gesture with her hand. Mingo said, "Give me ten minutes, step into the room, and tell me the test came back positive."

Mingo went back in with Valiant. "Well, it's been taken to the hospital lab. Won't be long now."

"What?"

"The cigarette butt with your DNA."

"Hey, you can't take my DNA without my permission," Valiant complained.

"You're a suspect in a killing."

"Not no people, I ain't."

"I guess we'll see what we'll see," Mingo said quietly and let his words stand.

"*Seriously*, a killing? Jesus, Mingo!" Valiant said, tapping his fingers on the table top, blinking furiously.

"*Did* you kill someone, Harry?"

"*Fuck* no, I din't!"

Mingo held out his hands the way Juney did when she wanted him to accept one of her assertions. "Hey, I have to ask, Harry. Nothing personal. Maybe it was an accident. You know, shit happens?"

"Listen, asshole . . . er, sir, I . . . did . . . not . . . kill . . . nobody!"

"Good to know, Harry. Outstanding. You didn't kill anyone, I can dig that, but you killed some *things,* right?"

Valiant tilted his head slightly. "I ain't talking about nothing till we get this killed-somebody shit straightened out and off the fuckin' table."

"Understood, Harry. We're working in that direction, we truly are. Like I said, twenty-seven forensic clues left at the average murder scene."

Valiant slammed his right fist against the table, his eyes wide and wild. "There *ain't . . . no . . . fucking . . . murder . . . site, dude!*"

"Yet there is a forensic evidence chain, and it will tell us the story, no matter what you contend."

"I don't contend shit."

"Contend, Harry. It means claim."

"Claim, shit. I ain't capped nobody, swear to God on my mama's sweet memory."

"You hated your mother, Harry. You used to beat the tar out of her."

"Just one time, man, and it weren't as bad as it looked. One time I missed pulling back one shot, caught her forehead, and she bled like a fucking pig is all, an accident, not my fault."

The conservation officer sighed. "Your fist, your fault."

"Old news," Harry Valiant said.

Brenda Joyntlet stepped into the room and said, "The test came back positive."

Colfax Mingo said, "They're certain?"

"Had them do the PCR twice," she said. "To be sure."

"What the hell's a PCR?" Valiant asked, looking panicky.

Joyntlet smiled at the prisoner, closed the door, and left the men alone.

"Okay, Harry, the test results prove you handled the bears in the Camaro's trunk."

"Big whoop. So what about all that murder shit?"

"We'll get to that."

"Jesus Christ, this is a nightmare, sir."

"DNA tells us you killed the animals and perhaps someone else. Powder from your shotgun gets on bear hair and into the animal's DNA. Then from hair to your skin."

"You ain't took no skin."

"Skin absorbs DNA from your bloodstream, Harry."

"You ain't took no blood neither."

"DNA goes all over inside your body, even into your spit." Mingo let the man contemplate this and connect dots for himself. "Spit or saliva gets on a cigarette. You know that, right?"

Valiant put his hands over his face and mumbled, "Faaa-uck," pushing the word into an elongated double syllable.

"DNA can tell us exactly when and where you did your killing," Mingo said.

Valiant was missing a couple of front teeth but showed the ones that remained. "That's bullshit."

"Don't believe me?"

"No way."

"Make a bet?"

"What sort of bet?"

"You write on a piece of paper when, where, and what you killed. I'll write what evidence says on another piece of paper. We'll trade notes. If they don't match, you can go, and we'll drop the murder investigation."

"I ain't heard no actual charges, have I?"

"Bet or no bet?" Mingo asked, pushing a pad of notepaper and a pencil across the table. Harry Valiant was eyeing him with deep suspicion. "What do you have to lose, Harry? If you haven't killed anyone, you're good to go."

Valiant said suddenly, "Hell, yes I'll take that bet," grabbed a pencil, and scribbled away as he gnawed his bottom lip.

The two men traded papers. Valiant wrote only that he had shot the bears, where, when, and with his shotgun, an off-book .20 gauge he kept at his girlfriend's house trailer.

Valiant looked at the paper Colfax Mingo gave him. "Hey, there ain't nothing wrote on here."

"You win, Harry; there will be no charges for murdering anyone, but those bears, we can't let you walk on that, hear what I'm saying? I mean, four bears beats hell out of a murder rap, yes?"

"I guess," Valiant said, chewing his bottom lip.

Mingo gave the man a larger pad of paper. "You know the drill, Harry; write us the story of the four bears, every detail, every moment."

"Do I get me a lawyer?"

"For what, murder charges?"

"I didn't murder nobody, and I just proved her, eh?"

"That's right, you did indeed, and I believe what you say, but do you really need a lawyer for some measly bears? I mean, we'll call one if you want, but do you really want to go to trial, have it in the paper how Harry Valiant killed three cute little bear cubs and their mama?"

"Who the fuck are you, Walt Disney's butt buddy?"

"Do you?" Mingo repeated.

Valiant shrugged and began writing.

Colfax Mingo stepped out of the room and rubbed his buzz cut. "You're a woman, right?" he said to Brenda Joyntlet.

"Is that, like, a trick question?" she answered. "You want me to show you undeniable proof?" she joked, reaching for a blouse button.

"No, no, I just want a female's point of view. My wife claims I sometimes don't know black from white, that my whole life is lived in gray. What's up with that?"

The state trooper grinned and pointed at the mirror. "You just lied to and faked that dumb bastard into a confession. And maybe violated his constitutional rights."

"That's my job," he said.

"I think that's what your wife's saying," the troop said.

"Huh," Colfax Mingo said. "Sort of a Mars–Venus thing?"

Brenda Joyntlet shook her head, patted his shoulder, and walked away.

Damn Near Russian

Manbear Faks studied his crew as they gathered around the fire at Corn-beef Junction. Manbear, twenty-eight, had served two weeks in the Marines before blowing out a knee and being dropped so he could reha-bilitate and return. But the recruit had chosen to not go back, and, hey, what was the big deal, once a Marine, always a Marine, right? Faks had lasted long enough to prove to himself that he had what it took. The rest of boot camp was just a detail. It was a matter of principle, right?

Manbear, despite his Marine Corps training and leadership abilities, knew his posse was less than impressive. None of them would have lasted two weeks in Boot the way he had, and all of them were skittish as girls when it came to possible confrontations with DNR officers like Loco Joe Traynor, who worked the south end of Chippewa County and treated the Gem of the Huron like his own damn personal crown jewel.

The only way forward here was to disabuse the little pricks of their fear. "You dudes afraid of Traynor?" he asked, spitting into the fire.

"Hell, yes," Clegg Pokryfyke said. "Two weeks ago Skateboard was practicing over to the Raber Bay boat launch, and Loco Joe come by and told him get the hell out, or else!"

Skateboard was Lance Ross, a small-time meth dealer who consumed more of his own product than he sold. He'd once been bigger than life. No more. Too many dead brain cells. "Or else *what*?" Faks challenged.

The man shrugged. "You know. Fucking Russians don't gotta tell you nothing specific. They just, like, grin, come back to your house at night, kick your ass, haul you off, and nobody ever sees your sorry ass again."

"Where do you *get* that shit?" Faks shot back.

Pokryfyke puffed up defensively. "Everybody knows, dude."

"*I don't know any such shit*," Faks said. "Fuckers come around my place after dark, I'm gonna shoot first, talk later, aim above the chest and below the waist. That'll stop that fuckin' Traynor right in his damn tracks."

"And what if the game warden's got on leg armor, you know, like a robo-cop man or something?" Holo Balum asked. Holo was short for Holomite, a takeoff on dolomite, the high-grade limestone that comprised the island's base. Dolomite eroded and became holey under weather, like Balum's brain, which had seen a few too many meth moments over his thirty-six worthless years.

"A fucking robo-cop man? Where do you come up with this shit?"

"Seen it in a movie," Balum said defiantly. "Like Iron Man, dude, in that one movie. That fucker had leg armor for sure."

"He was, like, a billionaire, man," Faks said. "Don't be such an asshole. We're talking serious shit here tonight. When we do our deal, the fucking Russian Commies in green ain't gonna touch us."

"How come if they're real Commies, they wear green?" Pokryfyke asked. "Commies is red, ain't they? Waddup widdat green shit?"

"Uncle Joe Stalin wore green," Faks said, "And he was the baddest Commie motherfucker of all."

"Your uncle Joe?" Balum asked.

"I ain't got no Uncle Joe," Faks said disgustedly. "Jesus, I'm talking frickin' history here, rock brain. Stalin was, like, governor-king-in-chief or some shit of all the Russian Commies. He killed thousands to get himself a job paid only one dollar a year."

"If he was Russian, how come they paid him American money?" Pokryfyke asked. "Don't they got their own money?"

"Too fucking dumb to figure out their own money, so they just steal ours—like the state does down to Lansing. They steal our fucking taxes and hire goddamn Russian Commie cops to hassle our asses."

"Lansing pays them Russian cops same as our American cops, you know, like state troopers?" Balum asked.

"More," Faks said.

"Well, that sure don't seem fair to me," Balum lamented, "Russian pigs getting paid more than American pigs. What's wrong with this damn country?"

"Not near enough damn guns is what, nor the will to use 'em," Faks said. "Face it, boys, and I hate to mention this out loud, but we have, and it even pains me to say this, we have become a nation of pussies."

"I ain't no pussy," Pokryfyke said with a growl. "I won't even *eat* that shit."

Nation of pussies, Faks thought, has a nice ring to it. He'd write it down later, keep it in his leadership repertoire. "You're right. *We* ain't no pussies, but look around. I put out the summons to battle, and it's just us three here."

"Kind of cold tonight," Balum said, stepping closer to the fire and folding his arms across his chest. "Just our luck Loco Joe will show up and beat da shit outta all of us."

"One against three?" Faks said incredulously. "You afraid?"

Pokryfyke said quietly, "Not afraid, cautious is all. It's okay even for brave men to be cautious. Otherwise them Navy Seals wunta got old bin Laden, sayin'?"

The three men heard a badly muffled four-wheeler surging northward on Glen Cove Road. Faks said, "Koney Tomarck. When's he gonna get that piece of shit muffler fixed? Can't work with people gonna hear his ass coming a mile off, for chrissakes."

The visitor turned out to be not Koney Tomarck, but his Hamtramck cousin's friend Gilbert Horseman.

"We thought you was Koney," Faks greeted the new arrival.

"His old lady got him throwed in the tank."

"What for this time?" Pokryfyke asked.

"I guess he knocked her around some, and she called the nine one one, and in come the storm troopers, led by Loco Joe Traynor, who just happened to be closest when the call come in."

Faks said, "Fricking Traynor, and everywhere we look we got Loco Joe and those damn Russians."

"Koney resisted," Horseman said, "but Loco Joe beat up on him real bad and real quick."

"Where's a man's rights?" Pokryfyke asked. "I once seen this movie 'bout a country where a woman fucked anybody but her old man, the law let him brand her head with a H for horticulturess, and if he wants, the old man can kill her sorry ass, all legal-like."

"You gotta stop watching movies," Faks complained. "They'll just tie knots in your mind."

"Yah, well, I seen the same damn thing on a video game, and everybody knows they can't put nothing that ain't true in video games, you know, the ones that are s'posed to be, like, real life. That's the law."

Video games? Sweet Jesus God. "Hank, shut your damn beer hole before we all kick your stupid ass."

Pokryfyke shrugged. "I try to enlighten you dudes, but you don't wanta know; ain't no sweat off 'n my balls."

Faks looked at his crew. Clegg and Holo he'd known his whole sorry life, but Gilbert Horseman was an outsider. He'd shown up a year ago with Koney Tomarck's cousin and come north now and then since that time. A union guy, he worked tool and die outside Flat Rock and seemed okay, but he was an outsider, and Faks couldn't get past that fact, which put his nerves on edge. As a leader, you had to be damn careful with so many Russian stooges and informers around.

"How long you up this time?" Faks asked Horseman.

"Month, GM's got model changeover going on. So, what we got going for giggles and profit?"

"We?" Faks shot back. "You ain't no we, Horseman. Leastwise not yet. And what's with that faggy name? You tribal or what?"

"Yeah," Horseman said. "Fuckawee tribe: Where the fuck are we, eh?"

Pokryfyke and Balum laughed at the old joke. Faks didn't. "How you know Traynor was first to get to Koney's place?"

"His old lady told me."

"Best stay clear of that stuff," Faks said. "She's trouble, calls the law over spilt beer and such."

"Beatin' on your old lady ain't no small thing these days," Horseman said. "Cops and judges downstate take that shit, like, serious, sayin'?"

"Fuckin' Russians," Faks said.

"Who?" Horseman asked.

"DNR, judges, all pigs, social workers, whole frickin' lot."

"I heard down to the shop the DNR has special federal money to pay snitches," Horseman said. "Couple million this year, the guys said."

"Snitches," Faks said, making a face in the firelight. "That's what I'm talkin' about, Russians payin' kids to snitch on their mommies and daddies, keep track of ever'body, ever'thing."

"I thought the Russians went broke," Balum said.

"You see that in a movie?" Pokryfyke asked.

"On the TV, I think. Fox mebbe."

"Nah, they still got money," Faks said. "Commies stole all the government's shit, mines, old factories and shit, and call themselves businessmen. Rob your ass just like corporate suits right here in America. Can't believe nothing on the damn TV. They all owned by corporations, says what the suits want 'em ta say."

Balum protested. "But it was Fox News, that Glen what's-his-face, looks like a prairie dog sucked bad lemons?" Balum made a face.

They all laughed.

"Heard something else," Horseman said. "Feds are afraid A-rabs got secret agents here by the hundreds. DNR's getting money to help Homeland Security root out towel-head spies, shoot their asses like wild hogs, no questions asked."

Faks said, "Ain't no frickin' A-rab spies up here in these woods. There was, we'd know."

"Boys in the shop said the DNR will use money to step on guns and violator crews. Feds think violators are supplying them Christ-hating Moslems with guns and ammo."

Deathly silence. "Fuck we want to give our guns to towel heads for?" Faks asked.

"Cash. You know them Moslems got all that damn A-rab oil money, man. That's a fact you can look up your Winkiepedia."

Faks said, "We ain't no terrorists, and we ain't no traitors. Not us. Hell, I was a *US Fucking Marine*."

"Drummond Island's gonna be a top target for the DNR and Homeland Security," Horseman said. "Just a short boat hop from Hockeyland across the lake."

Faks mulled over what he had heard. Logic here was unwarranted yet seemed reasonable. The Gem of the Huron was just across the lake from Canada. "Who down to your shop told you all this shit?"

"Lotsa guys, and it was also in the *Detroit Free Press*. You didn't read it?"

"Fuckin' newspapers is Commie liberal tools," Faks declared.

"Damn right," Pokryfyke chimed in.

Faks hadn't read or heard any of this shit, but it had always rolled around in the back of his mind that the feds and state boys could team up and, like, bring *major* heat. "Okay, boys, that's it for tonight," he announced.

"What about that job you got in mind?" Balum asked.

"We'll talk later," Faks said. "I got to gather me some more facts and intel first."

The men nodded, got on their machines, and headed into the darkness for their homes.

Faks used a shovel to knock down and extinguish their small fire. You couldn't shoot ducks, bears, wolves, or deer if the damn woods burned down. When the fire looked safe, he mounted his Polaris RAZr and raced away into the night.

• • •

Horseman ducked into a camp off Johnswood Road. The DNR truck was backed up the two-track lane. Joe Traynor was smoking a cigarette,

166

cupping it with his hand to hide the glowing ember. Horseman's real name was Kripp, a detective with the Department of Natural Resource's Wildlife Resource Protection Unit, and operating undercover as he had for the past three years.

"How're my boys?" Traynor asked.

"Dumb as bicycle chains," Horseman said. "I gave them the story, and they split. Faks is cagey and real cautious."

"Not cautious enough. His sister Engadetta tells me everything he's doing. She hates his ass."

"Why bring me in?" Kripp asked.

"To save me time. If I can neutralize Faks with disinformation, I can spend time doing important things, not chasing those idiots."

"Maybe those guys are right," Horseman said. "We might operate a bit like the Russians."

"Whatever floats their boat," Loco Joe said. "They know I'm on the island?"

"Told 'em you put the whoop ass on Koney Tomarck."

"Good, I'm gonna poke up into alvar country, spend the night out that way, catch the first ferry back tomorrow morning. You?"

"Last ferry tonight, head below the bridge, sleep with my wife; I hope she remembers how."

"Do *you*?" Traynor asked his colleague.

Tripp snickered. "Guess we'll find out, eh."

Last Night as a Secret Squirrel

All Buck Dudek could think about was the crew of thugs he had to meet tomorrow. They were bear houndsmen out of Kentucky, and he had worked them for two years and eased his way into their confidence, a sickening job because they were lower than pond scum. Unlike most violators, who saw poaching as a sort of game, the Kentuckians were out-and-out lawbreakers, raping everything; anything that threatened their bottom line was "handled rat quick," their leader once confided.

The Kentuckians guided licensed hunters, mostly from Michigan, but took gall bladders and paws from their "sports" kills, and from what Dudek could tell, unlicensed hunters in the group also had taken six to ten more animals each year for paws and galls to be sold to Korean middlemen in Mishawaka, Indiana.

Dudek knew this would be a major take-down and subsequent case. Or, if it went awry, he would be dead. There were no other outcomes between the two extremes, not with this crowd, and he was amped already.

Naturally, this would be another day Karna felt the need to do jumping jacks on his psychological trampoline.

"Good God, Buck, that damn ponytail makes you look like a fool. How long does this charade have to go on?"

Ten years in uniform, the last four as an undercover detective, and Dudek had made it a point to keep his wife as far in the dark as possible, which was a difficult balancing act because she was smart, curious, nosy, and downright assertive about what she wanted. Truth: She was too emotional and too impulsive to entrust with even small tidbits about his undercover work. His only choice: Lie and dissemble, which made him sick.

His ponytail, of course, told her something about what he might be up to, but he never revealed precisely what, with whom, or where. All Karna knew was that he was a detective and not required to wear a uniform.

"I swear," she said, "most wives in my situation would pack up and move the hell on. Out all hours—for days sometimes—comin' home stinking of cigarettes, cheap whiskey, dope, perfume . . . How am I supposed to know you're not fooling around on me, Dudek? Tell me that."

"Because I'm not," he answered, calmly eyeing his body armor. No way he could hide a Kevlar vest around the Kentuckians, but without it he felt naked and exposed. The hammerless Taurus .38 snubby in his calf holster didn't help his confidence, either. A gun was a matter of last choice, desperation. Having to reach for the weapon would mean he had failed, that the case was in the shitcan, and he'd be damn lucky to get out with his life and body intact.

There were times when he wished Karna could be calm and serene, and listen, but this just wasn't her way. She was a born drama queen in all things, large and small, and a legendary gossip. Actually, her being so gossipy helped his cover. If anyone came poking around, they'd look at Karna and think no way that woman's husband is an undercover cop.

"When are you leaving this time?" she demanded.

"Half hour. You know where the will and paperwork are, right?" He knew this would set her off, but it was part of their ritual, and he had no desire to change ways after they had helped keep him alive for ten years.

"Goddammit, yes. You say the same thing every time you leave, and it still just about floors me. It really, *really* creeps me out, Buck, this talk of wills and that damn silly ponytail."

"I said the same thing before every patrol when I was in uniform," he reminded her.

"It's different since you became a damn secret squirrel."

Dudek looked over at his wife. "Where'd you hear *that* term?"

Karna rolled her eyes. "I talk to the other wives, duh? They seem to know more about your work than I do, and that makes me wonder what you're really up to."

"What do they say?"

"They say they'd divorce their spouses if they took such a job."

"Is that what you want?"

Karna pushed his chest with the heels of her hands. "No, you big jerk. I just want a normal life, watching you getting into your patrol truck, listening to you bitch about your sergeant and Lansing, finding all the stinky evidence you left in our fridge and freezer, yelling at the kids for leaving toys in your boots, you know, a normal uniformed game warden's life."

"I doubt many would call that normal."

"They're not game warden families."

"And we *are*, you included?"

"Dudek," she said, "I'm the pilot of this mother ship, keeping us all on course while you battle the forces of evil."

Dudek made a sniffing sound toward her. She was a foot shorter, skinny. "You been hittin' on the bottle?"

She slammed his chest again and waved her hand at the back door. "Go on and get yourself shot, or have sex with some diseased swamp angel."

"Do I get to pick?" he shot back.

"Hell no, that's my job! Pushed to a wall, I'd prefer you do the flatbed tango with skanks than take bullets in your brainpan."

"I'll try to remember that."

"Git," she said. "When will we see you again?"

"Day after tomorrow, probably. Sometime."

Her eyes narrowed. "Really?"

"Yep."

"And when do you leave again?"

"Saturday."

"Well, at least you'll be home for a few days."

"Saturday you and I will be driving over to Crystal Falls to look for a house."

Karna Dudek stared at her husband, her mouth open, frozen between words.

"Promoted," he said. "Lieutenant for the district."

His wife whispered, "Ohmygod."

"You like?" he asked.

No words, but she nodded enthusiastically. "Can't you stay home tonight so we can, well, you know. Geez, Buck, can't they find another officer this one time? I mean, *good God*, Buck!"

"No can do, hon. You know better than that. You need to start thinking like a lieutenant's wife. There will be twenty families for us to worry about."

"You mean no gossip?" she said.

"That would be a fine start."

"Soap-on-a-rope, Buck, I don't know. Maybe you should have talked to me before you accepted."

"I can still turn it down, stay with what we have."

"No more gossip," Karna said, making a zipping motion across her mouth. "We got time to fool around?"

"I can't do you *and* a swamp angel in the same night. Don't have that kind of stamina anymore."

She leered. "You had it last Tuesday morning."

"The exception that proves the rule," he said, pulling her to him. "You know where the paperwork is, right?"

She pulled away and wagged her finger. "Tell you what, Dudek, you make that the last time you ask that, and I'll never gossip again, quid pro quo. Deal?"

"Deal," he said, pulled her close, and they had a lingering, tender kiss.

Out in the truck he called his lieutenant. "All set?"

The plan called for him to hook up with the Kentuckians. His truck was equipped with an electronic tracker and a disguised automatic vehicle locator panic button, hooked to his key fob. When an unlicensed hunter took an animal, he would sound the silent alarm, which would shoot a signal up to satellites and back down to his backups, who would come in hard and fast and make the arrests, including him. The bad guys wouldn't know he'd set them up until it got to a jury, if it got that far. Meanwhile, Kentucky officers would serve warrants at the homes of the suspects in the group, and several Michigan officers would converge on the Kentuckians' camp off Coast Guard Road, where they kept a freezer filled with illegally taken meat and animal parts.

• • •

Driving to the rendezvous with the hunters, his hands kept shaking, and he stopped and bought a pack of unfiltered Camels and lit up. One more time, he told himself. Keep it together. Deep down he knew Karna was right. No one could endure the life of a secret squirrel for years on end.

"Last night as a secret squirrel," he said out loud. "Keep your eye on the damn ball, Dudek."

Sisyphus Redux

At more than two score years, the callipygous, auburn-haired Gayfryd Davilla Fairlane Flood had the tight-packed figure of a woman half her age, an IQ in the I-shit-you-not-o-sphere, the temperament of Virginia Woolf, the insatiable sexual appetite of Cleopatra, and the moral compass of a snake.

Ten years on the bench in the Upper Peninsula, and District Judge Flood had built a fearsome reputation as a punitive jurist, an avenging angel some called "G-Bomb." She didn't just throw the book at her docket dogs, she used the book to pound them so deep into the system that they'd never get loose.

The severe sentencing practices of Gayfryd deeply disturbed Conservation Officer Ernie Fortier, though he could never admit it publicly. How could he? For going on eight years Ernie had compiled a remarkable and enviable record of never having lost a case that went to a jury, not once. This made him the envy of Upper Peninsula law enforcement personnel, a sort of demigod of hardrock copwork.

Admiration aside, Ernie wore his record like an albatross as he watched every arrest he made get the maximum sentence with no ameliorating or mitigating circumstances, the result being that Ernie The Ticket Machine rarely wrote tickets anymore because he couldn't stand to see the punishment meted out by his paramour, Gayfryd Flood. His lieutenant in Marquette and department higher-ups in Lansing looked at the fall-off in citations and figured it was because he had literally pacified his area, the goal of all peace officers, rarely achieved.

Ernie's relationship with Gayfryd began when she called him into her chambers before a contested illegal deer case. It was Fortier's second time before Her Honor, the first case having involved a tribal member with 800 pounds of walleyes, all the fish netted outside the area allowed by treaty.

That time, a tribal attorney had vehemently argued that the tribal court was the proper venue for the case, not a US or state court, but Gayfryd Flood had given the lawyer the evil eye, ruled for the state, and waved the attorney out of her courtroom. The steel and certainty in the judge's voice that time had given Ernie Fortier the chills. Thus, standing in her private chambers was akin to being naked in the lion's den.

"I see you've got fine big feet," she greeted him. "But stamina? No way to judge stamina, Officer Fortier. Do you have stamina to match those beautiful big boots, and what size are they, anyhow?"

"They're 16D," he said meekly.

"Lord have mercy," the judge said. "And stamina?"

"Stamina with regard to what, Your Honor?"

She narrowed her eyes. "Are you a naïf?"

"I don't think I know that word, Your Honor, so I can't really say."

"Only one way to find out," she said with a smile. "Drop your gear and let's get to this trial."

Trial? "Your Honor?"

Judge Flood yanked her robe over her head, tossed it upward to flutter down over her chair, stepped from behind her desk stark naked, helped strip him quickly, pushed him over to an oversize leather couch the color of aged red wine, and commenced what she would thereafter call the Mother of All Stamina Tests, after which she dressed without talking, put her hair back in place with an obviously shaking hand, pulled on her robe, and dismissed Ernie Fortier with a wave of her hand. "See you in court, Ernest. Now, shoo!"

Only when he was back in the hallway waiting for the case to be called did he realize she'd been naked under her robe before he arrived, which meant she'd planned the whole thing, and he wasn't sure in the least what exactly that meant, or how he felt about it, but *schtupping* a judge couldn't be good. Could it?

The defendant's lawyer was nervous, Judge Flood told him to keep quiet, and after less than five minutes Dento Salminen admitted to not just the deer Ernie Fortier caught him with, but to seven more, and Judge Flood sentenced him to a year in jail, $7,000 in fines, and another $1,000 in expenses, including the officer's time away from his job. When Salminen's attorney protested the jail term, Flood held up a hand. "The statute says one year mandatory," she barked. "If you have a problem with said statute, counsellor, I suggest you lobby legislators to change the law."

"But in our culture, it's customary," the lawyer protested.

"You are in *my* court, sir. *State* rules, no customs, no tailoring, by the book in every case, every time. Your client doesn't approve? Advise him not to break the bloody law. With eight illegal deer, he's stealing from every citizen of this great and currently impoverished state, and I will not have it, sir. Do you hear me, sir? I will not have it!" Her gavel came down like the report of a .44 Magnum.

Judge Flood then waggled a finger for Officer Fortier to approach the bench, and there in front of others she slid a card to him. It had a camp address and her private home and cell phone numbers, written in flowery script.

• • •

Ernie Fortier never became comfortable with how Gayfryd Flood's ways affected his attitude toward his job, and he was in a terrible quandary about what to do. He was afraid if he tried to break it off with her she'd retaliate with vengeance. And truth be told, the judge was a lot of fun in some ways, especially with her clothes off and a few liquid libations down the hatch.

Recently, it seemed, Ernie spent more time trying to figure a way to free himself from the judge than thinking about fish and game miscreants. He was working at bare minimum, and in an unhealthy situation.

Over breakfast one Wednesday morning at her camp, Gayfryd Flood said, "Ernest, you seem unhappy. Want to talk about it?"

It was the classic can't-win scenario. If he tried to talk, she'd bury him with cold logic and vocabulary far beyond him, and, in doing so, bring about the end she'd already decided. On the other hand, if he denied a problem, she'd smile, take his hand, lead him to the bed, and robustly celebrate by exercising his stamina. Decision time, he told himself, feeling sweat bead. He furrowed his brow and meekly gave her his hand.

• • •

Days of shame turned into weeks and months of worry, and one day Lieutenant Binky Muhlendorf called Ernie to the district office for a chat, about what, Ernie had no idea. Muhlendorf was a rising star in the state, from CO to El-Tee in eight years, and deserving of it. Some fast risers were political, but not Binky, who had been a great CO and sergeant, and had fairly earned the brown bars on his collars.

"Have a seat," his lieutenant greeted him. "Grab a coffee."

There was a thermos and two cups on the table, and Fortier helped himself.

"I'll cut right to the chase," Muhlendorf said. "No officer in the state has ever achieved the record you have for clean cases. The management team wants to promote you and send you around the state to train other officers in the proper way to write and substantiate violations. You'll also audit officers whose cases tend to get tossed or downgraded and see if you can analyze what went wrong. If there's a trend, what does it portend, and what as a department can we do, if anything? How does that sound to you, Ernie?"

"Like something I'm not qualified to do."

The lieutenant smiled. "You're kidding, right?"

"No sir," Fortier said, "I'm serious. This ticket thing of mine is just a fluke, and that's all."

His El-Tee shook his head in disbelief. "Eight years cannot possibly be a fluke, Officer Fortier."

"I'm sorry, sir, but it is, and that job you talked about. I'd hate it because it sounds like internal affairs or something, and you know how that goes down in the ranks."

Muhlendorf rubbed his face, perhaps an indication that he'd not expected the meeting to take this tack. "I'd like for you to think about it, Ernie. Take a week, and understand, this was the chief's idea. He thinks you walk on water."

"Okay, I'll think on it, sir. I can do at least that much."

"Good, good, you do that. The promotion would be to sergeant, and you can live anywhere in the state because you'll cover the whole state. The chief thinks you should plan on 75 percent road time, give or take."

"For how long?"

The lieutenant shrugged. "Open-ended. Permanent is my guess—if the audit supports the mission's assumptions."

"How do I do my do job when I'm going to be here only 25 percent of the time?"

Muhlendorf grinned benignly. "Given what you've accomplished here, you could probably do both, but the idea is for you to leave the field."

"You'd put somebody else in my place?"

"Yes, at some point," Muhlendorf said.

"Would I have a say in who replaces me?"

"That's not how we do things, Ernie, but I understand your commitment and attachment."

"This is a new job, so it ought to include some new procedures."

"I can't argue that logic, but what do you care?"

"It took me years to get this place into a delicate balance, and I'd hate to see that disrupted by a new officer who doesn't understand the rhythms here."

"I'll run that by the chief," the lieutenant said, "but I'm pretty sure that dog won't hunt."

"Yessir. Thank you, sir." Fortier quickly gathered his hat in a cloud of adrenalized hope. If he could swap a new man for himself, he could be clear of Gayfryd Flood and her controlling ways and get back to being just another lawman.

Who might replace him, of course, was an entirely separate and paramount issue, and he was quite clueless how to proceed except that he had a hunch the judge needed to first get accustomed to the idea of his leaving before he broached the issue of a replacement.

• • •

There was no reaction whatsoever from her when they met at her place three days later. Her total verbal response was "Oh." He waited for more, but nothing emerged. He did, however, think she rutted with increased gusto and energy that night, leaving him exhausted and her snoring softly on his sweaty shoulder. Not at all the way he thought it would go, and he went to sleep feeling encouraged.

At breakfast—after alarm-clock sex—Fortier's knees still rubbery, Gayfryd took a sip of coffee and asked him, "So what exactly is all this promotion nonsense about?"

He tried to explain that in part it was her support of him that paved the way.

"Pshaw," she said. "Weren't but two of those cases that were even close to a judgment call. High likelihood any jurist would have found same as I did."

"I guess Lansing sees it differently."

She took another hit on the coffee. "Won't fucking do, Ernest my boy, won't do a'tall. Took all these years to find what I want in one man, and I do not intend to willingly let go. Turn down the job, Ernest," she said, adding, "Are you taking this aboard, my sweet ? Tell them no way, Jose."

"I'm not sure I can do that," he said. "I'm guessing they think something's wrong here, and they want a new body in place to test their hypothesis."

Gayfryd Flood stared at her man. "You think they want you *out*?"

"It sort of occurred to me," he said. In fact, he'd just had the idea and gone desperately to it without giving it much thought. Still, it seemed a promising argument.

The judge kept her eyeglasses on a golden chain around her neck and now lifted the tiny specs into place like shiny binoculars. "You're a fine woods cop, Ernest, but you're no lawyer, so don't float some stupid-ass argument with hope as cheap fuel."

"I'm not arguing. It's just a hunch," he came back.

"I'll eat a brunch, officer, but not a hunch. But for civilized argument's sake, say they move you out. Where to?"

"Lansing."

"Thought you said the job serves all districts," she countered.

"The staff support is in the Mason Building."

"Nonsense. This is the epoch of the electronic office, work from home, all that new age computer happy talk bullshit." She paused and took a deep breath. "So there you are in Lansing. What do I do, diddle myself with an electroshock wand?"

"No, ma'am," he said. "You'd probably wear that out."

She frowned. "I wear you out, is that what this is all about?"

"My El-Tee called me in and laid this whole thing on me. That's what it's about, Gayfryd. We're talking reality here."

"As a jurist, it is I who will decide what the hell reality is, Ernest. Me, in my court, in my bed, up there on the bench, everywhere, me, not you, not them, me."

"Just saying," Fortier mumbled.

"Let me guess," she said. "You're having a little moral dilemma vis-à-vis us and your perfect professional results, and you feel the fix is in and your reputation isn't warranted, and that this leaves you feeling sullied, perhaps a little tawdry. Am I on the right track here, Ernest? Please enlighten me."

Ernie Fortier weighed options and shook his head.

"Don't bullshit a bullshitter, Ernest. Judges are, bottom line, primo bullshitters. You arrest shit, but we have to swim in it. So, you move to Lansing, and a new officer gets assigned; is that the plan?"

"No plan, just thinking out loud," he said quickly.

She stared at him with hard eyes. "Would you have a say in said replacement?"

"It's not done that way."

"Maybe I should call your El-Tee into chambers for a private Come-to-Jesus meeting."

"I don't think so," Fortier said meekly, his heart pounding, head beginning to thrum.

"But that's your idea, if I read you right, to place some other individual betwixt my legs."

"I'd never do such a thing," he said.

"You're right on that count, pal. Only one person makes that decision, and that's *ish*, you *capisce*?"

"I didn't mean—"

She cut him off. "You mean you didn't *think*, Ernest, so here's my counterproposal. If you take the promotion, I'll blow up your replacement. The DNR will never get another conviction as long as I'm here. I chose you, Ernest Fortier, though I am somewhat hard-pressed at this very moment to calculate *why,* other than the obvious carnal connection. So here's your choice: Take the promotion, and I bomb your operation, or you can stay where you are and continue your record of perfection and live in perfect bliss. It's a raw, cruel damn world, ain't it, bub?"

• • •

Judge Gayfryd Davilla Fairlane Flood owned him, body and soul, and when his week was up, Ernie Fortier knocked on Lieutenant Muhlendorf's office door and stepped inside. Binky had a small picture of an old man pushing a gigantic boulder up an impossible slope.

"That new?" Fortier asked.

"Judge Gayfryd Flood sent it over as a gift. She and my wife are old pals. So, how about the decision on the promotion?"

"I can't take the job, Lieutenant Muhlendorf."

"But it's the chief's idea."

"I'm sorry, sir. Really."

"Do we at least get a reason?"

Conservation Officer Ernest Fortier had never lost a trial or disputed case and knew he never would. He just pointed at the picture on the lieutenant's wall and took his leave.

A Good Little Lie

Anacota Quirt's first contact of the day was with Arne Sune Samuelsson, the six-foot-four vegan, card-carrying PETA member, Bible-thumping mental midget who sometimes wore a black satin cape and mask and appeared suddenly at hunters' blinds at nightfall, driving off game and sportsmen. Luckily, nobody had shot him. Yet.

Quirt had arrested the man three times already for hunter harassment. Each time, animal rights groups had stepped in with lawyers to represent Arne, whom she privately referred to as Ass, his initials. Quirt had lost six field days to Samuelsson's legal shit, and despite the maneuvering, he'd been found guilty in all three cases and given moderate sentences.

Early this morning a hunter called to tell Quirt that he'd seen a caped giant overnight near Beaver Dam Creek, north of Hermansville. Quirt called the Dickinson County jail and learned Ass had been released a week ago. This time she decided to undertake a preemptive strike and drove to his trailer on Waucedah Road in East Vulcan.

Samuelsson answered the door in camo boxer underwear and blinked into the morning sun.

"Mind if I come in?" Quirt asked and stepped inside. "'Course you don't, you having a clean slate and all. How were things over at the jail?"

"Don't like it there much," the man said gloomily. "Guys are bullies, and dey use bad language and da eff word."

"Really?" Quirt asked, trying to hide a grin.

"Ya know, fuck this, fuck that, that's all they say, dose guys in dere."

"Shoot the finger at you?" she asked.

"Sometimes," he said. "How'd you know? You want coffee?"

Quirt looked around. "Who kept your house while you were away? It looks nice."

"My *Moster* Solvig."

His aunt was a hardnosed spinster Lutheran lady who looked after her nephew when he'd allow it.

"That thing down to jail," Quirt said, "all those pottymouths?"

"Yah, what?" the big man said, putting a new filter into the coffee machine.

"They got the virus," she said.

The big man's eyebrows lifted. "You mean like the AIDS?"

"No, this virus causes something called DUPC. You notice how some guys shoot the finger at you more than others?"

Arne pursed his big lip as he thought. "Yah, some of them dudes do it a lot. I don't like it."

"Those are the advanced cases," she said, "got the old finger flag waggin' all the time, eh? Where's that coffee?"

"Couple minute," Arne said, looking at the pot like it was an undecipherable device and leaning down to listen for sounds in it.

The house does look pretty good, Quirt thought. "Is Solvig here?"

"No, she went back over town her house."

"You ever think about moving in with her?"

"She wunt have it, says I'm big scab on the family name."

"*Are* you?" Quirt asked.

"I ain't even sure what she means."

"She means your problems with the law affect your family's reputation."

"But I'm doing good, ya know, like God's work?" the man argued. "He said, 'Thou Shalt Not Kill.'"

"I think the commandment refers specifically to murder."

"The Book don't say them words like that," he said. "I can read, ya know?"

"I know, and that's good, Arne, but how many times have you been inside now?"

"T'ree," the man said sullenly.

"The deal is this," Quirt explained, "every time inside increases your exposure to the DUPC virus. Sooner or later you're gonna come out sayin' fuck this and fuck that."

"Fuck I am!" the man thundered, paused, and his face collapsed into shock and disappointment.

"See?" Conservation Officer Quirt said. "The virus may already be inside you."

"How can that be? I ain't done nothing dirty ta get it."

"It's airborne in there. You breathe it in, and, if it likes what it finds, it stays and over time takes over your body."

"How do *you* know?"

"Gimme your hand, Arne."

The man held it out. It was massive, larger than a dinner plate, with broomstick-size fingers. Arne Samuelsson was a pulpie, a logger who worked in the woods, and his battered, scarred hands showed it. "All those bumps," Quirt said, poking the huge calluses," they're what doctors call palmar fibromatosis. Your hands get banged up all the time, and that causes inflammation in your fascia."

"Feces, youse mean, like, poop?"

Geez, she thought. "Fascia. It means stuff inside your hand."

"You mean logging's doing this to me?"

"No, but logging *preconditions* you as a viral host."

"Huh," the man said, studying his hand as if he'd never noticed it before.

"You're a Swede, right?"

"Yah sure, you betcha," he said beaming.

"DUPC is also called Viking disease."

"But I ain't no Viking; I'm a Packers man all the way."

Some men were dull as dirt. "Not football, Arne. Real Vikings are no doubt somewhere in your family history. That means you have some of their genes in you. Swedish heritage, Viking genes, you work outdoors, you're over forty, and you drink a bit too much on occasion."

No response. She knew she had his attention. "The good thing is you can stop Dupuytren's disease from developing."

"What's that?"

"The disease the virus causes. Eventually it will curl all your fingers until just the middle one is sticking up all the time—a permanent finger."

"You think I got that thing?" he asked, his eyes pleading.

"Only a touch, but it won't get worse if you do the right things."

"Such as?" Samuelsson asked.

"Such as not go back to jail, and stop drinking. I know a program, people who can help you."

"I ain't no drunk," he muttered.

"Never said you were, but alcohol opens pathways for the virus, any alcohol." Every time she'd arrested Ass, he had exceeded a blood alcohol concentration of .08 and was legally intoxicated. His BAC wasn't outrageous, but it was always over the limit.

Arne Samuelsson squinted down at his coffee.

Quirt sipped hers. It tasted good. "Not too bad. You want to talk?"

"'Bout what?"

"DUPC."

"I stay out of jail, I'm safe?"

"Should be."

"But logging?"

"That and booze only make it easier for the virus, but if you stay away from jail, the virus will have no way to get to you and take over. Jail is where the virus waits, Arne. If you go back, it'll get you."

"Don't want that fucking virus," he blurted and immediately covered his mouth with his hand.

"Your choice," Anacota Quirt said. "Stay out of the clink and maybe your Solvig will let you move in with her. That could make your life a whole lot easier."

"'Cept all them church biddies she hangs with," he complained. "Buncha clucky hens, sourpuss old women."

"That's for you to work out, Arne. But you show up in that black cape outfit again, and you're going back to jail, and the virus will pounce on you like a bear on honey."

"I ain't ever going back," the man declared.

"You were seen over near Beaver Dam Creek last night. In your cape."

"I ain't gonna do that no more."

"No?"

"No, ma'am. There a cure for that Viking thing?"

"No cure, Arne. You have to avoid the virus. Remember?"

"Which is only in jails, right?"

"Yah," she said.

Samuelsson seemed to cogitate for a long time. "You could be lyin' ta keep me from doing God's work," he said.

"I could, or I could just be trying to spare you from falling into the ranks of the infected."

"How I'm ta know?"

"Get arrested again, contract the virus in jail, then you'll know, but then it also will be too late."

He raised his eyebrows. "You think I'm stupid?"

"Not in the least, Arne. And I've got to go."

A mile from the man's trailer she pulled her truck up a two-track, got out, and lit a cigarette. She had lied to the man, made it all up, but it was for his own good and to spare her wasting time with him. If he kept getting arrested, he risked being labeled a habitual offender, with lengthier prison stays. Hunter harassment was a misdemeanor, but there was no doubt in her mind that if he continued the confrontations, one of them would elevate to a felony. Sometimes it took a few small lies to encourage good behavior.

The cigarette tasted like shit. How did I end up in this business? Quirt wondered as she got back into her truck and picked up a microphone. "Central, DNR One One Fifty is clear of the last," meaning she was back in her truck and proceeding on patrol.

Rampike

Wind had reshaped the heavy snow into twenty-foot drifts in less than a day. CO George Gabriel looked at his partner, Ellis Madorski, shook his head, and said, "Anybody caught in this crap is a goner."

The two men had barely made it to the safety of Lemmings Corner themselves when the Lake Superior storm exploded, burying everything for miles around. In their low-slung new Plymouths, the officers knew they both would have been stuck in the bush and trapped until the storm blew itself out, which it would—eventually. Only *when* was the question and the answer known only by God. By pure chance the officers had arranged to meet for coffee, and that had saved them a lot of worries, troubles, and headaches.

Most people didn't give much thought to the time game wardens lost to being stuck, or how often they broke their backs with jack-and-jumps or by inching their vehicles out with come-alongs. Gabriel thought someone ought to figure out precisely how many hours, days, even weeks officers lost because their vehicles weren't designed for bad-road or off-road use. Every officer knew game wardens ought to be driving four-wheel-drive Jeeps, not bloody Plymouths. What the hell good was a 350-horsepower engine on a two-track? But driving a state-owned vehicle beat the dickens out of having to use your own personal ride, which—up until 1966, just two years ago—was the way it was. Nope, this wasn't ideal, but it was a definite step forward.

The two officers holed up in Avro's Roadhouse after working on nearby roads getting people unstuck and to safety. Phone lines were down from the furious ice storm that had preceded the November blizzard, and radio reception was intermittent. Avro's didn't have a television because Old Man Avro "didn't want to spend money on a dang aerial for a dang toy for a bunch of dang fools."

Madorski looked at the world turned virginal white and said, "I'll guess she'll blow another twenty-four hours before she's had her way with us."

Gabriel nodded. "At least, eh. Hope Avro's got enough grub for all of us accidental refugees."

"And blankets," Madorski added.

"And blankets," Gabriel agreed. "You got snowshoes in your squad?"

"In the trunk," Madorski said. "With ski poles."

"Me, too."

If they had to go help someone in an emergency during this storm, it would be on foot in snowshoes, but not until the storm let up. At full blow, this storm was a stone killer to almost anyone caught outside, even experienced bushmen like the two game wardens.

"Schnapps?" Madorski asked.

"Vodka," Gabriel said, "neat and cold. This storm blowing, nothing we can do outside, so might as well have us a couple of belly warmers."

"And eat," Madorski said.

"Food and a little drink," Gabriel agreed.

"Could be worse," Madorski said. "We could be camping out in some darn snow cave, eh."

"Yah, youse got out in your cruiser some candles?"

"Whole box, store-bought."

"Borrow me some, eh?" Gabriel asked, thinking about a blizzard he had endured by piling up a mound of snow, tunneling inside, making a platform, poking a hole through the top for ventilation, and setting up a candle. The lone candle and his body heat kept him alive, not warm, but alive. He'd learned the trick from a retired state trooper.

Old Man Avro came over to jaw. "You boys pretty damn comfy, inside all toasty warm, drinkin,' eatin,' living high on the state tit." Avro was forever complaining about state government and how his taxes got wasted. He could and would talk on such subjects for hours.

Gabriel said, "We were city cops, you'd be serving free grocks. Up here, at least the state pays."

"With my own damn tax money," the proprietor said.

"Go play in the snow, Avro," Madorski said. "Not one hour ago we towed your waitress outen a snowbank down road dere, eh? She wunt here now, you'd have to take care of all these customers alone, you ungrateful old bolt."

• • •

Thirty-six hours later the storm finally began to taper, and miraculously the phone began operating again and radio reception came back, sort of. The entire Upper Peninsula was pretty much closed, airports, highways, trains, even the Mackinac Bridge, which linked the state's two large peninsulas.

Nobody had shaved for three days, and the toilets in Avro's were miraculously holding up, while the interior of the bar had begun to smell vaguely like a human cattle car.

Madorski and Gabriel had fought in World War II, both in Germany, and both had helped liberate concentration camps. Neither man would ever forget what he had seen. "Cars the Nazis moved Jews in smelled a bit like this joint," Madorski said, sniffing the air.

"This will end better," Gabriel said, walking toward Avro, who was holding a phone out to him.

"Gabriel," he answered.

"Geez oh pete," Justy Kona said. "Madorski with you?"

Kona was their area law supervisor, sort of their sergeant. The two war vets compared all state matters to the military.

"Yah, we're nice and comfy here at Avro's."

"I just talked to the troop post commander in Newberry," Kona said. "Says some folks name of Lundquist with a camp over on Minky Lake called relatives in the Soo when the storm was starting and said they were coming out, right as the snow hit. Said the roads were closing fast, and they had to scoot. Family's not heard nothing since, and they're worried."

"We just got phones back up here, Justy. They're probably holed up. If they stayed put, they should be fine."

"Family says they're headstrong sonsaguns, in their seventies. Any way you fellas can poke east and take a look around?"

Gabriel pulled up his mental map. Minky Lake was part of the Little Two Hearted group, about ten miles east, but there was no direct route from here to there, and with this snowfall Gabriel wasn't confident enough to cut cross-country. They'd have to follow the roads and wend their way north, then east. "They probably tried to run down south to the North-western Road out to the state highway," Gabriel told his supervisor.

"Highway's open some, but the Northwestern Road is shut tight and packed in, snow drifts ten feet deep. Family says the couple always goes north and loops west. They should've come right through Lemmings Corner, but I talked to Avro, and he ain't seen 'em."

"Drifts here are as bad or worse," Gabriel said. "Locals?"

"No, but their local connections and relatives over to the Soo are worried. Youse guys take a look?"

"Where are you, Justy?"

"Town, storm caught me at home."

Meaning Engadine. Justy never strayed far from his hacienda or his old lady.

"Snow bad down that way?"

"Not like what youses got up there. US 2's open, bridge too, traffic's movin' slow, but at least it's movin' again."

Gabriel took a deep breath. "Okay, Justy, we'll see what we can do."

Madorski lifted an eyebrow as his partner came back. "Justy," Gabriel explained. "Coupla Swedes from Minky Lake bailed out as storm come in, and nobody's heard from 'em."

"Northwestern Road south to the state highway," Madorski said. "Should've made it easy to Paradise or Newberry."

"Turns out these folks like to go north and come west through here. Avro hasn't seen them."

"People," Madorski said. "How come they always got to do stuff the hard way?"

"Just how some are wired," Gabriel said. "The name is Lundquist."

"Norm and Naomi," Madorski said.

"You know them?"

"Yah, sure, she ferried planes during the war, and he flew B-17s against Ploesti. Headstrong and tough, da bot' a dem."

"Justy wants us to go take a look."

"With what? Our magic carpets?"

"Our choice of transportation," Gabriel said. "Justy can't make tactical decisions from home."

The two men laughed.

Madorski said, "Could use one of them damn new snow machines, I t'ink."

"We could ask Avro if anybody hereabouts has one."

"Helluva long way out to Minky Lake," Madorski pointed out.

Gabriel said, "Guess we could strap on the racquets and tramp our way east. If they aren't close, we'll assume they stayed put or found safe harbor. Nothing else we can do, eh? If they came east, they'd have to come by Stumpy Shamp's place over Pike Lake way."

Gabriel called over to Avro.

"Call Stumpy Shamp, Avro, see if he's got the Lundquist castaways at his place. Anybody around here got a snowmobile?"

"Ain't that kind of money out this way, George. You know that. Only goddamn state employees earn that kind of money. I know a guy in Grand Marais got one—when it works. Canadians make the damn things, and all they give us is damn snow and a buncha goofball hockey players."

"Call Shamp," Gabriel told the man and went out to join his partner. "Guess we were too cozy for it to last, eh?"

"State ain't happy 'less we're freezing, drowning, or burning up."

Avro called them over and said, "Stumpy ain't seen 'em, says it's real bad over his way, most roads drifted completely shut."

"Hooray for us," Madorski said sourly. "We get to be the cavalry."

Gabriel thought, *As long as we're not Custer's boys.*

The two men suited up, got out their snowshoes and poles, emergency packs, blankets, and sleeping bags, and looked at each other. "We few," Gabriel said.

"We ain't no few," Madorski said. "We're just two, that's all. A few is three."

Literalism, enemy of all romantics, Gabriel thought. "Okay, Ellis, I'll start out front. Rest every twenty to thirty minutes, and switch leads."

"Sounds good, partner. Shunt be no crust on dis crap. We'll have to plow through like winter moose."

State the obvious, that was Madorski's way, and Gabriel knew his partner was as nervous as he was. This was a very dangerous thing they were being asked to do.

It took them about four hours to get no more than a mile from the start point. The snow drifts were too deep and expansive to measure depth, but at least the storm seemed to be starting to let go. The two men were sweating heavily.

Their first big concern had been Ruthie's Creek. In deep winter you couldn't make out the wooden bridge from the sides, and plenty of vehicles had plowed down the little drop-off over the years. But they found big puffy drifts, like piles of divinity, at the bridge and made it across quite easily. Then the going got tough and remained that way.

"Don't know if my legs can take much more of this," Madorski admitted as they rested. "Ain't in the shape I used to be."

"Me neither," Gabriel said. "This is crazy. Let's duck into the hardwoods here, make a fire, and get us some tea with sugar, assess our situation."

"They're not in a cabin somewhere," Madorski said, "this ain't gonna end happily ever after."

Gabriel knew. As fit as he and his partner were, the four hours had sapped both of them. "Let's find us a place where a drift tapers and get down under the thick trees. Shouldn't be as much snow under the canopy."

"Looks like we're gonna spend the night in the woods, eh?" Madorski said with a flat voice.

"Looks like. I don't want to backtrack through this crap in the dark. Storm picks up again, we'd be screwed, blued, and tattooed."

Madorski exhaled a heavy breath. "She's a tad nippy, eh."

"Ya, let's get to cover."

They found a helpful snow contour and battled their way down and into the trees. Drifts were high along the edges, but there was much less snow underneath in the woods. "I'll find us some dead wood, get a fire going," Gabriel said. "See if you can find some birch bark. I usually got some in my ruck but don't know where it got off to."

Thirty minutes later they had a fire and a wood supply, made tea, and cut some boughs to put under their sleeping bags and blankets. "You ever use a fart sack in the war?" Madorski asked his partner.

"Once maybe," Gabriel said. "We slept in the dirt most of the time."

"Mud for my outfit," Madorski said. "Snow mixed with mud."

"No mud here," Gabriel said. "Good luck for once."

"I'll keep the fire," Madorski volunteered. "You sleep. Wake you in a couple hours, eh. We got plenty smokes?"

"I got three packs," Gabriel said.

"Me, too, we're good. Bring Boy Scouts out in this shit, they'd never camp again."

"I just might not either," Gabriel said, laughing.

• • •

No dreams, but Gabriel thought he felt the ground shake and wondered if it was an earthquake or blast from a new blizzard. End of the world, maybe. Could be anything out here in this Lake Superior country.

"Wake up, Gabriel."

Gabriel peeked out, tried to push away sleep. "*My* watch?"

"First light, you'd better have a look."

Gabriel used a finger pad to dig sleep out of his left eye and Madorski handed him a cup of tea and said. "She's hot. Look over dere, eh?"

The snow seemed finally to be done, though flakes continued to flutter like confetti out of the trees. They were in blue-gray twilight. Gabriel saw a snowy silhouette, looked like the remains of a tree that had been struck by lightning, maybe. "That a rampike?"

"Let's go look," Madorski said.

"Oh, God."

The rampike turned out to be two people intertwined, frozen solid, a macabre sculpture, dusted and caked with snow.

"Had same idea as us," Madorski said.

"Where's their car?"

"Hard to say. May not know till there's a thaw. Could be forty feet or four miles from here."

"You check them?" Gabriel asked.

"Gone," Madorski said. "Pretty sad, clinging on each other that way."

"Never should have left their camp," Gabriel said.

"Or their damn vehicle," Madorski added. "Pilots should know better. Stay with the damn plane. You think we ought to dig them out, cut a travois?"

"No point. I'm sure coroner will want see this one as it is. Make tea, eat some breakfast, snowshoe out, report it, let others clean this up," Gabriel said. Avro had given them hunter sandwiches, peanut butter, jelly, honey, dry oats, big energy smeared between two thick bread slices. They ate in silence, hung some ribbons on tree branches by the road edge to mark the location, adjusted each other's packs, put ski pole straps over their wrists, and looked back at the couple.

"Hardheaded Swedes," Madorski said in a flat voice.

"Damn pilots," Gabriel said with a grunt. "Think they're bulletproof. Same as in the war."

The Fifth Ace

Sitting beside three gut piles in a Drummond Island clearing, the game warden came as close to tears as he ever had, but the feeling quickly turned to cold rage. Sandy Macbeth vowed that he'd bide his time and find a way to bring down Francis Brush, longtime scourge of the Gem of the Huron.

Several years passed, no opportunity came, and Sandy Macbeth eventually guessed that someone on the ferry boat crews was letting islanders know when he crossed. At first he thought it could be the owner of the Star Queen Tavern right next to the ferry dock in Detour but then decided a crewman made more sense.

Early September in their garden patio, his wife, Glamis, was reading the newspaper. "Says here Astel Balcers died down to Drummond."

Glamis read every word in every newspaper every day, saving Macbeth the trouble and time. As she read, he watched their cat Thumbprint crawling through empty boxes and jumping out on their older cat Lardass. He'd watched the two cats do this for years, and the older one never seemed to figure it out. Ambushed once, Macbeth could understand, but to be fooled years on end? Glamis insisted cats were among God's most clever creatures, while he had his doubts. But he kept his own counsel because Glamis, undoubtedly a fine wife, insisted on being right about all things, small and large, every time. Never wrong, but she kept a clean house, spent money frugally, took good care of their kids. . . . What more could he want in a spouse?

"You think Brush will pay his respects?" she asked.

"Not a chance. Balcers stole Brush's wife, and they hated each other."

"So Brush will be glad to be shed of competition," Glamis said.

Sandy Macbeth looked from the cats to his wife. "When and where's the service?"

Glamis rattled the newspaper. "Says Friday at Saint Filippo NeriFillipo's."

"Which funeral home?"

"There's only one out to the island," she reminded him.

"That one belongs to Sepanu," he reminded her. "He's married to one of Brush's daughters. The Balcers clan won't turn to Sepanu."

Glamis scanned the paper. "Payment out of Cedarville," she said. "You think this is an opportunity to get Brush? I don't think so."

Sandy Macbeth said nothing. His mind was in overdrive with possibilities.

· · ·

The hardwoods had a lot of beech trees, and the ground was littered with nuts down toward the old fort ruins. This time of year the area was over-run with deer, including some big bucks that moved out of thick cedar swamps just for this annual feed.

Macbeth headed for a major intersection of deer runs he knew Brush sometimes frequented and stashed himself in a pile of browned ferns, pull-ing a lightweight camouflage tarp over top. The cover was made of mate-rial that let him see out but kept anyone from seeing inside, and it had cost him a small fortune from a military catalog outfit. Glamis had made him a lunch and dinner and gave him two thermoses, one containing coffee, the other soup. If Brush didn't show, Macbeth had decided to turn in his badge and retire. Going on twenty years he'd chased this scoundrel, and this night he was going to nail him. Been oh so close lots of times, but not one arrest. Until now. He was almost certain.

Peak full moon would leave the woods nicely lit, not quite as bright as a sunny day, but as good as some cloudy days and better than most twilights. The trip from Cedarville had been made in total darkness and stale air that left him nauseous. His eyes were still trying to adjust, but he was damn proud of his ingenuity and hoped it would pay off. If not, it was just another stupid trick wrought by desperation, old ground revisited, and maybe it was time to call it quits.

Sandy Macbeth ordered himself to not dwell on the past, only on the present, only on tonight. He was fairly certain Brush would work alone; it was his MO, and he knew to keep his yap shut when deeds were done.

A few moments before midnight Macbeth heard four spaced shots. There was one brief flash of light before each discharge. He also thought he heard at least one animal crash to the ground and thrash momentarily. No sign of Brush, of course. He'd killed, would come back later to collect his meat, no doubt from a different direction.

Macbeth found the deer, three does and a June fawn, still spotted but putting on weight. Each animal was missing an eye. Small caliber, .222 or .22 Hornet, Brush's caliber. Macbeth made a new hide for himself and crawled inside, pulling the camo cover over the top. He ate a chicken sandwich and sipped coffee, told himself Brush would come back around zero four hundred when most people were in their deepest sleep. Brush played odds. No way it would be earlier than that.

Macbeth settled into the half-awake, half-sleep mode all game wardens and combat soldiers came to rely upon. He'd fought in Korea and nearly frozen to death, but he knew the trick of suspended animation and slowed metabolism, like a snake. That trancelike awareness and luck had kept him alive. Now here he was, seventy-three years old, forty years as a game warden, conqueror of every violator he'd ever gone up against. Except one.

Macbeth debated what to do with Brush if he pinched him. Were this not the island where the man had a few friends, he might thrash the tar out of him and leave it at that, but this case needed to get to the JP and into the paper. The game warden prayed Brush would want a jury trial so the whole thing would be known by everyone.

Unsure whether such thoughts qualified as dreams or nightmares, Macbeth's meditative state brought familiar, disturbing images. T.J. Fowler sitting next to him in North Korean snow, an airburst ripping nearby trees, and T.J. still sitting there, minus his head, which had somehow been vaporized, covering Macbeth with tissue and blood, and there he'd sat all night until someone brought hot soup at daybreak.

This was not the sort of thing he shared with Glamis. Dirty work was dirty work. Soldiers went to war. Game wardens found the lost and the dead. No need to plant seeds of distress in those who were fortunate not to have to deal with such ugliness.

Macbeth desperately wanted a cigarette, but in the still night air Brush would smell it a hundred yards out and not come in to collect his prizes. Game wardens and violators alike learned that noses and ears were better than eyes after nightfall, and Brush was a cut above most violators in his woodcraft.

Given other circumstances, Macbeth thought, their roles might have been reversed. In fact, Macbeth believed ardently that as many game wardens as possible should come from the ranks of violators, and because of his outspokenness Lansing had left him where he started. He told himself he didn't care: Promotion in this outfit was a curse.

● ● ●

Brush came in much later than the warden expected, oh-six-thirty, just morning twilight, pushing a wheelbarrowlike contraption with a box built up so he could carry bigger loads, and with two larger than normal front tires to make the thing go better through the woods. Damn clever, he thought begrudgingly. The man could patent it and make a lot of money and not have to poach. But then, Brush's violating wasn't about food or survival or profit, it was just about flaunting the rules and never getting caught.

Macbeth let the man eviscerate all four animals before stepping out from cover and grasping his arm. "You're under arrest, Mr. Brush."

The man stood mute, staring before mumbling, "Okay I light up, Sandy?"

"Suit yourself," the officer said magnanimously, and when the poacher held out the pack, Macbeth took one and also lit up.

"Clever as the devil," Brush allowed after a few puffs. "I'll give youse that."

"Long time coming," Macbeth said.

"Guess it was," the violator said, chuckling softly.

"You didn't look the least bit surprised when I stepped out."

"Always assumed it would happen. You've been close too dang many times to count. Saw me shoot these, did youse?"

Macbeth said nothing.

"I figured it would happen the time I was certain you couldn't be here. Last night I had one of dem feelings and almost stayed home."

"Probably should have."

"Care to tell me how you pulled it off?"

"When the time's right, Francis."

"I'd offer a trade. Name my crow."

Macbeth heard in the man's voice an anger over someone failing him. "You first," the conservation officer said.

"Take out my wallet?"

The warden nodded. Brush dug a faded photo out of the billfold, held it for the game warden to look at.

Macbeth's heart juddered and sank. He stepped toward Brush with malice, but Brush stepped back and held up his hands. "You wanted to know, Sandy. Now youse do, and it's your turn."

"No deal," the game warden said through clenched teeth.

"You started coming out here, what ten years back? Nobody even knew who the hell you were, eh? Think about it, Sandy."

Macbeth was visibly shaking. *How could this be?*

"Grew up together, neighboring farms. You probably never heard dat fum 'er, I'd bet. I got tagged as the black sheep early on, was encouraged to get on with life on my own, which I done, I guess. Your turn, Officer Macbeth."

"Astel's coffin," Macbeth said. "Nobody knew."

Brush showed a toothless grin. "Coffin, eh. That musta been one creepy ride, eh?"

"Not one I'd recommend."

"Pinched me, though."

"I suppose." A major arrest and a major, crushing revelation. It wasn't supposed to feel this way.

"We gonna go see Essie?" Brush asked.

Esther Magnum was the island's longtime justice of the peace. "Got to."

"Help me move dis meat?" Francis Brush asked.

"You won't be keeping any of it."

"I know dat. Essie'll give it to folks can use it."

"No shenanigans," the game warden said.

"Nope, I guess you got me good, unfair and unsquare. I even thought about coffins, Sandy, and I called Sepanu. Payment couldn't bury nobody widout having rep on the island. He said he meet the ferry hisself, and I told him make sure he meet dat Payment out in the open and keep his eyes open."

"Was a crowd of cars," Macbeth said. "Payment pulled over to the woods to be courteous. I was out of the truck quick and gone while Payment talked to your son-in-law."

"Young'uns, dey just don't listen," Francis Brush said, adding, "Pretty darn smart of you. Gotta give you dat, by gott."

• • •

Home, late afternoon, Macbeth stormed inside, shooed the cats away, got out a suitcase, began pulling out drawers, and began packing haphazardly. Glamis came out of the bathroom in her ratty terrycloth robe. "What's going on in here, Sandy?"

"I *got* that sonovabitch!" he said angrily.

"Brush?"

He glared at her. "*No thanks to you.*"

Glamis's face tightened. "And what's *that* supposed to mean?"

"I went across in an empty coffin. Never told nobody, even you. Was there when he put down four animals, pinched him at first light. *No thanks to you.*"

Her eyes widened, then slowly closed. "That damn Francis," she said. "Let me guess. You pinched him, and he hauled out an old photo of me."

"All these years you knew him and never said a bloody word!"

"There was nothing to say a word about, Sandy. He was a neighbor boy, nothing more. Mothers in those days gave class photos to other families. I hardly knew him before his family gave him the heave-ho."

Sandy Macbeth sort of wanted to believe his wife, but he couldn't—at least not now.

"You realize," Glamis said, "he's beaten you again. You arrested him, and he showed you an old photo he's been carrying like a fifth ace for God knows how many years. You undo him, and now he tries to undo us. What kind of husband throws away his wife on the words of a known violator?"

She had a point, but he couldn't stand the thought of her being right again.

• • •

Things were never again the same between the couple, and a year later Macbeth came home to find Glamis moved out, cats and all. She left a note: "You swim in filth with vermin, and think it's real, but it's not, Sandy. I pity you."

• • •

One year after that, Sandy Macbeth retired quietly, sour and wounded.

To the exact day, one year after retirement, he died of a brain aneurysm. By then the old game warden had alienated everyone in his personal and professional life, and only one person came to the graveyard.

Francis Brush watched dirt thump on the casket lid and nodded. "It's poker, Sandy," he said out loud. "Got to always think two lay-downs ahead. You, of all people, should have known that."

Dancing for the Dead

Night, black as the inside of a cow, and Conservation Officer Joseph "Shaky" Jolstaad had his truck aimed down a grassy two-track so tight that jack pine branches clawed at the truck and scraped the windshield as he motored slowly along, running dark, an invisible steel creature prowling silently. Jolstaad liked being alone, even if he was afraid most of the time, which he was. Petrified sometimes.

His last-phase field training officer had been the legendary Army Kelley, murdered six weeks ago. First phase, recruits watched their FTO do the job. Second phase, the recruit did the job and was coached daily by the partner. In phase three it was up to the recruit to do the job, the FTO there solely to evaluate the recruit's ability to cut it. When Jolstaad's last patrol in phase three ended, Kelley looked at him and grinned. "You pass," the experienced officer said. "You done damn good."

Kelley then drove them to a stream with a six-pack of beer and some small cigars. "I think you're gonna be great CO, Joey. I know you're afraid, and sometimes that shows when we're alone, but you never let the public see it. That's good, *really* good. Don't worry about the shakiness. We each prepare and funnel adrenaline and nerves in our own way. You did good, Joey. You could be my partner any day, any time. I'd damn well go to war with you."

They each took a slug of PBR and puffed a Swisher Sweet cigar. Kelley pointed up at the night sky. "Belt of Orion, those three stars up there in a line. Orion was a hunter, according to the Greeks. That belt holds him together. Every morning you put on your duty belt, think about Orion. We're the hunters, Joey. That's our job."

Jolstaad said, "I can't shoot for beans. I struggle every time on the range."

"Practice shooting, practice drawing, make the weapon part of you so you don't have to think about it. It's a tool, like a hammer, nothing more. You'll get better. Trust me."

At first Jolstaad had been elated to have passed, then he was relieved by not failing, and finally he was terrified by the reality of what lay ahead. That had all been four years ago, and from the start his colleagues called him "Shaky" but always to his face, never behind his back. Hell, he didn't mind. After all, it was true.

Still, he'd never shared with anyone what Army Kelley had told him that night on the creek bank.

Now Army was dead. The mere thought made him tear up and feel angry like he'd never felt before. Tomorrow there would be a memorial service in Grand Marais, where Kelley had grown up. Jolstaad was supposed to be done at 10:00 p.m. tonight, but he'd stopped for gas in Bergland, where a logger named Valk ambled over to him and told him he'd seen some fresh timber cuttings southwest of Porcupine Mountains Wilderness State Park, an area where no contracts had been let. Jolstaad decided to go take a look. Illegal logging was endemic nowadays.

If he got into something, he'd rejigger his daily report to reflect the longer day. As it stood, he was out of hours for the pay period, but Valk was a solid guy, not one to bullshit. If the ride turned out to be nothing, he'd eat the extra time himself. Not the first time he'd donated his time to the state. No biggie; it was the work that mattered, not the accounting.

• • •

Cara O'Brien Kelley sat on the edge of her bed, staring at her husband's urn. It looked a lot like the old dented thermos he took in his truck every day. His ashes, she had decided, would remain with her, go where she went. Selfish, maybe, but the urn was all she had left of her Army. They'd known each other only two months when they married. It had lasted five years. There were supposed to be so many more.

The first morning after they'd slept at her place, she had watched with horror as he suited up, putting on his bulletproof vest and gun belt. She must've made a face because he said, "Here's the deal, hon. I'm a cop. I make enemies. And some assholes just don't like badges or what they stand for. Overall the job's pretty safe."

"Overall, but?" she said.

"You know," Army Kelley said, and she did. He was telling her a day or night might come when he'd not come home from a patrol. She remembered shuddering then, wondering if she could handle that. But she also knew the day he walked into her eighth grade social studies class that he was not just special, but the one. He came with his fur kit, and the kids loved him. He didn't talk down to them, but talked to them with lots of give and take and smiles and jokes and laughs. God, he was funny! She was forty then, same as him, neither of them ever married before, and she just knew. That afternoon when she walked out to her car his green patrol truck slid silently up beside her, his window down.

"Dinner sometime?" he'd asked almost sheepishly.

"Tonight would be good," she answered.

He smiled and said, "Pick you up at six, which for a game warden is pretty much of a very approximate time."

But there he was at six sharp, all showered and shaved and smiling, and things progressed in lockstep from there.

From a day in class with eighth graders to married in what amounted to a blink. God, he was such a man's man, tough as seasoned hemlock, yet sensitive, meticulous, precise in all things. When they picked blueberries, his bucket was all berries, not a single piece of extraneous debris.

Five short years, she told herself, as she sat there on the bed. Not fair! But I should be glad for what I had, not what I don't have. Tomorrow is his memorial. No tears. You're Army Kelley's wife, and you have to act like it, be worthy of him. She lay back on the bed but knew she wouldn't sleep.

Murdered, no suspects, the whole thing sudden, out of the blue. No clues. Alive in the morning, dead that afternoon. What had followed were endless interviews with DNR personnel, state police detectives, deputies, questions, questions, questions. Did he have enemies? For God's sake he was a game warden in the UP. Of course he had enemies!

On and on, and never a word or hint about the progress of the investigation, which meant they'd hit a wall. Army had taught her to read cops' words and silences for real meanings. He was so damn smart, so aware. How the hell could he let himself be killed?

She had learned about Army's death from his lieutenant. Army had been found shot.

"But he wore a vest," she'd said.

"In the head, Cara. I'm sorry," the lieutenant had said, staring at his boots.

Soon after, Chief Cameron Campbell had told her, "We'll get him, Cara, by God we *will* get him."

It had been a less-than-convincing statement, but what else could he say? The chief was a fine man and not to blame for Army's death. The only blame lay with the killer. She stared at the urn. "They'll get him, Army. I know this for certain." It was all she could think to say as she tried to will herself to stop thinking at all and get some sleep.

• • •

Jolstaad's nerves were frayed as he drove on. The grassy section turned to rock, and with all the windows down he could hear small rocks popping off the tires and pinging off the undershield of the truck. He tried to will the road back to grass, but it remained rock, and he kept driving.

At one point he stopped, got out, and thought about advancing on foot. Valk's description put the cutting site a quarter mile or less ahead, but it was hard to judge because the logger shared no coordinates.

Jolstaad was about to get back into the driver's seat when his windshield exploded, showering him with glass shards and stinging his face. Not thinking, he ducked low, pushed open the door, reached over with his right hand to activate the panic button, turned on all the vehicle's exterior lights, including the spotlights, which were pointed straight ahead, crouched behind the open door, his .40 caliber Sig Sauer in hand, and saw a man with a long gun, which thundered again, the round hitting the steel deer guard and some of the grill, to his right.

The spots and brights lit the man. Forty yards, max. A third round pounded through the door by his left leg, but Joey Jolstaad carefully aimed and fired twice, saw the man go down. He waited for more movement, his heart pounding, saw none, put the truck into gear, and let it move forward with the wheels in the ruts until he got closer and reached over to turn off the key, his hand shaking.

Automatic in hand below his SureFire, he approached the man. No movement. Rifle beside him. Jolstaad got the sling of the long gun and tossed it back toward his truck while keeping the pistol aimed at the man. He knelt, felt for a pulse, found none, and began to shake violently, willed it away as best he could, got on his radio, and called county dispatch and Station Twenty in Lansing.

"DNR One, One Thirty-nine, shots fired, one down, requesting backup and EMS," he said without a hint of tremor in his voice.

Both the county and state told him backup was en route, and Joey Jolstaad hunkered between the body and his truck, keeping his Sig pointed at the man on the ground, just in case he came back to life. He had searched and found no other weapons, just the .308 rifle, identical to the one in his truck. This coincidence passed through his mind, but he was too scared to lock onto much except wanting help to get there.

The man had long, unkempt white hair, a bushy white beard, and faded, filthy military fatigues, like he lived in them.

Off in the distance sirens wailed, converging on him like avenging furies. Army Kelley would have had a better word for this. He always had the right word, read all the time, seemed to know everything, could remember details like a subject's eye color from a stop fifteen years before. Army's memory had been astonishing.

Jolstaad's shaking turned to tremors. His body shuddered so hard he thought his heart might stop, and this time he let it go. He'd just done something he'd hoped he'd never have to do. At least three sirens, he told himself. Not that close yet. He wished they'd hurry.

• • •

Cara Kelley sat up in bed, rigid, electrified, certain she heard Army's voice, clear as could be, "It's over, hon." *Good God!* She swung her feet to the floor, went into the bathroom, and looked at her alarm clock: 12:05 a.m. In bed two hours, and now you're having nightmares, she told herself. *You'll be in shambles tomorrow.*

She got into her shower and stayed under the water a long time, letting the heat melt the knots in her neck and shoulders until she heard pounding on the bathroom door and a frantic voice yelling, "Cara, are you okay? Talk to me, honey!"

The widow got out of the shower stall, draped a towel around herself, and opened the door. "It's okay, Mom. I had a dream, and I thought a shower might help me get back to sleep."

Her mother was seventy-nine, feisty, cool under stress, and stared at her.

"Sleepy tea," her mother said. "It'll help the both of us. I can't sleep, either."

The two women embraced, stood there a long time, mother and daughter, now both without mates. "Don't forget the disc, hon," a voice said in Cara's mind. She didn't share this with Mom.

• • •

Sergeant Nick Carter was first on the scene, jacked up, ready to jump into the fight. He came slithering up the side of Jolstaad's truck, found him by the body, and looked him over. "You hurt, Joey?"

"Windshield," Jolstaad said. "Just some dings."

"Man, your face is all blood. Let me get my kit, clean you up some."

"He opened fire on me, Nick. No warning."

Carter checked the dead man. "Well, his shootin' days are over now, so let's just take care of you, okay, Shaky?" The sergeant snapped a photo with his digital.

Joey Jolstaad laughed. "You think a drink would stop this shaking, Nick?"

Carter held out his own trembling hands. "Not the kind of shakes we have, partner."

• • •

The Methodist church was a box, small, neat, well kept, very Methodist. There were cop cars and CO trucks everywhere, the small village overrun by an occupation force of crisp green uniforms. Cara and her mother drove over from Newberry, just the two of them. No pass-the-time chit-chat; each woman was lost in her own thoughts. Oddly, Cara felt almost lighthearted, didn't bother to try to examine the feeling, just let it wrap around her. She glanced at her mother, who stared straight ahead, her jaw set, eyes slits.

"It'll be okay, Mom," Cara finally said.

They pulled up to the church around 2:00 p.m., an hour before the service would begin.

Chief Campbell met them and escorted them into the church, down one of the two middle aisles. The chief's face was lined with concern. He had wanted to form a line of officers for them to walk through with the urn, but Cara had rejected this. "He'd hate that, Cam. You know how he was." Army preferred the background in almost everything, except at parties, where he usually emerged as the most boisterous troublemaker, putting the spotlight on him and revving up the crowd with endless darts and jibes and an Irish laugh that shook walls harder than his snores. Cara took the urn to the altar and set it on a small table.

Reverend Polly Wade putzed around the front of the church. There was some sort of CD player, and Cara caught Polly's attention and handed her the disc. "When I say, okay?" *If I can do it.*

The disc was the only unusual thing in Army's will.

The Kelleys, when they went to church, which was rare, came here. Army had been born and baptized Catholic, and he was a deeply spiritual man but not a joiner, and he was always skeptical of all organized religions and the petty bureaucracies they spawned.

All that aside, Cara knew he had loved this little church, always told her it made him feel, albeit briefly, that mankind had a chance. He never went beyond that, and she didn't ask, but she also knew that while what he said was heartfelt, he liked the fact that there were two small-caliber bullet holes in the stained glass windows on both sides of the church, evidence of an errant shot that had come down the hill and gone through the church without striking anyone. She was sure the bullet holes were the main reason he like the church so much.

• • •

Jolstaad was stitched in the local emergency room in Ontonagon. The state police took a preliminary statement, and his El-Tee talked to him. Everyone was polite until he said he had to get to Grand Marais for Army's memorial service. The doctor raised hell. "Thirty stitches in your damn face and a small fracture in your left forearm. You can't drive. The drugs will dope you up."

Sergeant Nick Carter stepped forward. "He ain't driving. I am."

This ended any opposition. Carter handed Joey a Guinness, and Jolstaad looked at this sarge. "Yeah, he was my final-phase FTO, too." Carter looked at his watch. "We can make this run in five flat, I think. Three hours to Marquette, two from there to Grand Marais. We'll scoot across the Adam's Trail, and we ain't stopping for shit," he declared.

It was ten till three when they pulled up in front of the church. There were more than a hundred officers milling around outside. Carter handed Jolstaad a small brown envelope. "Give that to Cara, eh," he said before looking at the other lawmen. "Get your spiffy butts out of the way of two working officers." Carter led his man to Cara Kelley and pointed to a seat beside her.

Cara whispered, "Joey, you look like you just wrestled a damn bear."

"Something like that," Jolstaad said, trying to grin. This was Army's moment.

Cara patted his leg. "He thought the world of you, Joey."

Jolstaad fought tears, kept his eyes straight ahead on the simple urn.

Chief Campbell materialized in the front of the church and said, "Reverend, may I say something?"

Polly Wade gestured toward the congregants and stepped backward.

The chief took out a piece of paper, unfolded it, and began to read. "Just after midnight this morning, Conservation Officer Joseph Jolstaad was fired upon without provocation in Ontonagon County. The perp fired three rounds. Officer Jolstaad returned fire with two rounds, striking the shooter twice and killing him. The shooter has been identified as Clarence Carl Boost, a man wanted for murder and numerous other crimes in eighteen states, and third on the FBI's most wanted list. Boost had no known history in Michigan." Campbell looked down at Joey. "Officer Jolstaad, I believe you have something for Mrs. Kelley."

Joey had forgotten the envelope, but dug it out of his pocket and handed it to her. Cara opened it, looked inside, and began to sob.

The chief continued. "An investigation of Clarence Carl Boost's camp turned up a .40 caliber Sig Sauer, a .12 gauge shotgun, and a .308. Investigators found Conservation Officer Army Kelley's wallet, badge, and bulletproof vest. The perp was not wearing the vest when he expired." The chief paused, looked out at the uniforms in the pews, and said, "You are hard men and women, walking hard ground. Cara, would you hold that up, please?"

Cara Kelley raised her husband's gold badge, and Polly Wade said, "Vengeance is mine, sayeth the Lord." But the chief corrected her. "Not vengeance, Reverend, justice."

The air went out of the congregation with a collective gasp, followed by applause that morphed into a colossal cheer, pumped arms and fists, hugs, high fives, fists and shoulders banging together, instant total chaos heard by townspeople a quarter mile away and wondering what the funeral ruckus was all about.

The chief had to shout to regain control as news raced out of the church to those listening outside. Nick Carter got to his feet and pointed at Jolstaad, "We thought you was a toad, Shaky!" It was Army Kelley's favorite line from his favorite movie, *O Brother, Where Art Thou?*. Cara Kelley pointed at the minister, shouted, "Now," grabbed Jolstaad's hand, and jerked him to his feet as the boom box began to blare "Sunny Side of the Street," with Irish madman Shane MacGowan's boozy cigarette voice slurring words and rasping lyrics with the Pogues, Army's favorite group and song, the one he had called his battle hymn.

Cara Kelley began to dance, steering Jolstaad this way and that. Chief Campbell danced with the minister. Every person in church danced, partners irrelevant. As did those outside. There was a time to live and a time to die. And on this day hard men and women rejoiced.

Cara pulled Joey close. "He's so proud of you," she said.

Joey Jolstaad didn't ask how she knew, and when she handed Army's urn to him, he began a frantic, spastic jig of jubilation officers would spend the next few years trying unsuccessfully to describe, finally settling on the day Shaky shook the world. As he danced that day, all Joey Jolstaad could think about was the Belt of Orion and the kind words of his friend, Army Kelley.

About the Author

Joseph Heywood is the author of *The Snowfly* (Lyons), *Covered Waters* (Lyons), *The Berkut, Taxi Dancer, The Domino Conspiracy*—and all the novels comprising the Woods Cop Mystery Series. Featuring Grady Service, a detective in the Upper Peninsula for Michigan's Department of Natural Resources, this series has earned its author cult status among lovers of the outdoors, law enforcement officials, and mystery devotees.

Heywood is also the author of *Red Jacket*, the first historical novel in a series featuring Rough Rider-turned-game warden Lute Bapcat.

Heywood lives in Portage, Michigan.

For more on Joseph Heywood, visit his website at josephheywood.com.

Set in 1913, Rough Rider turned game warden Lute Bapcat confronts a violent miners' strike, deadly sabotage, and the intentional destruction of wildlife

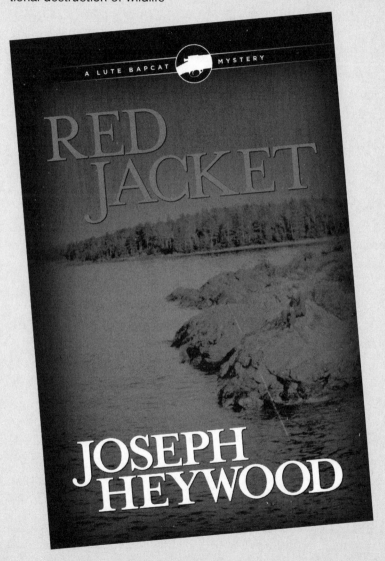

"A truly wonderful, wild, funny and slightly crazy novel about fly fishing. *The Snowfly* ranks with the best this modern era has produced."

—*San Francisco Chronicle*

"A magical whirlwind of a novel, squarely in the tradition of Tim O'Brien's *Going After Cacciato* and Jim Harrison's *Legends of the Fall*."
—Howard Frank Mosher, author of *The Fall of the Year* and others

"*The Snowfly* is as much about fishing as *Moby Dick* is about whaling."

—*Library Journal*

"Fly-fishing legend meets global adventure in Heywood's sparkling, ambitious novel . . . an engrossing *bildungsroman* . . . part Tom Robbins, part *David Copperfield*."
—*Publishers Weekly* (starred review)

"If *The Snowfly* becomes a movie, it will blast *A River Runs Through It* out of the water."

—*Fly Angler's Online Book Review*

One legendary insect—enormous, white, and exceedingly rare—attracts trout of such size that they couldn't possibly exist in the world as we know it. But in Heywood's classic novel, such things can and do exist. Richly imaginative and sensual, the world of *The Snowfly* has more mystery lurking beneath the surface than our own. Or does it?

JOSEPH HEYWOOD

THE
SNOWFLY

A NOVEL